Tribute

A BITTERSWEET CELEBRATION

By

Madalyn Morgan

CW01497554

CHAPTER ONE

1970

Ena opened the door. The lights went out and an air raid siren began to wail. As she stumbled into the darkness, searchlights criss-crossed overhead, probing the night sky for enemy planes, and her ears were assaulted by the sound of Ack-Ack guns that were soon drowned out by the mechanical drone of Messerschmitts and Junkers.

During the war there were no streetlights, and people's homes were shrouded by thick black-out blinds, pulled down or across in advance of regular curtains being drawn at dusk, but the moon shone on the Thames, illuminating it like a beacon to guide the German Air Force into the heart of London and beyond.

Ena shivered as she remembered the Coventry Blitz. The engineering factory in Lowarth, where she had worked, was twelve miles south of the city, and on November 14th 1940, the day of the most devastating attack on Coventry, a stray bomb had fallen on the factory's boundary wall, exploding on impact and destroying part of the building. Fortunately, it was the only bomb to go astray.

The following day, Ena's boss asked her to take vital equipment to Bletchley Park in Buckinghamshire, and while travelling on the 9:45 train to

Bletchley, Ena had been drugged, and the top-secret disks and dials she was charged with delivering to Britain's top code-breaking centre were stolen. A feeling of terror ran through her as she remembered the danger she had been in. Under suspicion by those she was trying to help, she didn't know who to trust. Haunted by the robbery and the possibility she had been betrayed, and with her closest friends accused of being involved, she had begun her own investigation to prove her innocence.

The sounds of war echoed in her head and she put her hands over her ears and squeezed her eyes shut. It had been twenty-five years since the Second World War ended, yet the memories and her fear of the Blitz had never left her, had never left anyone who had lived through that terrifying time.

'Ena?'

Someone was tugging her arm. She took her hands from her ears and opened her eyes to see her friend Natalie Goldman, the owner of the Prince Albert Theatre, by her side. At that moment, the deafening sounds of war stopped and the house lights came on, illuminating the theatre's auditorium. The stage curtains began to open, and the show's director, Connor Wolf, jumped up from his seat and jogged down the centre aisle.

Taking the steps at the side of the orchestra pit two at a time, he shouted from the apron, 'Thank you, Sound! That's more like the level. What did you think, Joe?'

Joe Singer, the stage manager, appeared from the wings, stage right, and put up his thumb. 'Sounded good to me.'

Wolf looked to the back of the stalls, to the guys

in the sound box. Silhouetted in the beam of a spotlight, he put his hand up to his forehead to shade his eyes and shouted, 'If you're happy, Sound, mark that!'

'Got it,' called a voice in the darkness somewhere to Ena and Natalie's left.

Wolf brought his focus from the back of the auditorium to his assistant, who had remained seated several rows back from the stage. 'Make a note of that, Charlotte.'

'Will do,' she replied.

Hearing Charlotte's confident reply to Connor Wolf made Ena smile. Charlotte was her brother Tom and sister-in-law Annabel's daughter, and the oldest of her nieces. An intelligent young woman, she had studied English literature at university and was looking for a teaching job, but when the opportunity to work on a theatre project about her Aunt Margot's rise to fame in World War Two came up, she jumped at the chance. Working as assistant to Connor Wolf, who had an excellent reputation as a theatre director, was a dream come true for Charlotte.

A Tribute to Margot Dudley was quite the family affair, Ena thought. Almost all her nieces were involved. Nancy, Bess and Frank's girl, who also had a degree in English literature, had co-written *Tribute* with Georgina Derby Bloom, known as George, and her friend Betsy Evans. Both were Margot's friends, and both were part of the Prince Albert Theatre Company during the war. Margot and Bill's daughter Natalie, the youngest of Ena's nieces, had been educated while attending the Margot Dudley Dance Academy. Now seventeen, she was playing the part of Margot in the musical and, from what Ena had seen of

Natalie in rehearsals, she was as talented as her mother. The exception was Aimee, Claire and Mitch's daughter. She had spent the first five years of her life in France and had taken a year out of her job as a librarian to return and visit the family that brought her up while her mother, who was with the Resistance, looked for her father after he was imprisoned by the Gestapo.

'If we can build the sound to that level and maintain it, as we just did,' Wolf said, '*Tribute* will have a cracking opening.' He turned to Joe. 'We'll block the first act later.' Then he checked the time on his wristwatch. 'We're late for the company meeting. See you there,' he added, heading for the exit stage left before Joe could reply.

Charlotte grabbed his script before scooping up her own from the makeshift desk: a couple of lengths of wood attached to the backs of three seats, cobbled together by one of the chippies.

Ena followed Natalie Goldman along the walkway at the back of the auditorium, down the side aisle, and through the exit leading to the bar and box office. 'The meeting is in the visitors' room,' Natalie said, turning into the corridor where her office, the production office and the meeting rooms were located.

Ena knew the visitors' room well. When her husband Henry was accused of murdering a spy who was found dead in Ena's office in Covent Garden, her sisters Margot, Bess and Claire came down to London to support her. Margot and her oldest sister Bess had stayed with Natalie at her home in Hampstead, and Claire had stayed with Ena in her and Henry's flat in Stockwell, South London. They had met in the visitors' room to discuss what had happened and plan what they would do.

A wave of cold dread washed over Ena as she remembered Frieda Voight, the reason Henry had been arrested. Frieda was a spy who Ena believed was her colleague and friend in the war. She had come into Ena's life again with a vengeance, and when Ena exposed her, she killed herself. Frieda's death led to Helen Crowther, personal assistant to Henry's boss at MI5, killing herself and framing Henry for her death.

Ena had also been instrumental in capturing Director Richard Bentley, the top German agent and her boss at the Home Office. Bentley had recruited several German spies and promoted them to powerful political and military positions during the thirty years he'd been in a position of trust. At the time, what should have been a huge scandal had been hushed up. Eventually, Bentley was tried for treason, found guilty and hanged; the others had German passports and were imprisoned. Ena had been called as a witness for the prosecution at Dick Bentley's trial. Although the trial had taken place behind closed doors, the newspapers got hold of the story, after which Ena kept her head down, first spending time with her family in the Midlands, and then staying at home with her husband. She had enjoyed it at first, but being a housewife wasn't enough for her. Sick of lies and bureaucracy, Henry left MI5 and went to work for GCHQ, and Ena set up her own investigating agency, Dudley Green Associates.

CHAPTER TWO

Ena felt a chill run through her as she entered the visitors' room. The ghosts of war, she thought, and shivered.

The father of Margot's dancer friend George Derby Bloom ran a network of people who helped Jewish students to escape Nazi Germany via Geneva, where George had been at finishing school, and the visitors' room had been a place of safety for them. Transported in a variety of vehicles, they were taken from Switzerland to France and then across the English Channel by boat. Once in England, they were given food and shelter before embarking on the journey from Dover to London. While they waited for new passports and travel permits, they worked in the theatre's wardrobe department, backstage, in the chorus as singers, or as statues in friezes, posing as Egyptian Gods or Greek maidens.

Young people came and went all the time in the theatre. No sooner had a new dresser, stagehand, cleaner or seamstress got the hang of the job than they would be called up, so new faces were an everyday occurrence and didn't cause comment. At first, students stayed with the Goldman family, but once the children and their nanny had been evacuated to Foxden Hall with Bess and the land girls, the smallest chink of light showing through the curtains of their supposedly empty house in Hampstead would have invited questions.

'Here we are,' Natalie said, as she waited for Ena, who had dawdled to look at the photographs of famous artists from the war years that lined the walls of the corridor.

At that moment, Natalie's secretary, Hilda, dashed out of her office. Flustered, her eyes widened as she said, 'Mrs Goldman, the foreman from the Young Albert Theatre would like to speak to you. I've put him in your office.'

'There must be a problem. Did he say what it was?' Natalie asked.

Hilda shook her head. 'He said he had tried to telephone you from the telephone box near the theatre but couldn't get through.'

Turning towards her office, Natalie stopped and looked back at Hilda. 'Telephone box?' she said. 'Why didn't he use one of the telephones at the Young Albert?'

'He said the telephones at the theatre aren't in service yet, and, as he can't work, he thought he'd better come to see you in person.'

'Can't work? That sounds ominous. I'd better see him and find out what's going on. You go to the meeting with Ena. Tell Connor to start without me. I'll catch up with him later.' Natalie took a notebook from her briefcase and opened it a few pages from the beginning. 'Everything he needs to know from me is in here. When you've told him what's in place so far, take notes for me, will you, Hilda? I shouldn't be long. Whatever the problem is, I expect it will be easily sorted.'

Natalie left to go to her office, and Hilda tapped on the meeting room door. A voice shouted, 'Come in.' She opened the door and stood to one side to let Ena enter first. They took the only two empty seats at the large oval conference table. Ena caught the eye of her sister Bess's daughter Nancy, and Margot's friends, George Derby Bloom and Betsy Evans, and smiled. She was there to observe and advise if she was asked about her sister's life when she was a child and when she worked as a dancer during the war. She hoped she wasn't asked too many questions. Ena knew all about Margot's childhood, but when Margot was dancing in the West End, Ena was working in an engineering factory she only knew as Station X, making secret components for Bletchley Park. It wasn't until later that she discovered it was the central location of British code-breaking operations during the war. With Ena working in Lowarth and Bletchley, and Margot working in London, they rarely saw each other. Now crippled with arthritis, Margot was no longer able to dance and Ena felt guilty and regretted not seeing her sister perform in her heyday.

She looked around the table. The Dudley sisters had once been so close, but during the war years, when Margot was in London, Natalie, George and Betsy knew her best. Not only had they worked as dancers with Margot in the theatre, but they had joined the Entertainments National Service Association (ENSA) with her, touring aerodromes and army camps to entertain British troops, and later entertaining American armed forces personnel. And it was Natalie who looked after Margot when, exhausted and addicted to prescription drugs, she had a breakdown.

There had been heated discussions about the scene where Margot made her debut performance at the Prince Albert Theatre. Two versions had been written. One was a funny sketch where cheeky, ambitious Margot learned all the songs and dances and took her chance when one of the dancers was called up. The truth was, Margot had taken a dancer's place on stage after her Nazi boyfriend had beaten her so badly she wasn't able to walk, let alone dance. While Margot sang and danced as Goldie Trick, Natalie and Anton Goldman looked after the young Irish dancer. By the time her boyfriend Dave Sutherland realised it wasn't Goldie on stage, she was safely in Ireland with her family.

Ena had agreed with Natalie that there was no need to shine a spotlight on Goldie's tragic story, but Connor Wolf, as the show's director, said it was an important part of Margot's rise to fame. Performing every night, knowing she was helping someone escape an abusive relationship while putting her own life in danger, showed strength of character and bravery on Margot's part. Without the tragedy that befell Goldie Trick, Margot may never have been the sensation she was. Everyone agreed that both scenes should be rehearsed, and the decision of which would be performed in the show would be made nearer to opening night.

Idly, Ena sketched a pair of stage curtains and a spotlight and wrote "Margot" in her notebook. For as long as she could remember, her sister had wanted to be a dancer. She smiled as she remembered how, on Saturday mornings when the village children played down in the brook, paddling in the shallow water and scooping up minnows and catfish in their hands, Margot would be at home doing jobs around the house for a farthing or a ha'penny.

Bess and Claire, older than Margot and Ena, often

worked at Foxden Hall, where Lord and Lady Foxden hosted autumn and winter balls, garden parties in the summer, and a grand New Year's Eve party. Because the Dudley girls' father, Tom, was Lord Foxden's head groom, their mother was called upon to work in the kitchen at big events and Bess and Claire were often asked to work as waitresses. They always gave Margot a penny out of their wages to add to her chore money. She hid it until she had sixpence, and then spent it on dance lessons at the village hall.

CHAPTER THREE

Margot, or Margaret as she was then, was the first of the Dudley sisters to get married. The summer of 1939 was one of the hottest on record, and July 1st, the day Margaret married her sweetheart Bill Burrell at Mysterton Church, was no exception.

Bill had had scarlet fever as a child. He didn't pass any of the armed forces medicals and couldn't join up but, because he was an experienced motorcyclist with a clean licence, Lord Foxden thought he would make a good special courier for the MOD in London. Even before war was declared, Bill was taking confidential and sensitive documents from the Ministry of Defence in Whitehall to top-secret locations all over England.

It was during a traditional Sunday afternoon, after tea, when the Dudley family gathered in the front room to tell each other their news, that Margaret made her announcement. 'I'm going to live in London with Bill.'

Margaret's mother was horrified. 'Being the capital, it'll be the first place the Germans bomb. You're not going to London. It's not safe!'

'What about your job?' her father asked.

'I've handed in my notice. I'll get another job when I get to London.' Margaret planned to work in a theatre, and the first place she would try was the Prince Albert. She'd heard about the theatre from her older sister Bess, who was a friend of the owners, Natalie and Anton Goldman.

Margaret got her way, as she usually did, and within a few weeks she moved to London. When she got a job as an usherette, she and Bill agreed that when the war ended, they would return to Lowarth, settle down and start a family. But when the time came, Margaret Burrell had become Margot Dudley and she did not want to give up her life in London, or her career as a West End star.

When Bill left London to find them a house in the Midlands, Margot was already drinking heavily. Eventually, she became unstable. The fear of losing what she had worked so hard for made her work even harder and push herself more. After performing on stage every night, she sang at the Prince Albert Club. She was burning herself out, and it was Natalie Goldman who looked after her when she suffered a breakdown.

Natalie saved Margot's life. Not only was Margot dependent on alcohol, which Natalie weaned her off, but she was addicted to sleeping pills. She took pills to go to sleep at night and pills to get up in the morning. Again, Natalie got Margot the help she needed by having her hospitalised. Yes, Ena thought, Natalie knew Margot better than anyone.

Natalie and her late husband Anton had also been good to Ena's oldest sister, Bess. They helped her when she'd had her handbag stolen on the train from Rugby to Euston while at teacher training college, and again when she was assaulted by a Nazi sympathiser who, two years later, beat up Goldie. But Bess was not in London when Margot was at the Prince Albert Theatre. Shortly after the war started, the school where she taught closed, the children were evacuated, and Bess returned to Foxden, where she and a team of land girls turned Foxden Estate into arable land.

Claire couldn't have seen much of Margot, either. She joined the WAAF, was recruited by the SOE, and was sent overseas. Ena found out some years after the war ended that Claire had been in France, where she met Mitch, her husband. It was possible that Claire had spent time in London, Ena mused, but if she had, she wouldn't have seen Margot.

Ena was the only sister who lived at home during the war, as the engineering factory in Lowarth where she had worked was only a couple of miles from Woodcote. She had met Henry, her husband, while taking components to Bletchley Park. Ena smiled to herself as she remembered how Henry and her sister Bess had walked out when they were young. Although she had known Henry Green for years, it took a war to bring them together.

After the war, her sisters went home to the Midlands and settled down, while Ena and Henry left to work and live in London. By then Ena, the youngest of the Dudley sisters, the little factory girl, was no stranger to top-secret information, espionage and spies. Her sisters did exciting work in the war, but so did she. No one knew about what she had done for Bletchley Park, and they probably never would. And since then, she had been a spy catcher. Who would have thought it?

Ena felt Hilda, Natalie's secretary, nudge her. She had been miles away, thinking about the lives she and her sisters had led during the war. She looked up. The meeting had begun.

'Thank you for coming at short notice, ladies and

gentlemen.' The artistic director, Connor Wolf, ran his fingers through his thick hair, pushing a lock off his forehead, before stretching out his arms. 'The opening music has the right atmospheric feel and the sound effects, the planes, guns, bombs... Well,' he said excitedly, 'everything that goes with the blitzing of London in forty-two has been replicated, and it sounds pretty authentic. So,' he looked around the table, 'can anyone bring me up to speed with what else is happening?' He looked at Hilda. 'Is Natalie not joining us?' As the owner of the theatre, Wolf was being respectful by asking her first.

'Natalie has been called into a meeting, but I have her notes.' Hilda cleared her throat and began to read. 'On the first night of *Tribute*, Natalie will be on duty at the Young Albert all day. The front-of-house staff will be on duty from three o'clock to cater for early arrivals. Because people will be coming from all over the country, there are bound to be some who have come straight from the transport that brought them to London, so the bar will also open early.' She paused and looked down at the notes. 'No time is given.' She carried on. 'The staff will double-check that they have enough of everything. Natalie has ordered champagne for opening night and the first night party at The Albert Club.'

Rebekah Goldman, the theatre's company manager, turned to Hilda. 'Do we know how many people to expect at the Albert Club after the show?'

'I understand your mother has the names of everyone who has replied to the invitations. The list is in her office. I'll ask her to let you know.'

As company manager, Rebekah worked with everyone involved in putting on the production. She was the link between the theatre management, which in this case was her mother, helped by her brothers Benjamin and Samuel, and the company – the artists, director, and stage management.

'Is stage management ready for opening night? Joe?' Rebekah looked across the table.

'Yes, ready. I'll be on the book for every rehearsal from now on. Backstage ready?' Joe gave his assistant stage manager, Lilian Truman, a questioning look.

'Ready. The space we have to work in has been marked out on the stage here, so the artists can get used to it.' Lilian bit her lip. 'We hope to get into the Young Albert to do the final tech and dress rehearsal. The backstage crew, stagehands, carpenters, electricians and technicians are all set.' She consulted a list. 'Props, scenery, lighting and sound are all good to go,' she announced with certainty. It was only the second time she had been Joe's assistant stage manager at The Prince Albert Theatre and she was nervous. She had no reason to be – she was good at her job – but, as Joe Singer's right hand, she needed to be.

'Wardrobe is on standby in case there are any alterations,' Rose Allen, the wardrobe mistress, put in.

'We're blocking today, Rose. I don't want the artists in costume,' Wolf said.

'Which is why *I* said wardrobe is on *standby*!' Rose replied, bristling. 'You know costumes aren't taken to the artists' dressing rooms until the dress rehearsal. And I'm hoping, as we all are, that the dress rehearsal will be at the Young Albert.'

CHAPTER FOUR

After the spat between the director and wardrobe mistress, everyone fell silent. It seemed to Ena that there was a mutual dislike between Connor Wolf and Rose Allen. She wondered why, and whether they'd known each other before they began working on *Tribute*. The theatre industry was a small world. Everyone knew everyone, especially those who worked in London's West End, and it was likely they had worked together at an earlier time in another theatre. Both sounded bruised, as if something or someone had hurt one or the other of them before they joined the Prince Albert Theatre Company.

Wolf looked away from Rose and focused on Rebekah Goldman. 'Music?'

Rebekah gave Charlotte Dudley a warm smile. 'I've called the orchestra in for 12 o'clock,' Charlotte said. Rebekah looked across the table at Wolf and raised her eyebrows, seeking confirmation without asking.

'Twelve is fine. Thanks, Charlotte, Rebekah.' Looking around the table again, Wolf said, 'Is there anything else?'

'Just one thing,' Hilda said, turning the page of Natalie's notebook and then looking up. She waited until she had everyone's attention but directed the question at Rose Allen. 'Natalie has provisionally booked the theatre transport company to take the costumes to the Young Albert in advance of the dress rehearsal.' She ran her finger down the page. 'She will need to give the company three days' notice.'

'Hopefully we can let her know five days in advance,' Wolf said.

'Thank you, Hilda,' Rose said, sighing.

Hilda made a note on the removal company's timeline. She smiled again at Rose but didn't look at Wolf.

'Right! Any other business?' After mutterings of no, and not at the moment, Wolf said, 'Is everyone happy?' Except for Rose, the theatre company members were smiling, and the collective answer came in a loud and excited, 'Yes!'

'Then take an hour, people.' Consulting his wristwatch, Wolf looked at Rebekah and, taking in Joe and Lilian, said, 'Everyone on stage to block the opening scene at twelve.' He left the visitors' room with Charlotte.

Stacking the pages of his script, Joe picked up his notepad. 'See you in an hour, everyone.' He left the room, followed by Lilian.

'Ena?' George called, as she got up to leave. 'Betsy and I are going to have a sandwich in the green room. We'll be there in ten minutes. Why don't you join us?'

'Thank you, I'd love to. I'll see you in there.'

'Aunt Ena?' Nancy threw her arms around Ena.

'Nancy! How are you? Are you enjoying writing?'

'I'm well, thank you. And yes, the script of *Tribute* is really coming together.'

'How do you like being in London?'

'It's great. I loved living in London when I was at

college but working here – well, sort of – it's even better. I loved every minute of working on the script with George and Betsy. It's more about watching rehearsals and taking notes now, but it's still exciting. The show is going to be spectacular. Aunt Margot will be blown away when she sees how our Natalie portrays her. I didn't realise how good Natalie was until I saw her in rehearsal. Aunt Margot will love everything about the show.'

'I'm sure she will,' Ena said. 'And what an accolade; a musical to celebrate her life in theatre during the war, and in a brand-new theatre.'

'A theatre in London's East End for underprivileged young people who want to be actors, singers and dancers,' Nancy added. 'I can't think of anything better. The scenery dock is vast. It could hold the scenery for dozens of plays. I'm going to suggest that the space beneath the stage – the trap room that was used to elevate artists in the days of the music hall, and is now a storeroom – is used for workshops.'

'So, you've already been down to the Young Albert?'

'Yes, several times. The stage is a different size, it's wider and not as deep as the stage here, so I work with stage management to make sure the artists stay within their lines. Have you been there yet, Aunt Ena?'

'No, not yet.'

'You must go down. It's going to be amazing when it's finished. It's very modern. The main auditorium, the Dudley Bloom theatre, is huge. It's as big as any of the West End theatres. And because it was an old music hall there are lots of dressing rooms. The front of house – box office and foyer, part of the main auditorium and the Margot Dudley Studio – were badly damaged when the street was bombed in the Blitz, but the dressing rooms, green room, theatre bar and the stage door area survived.

'The Margot Dudley studio was originally two large rooms where comics did matinees for children. Someone said they held socials in the rooms, whatever they were.' Nancy's face lit up. 'The studio is unique. Very special. One day, I want to write a play for the studio, a modern, down-to-earth play, you know, a play about real people, working-class people. It might even be a bit raw, something the people of Whitechapel can relate to. The West End has glamour, the East End has grit!'

'Is that what you want to do?' Ena enquired.

'Yes, it is. Until I worked with George and Besty, I wasn't sure what I wanted. I've always written, but I hadn't decided what I wanted to write about. And I have always secretly wanted to work in theatre in some capacity, but after co-writing *Tribute*, I know now that I want to write musicals and plays.'

'Theatre is in your blood, love.'

'I expect it is.' Nancy pulled a comical face. 'I don't want to be a dancer. I don't have the passion for it. Nor do I have the talent; I'll leave dancing and singing to my cousin Natalie. She's a natural.'

'Natalie is her mother's daughter, that's for sure!' Ena said.

'Connor Wolf says she's perfect as Margot in *Tribute*.' Nancy checked her watch. 'Oh, I had better get a move on. I'm fed up with tea, so I'm going to get a milkshake and a sandwich from the café next door. I don't want to be late for the band rehearsal at twelve.'

Kissing her niece goodbye, Ena set off to the green room.

19

CHAPTER FIVE

'Ena?'

Ena looked round to see Natalie Goldman coming out of her office. 'Natalie, you look worried. What is it?'

'I need to speak to you.' Natalie caught up with Ena. Taking her by the arm, she steered her back along the corridor. Opening the door to the theatre manager's office, she stood back for Ena to enter. 'Take a seat, I won't be a minute,' she said, turning on her heels and leaving.

Ena heard her knocking on the next door along the corridor, where Hilda worked.

'Hilda isn't there,' Natalie said, returning with the notebook her secretary had been writing in during the meeting. She crossed the room to her desk. Before sitting down, she said, 'Did I miss anything by not being at the meeting?'

Ena struggled to remember. 'It was mostly technical stuff, for sound and stage management. They agreed on rehearsal times with the orchestra, and that was about it.'

'If that's all, I won't bother checking in with Connor.' Natalie sank into her chair, put the notebook on her blotter and took a long breath. 'Ena, we have a problem at The Young Albert, and I need your professional help.'

'Of course, Natalie, anything,' Ena said. 'What

can I do?'

'Their sound system has been stolen. It wasn't delivered until late yesterday afternoon; it hadn't even been unpacked.'

Before Ena had time to reply, there was a tap on the door, and Hilda entered. 'I'm glad you found the notebook,' she said. 'I was at the stage door, signing for the champagne you ordered for the first night of *Tribute*. Stan's going to get someone to take it up to dressing room seven. I thought it best to keep it here after the robbery at the Young Albert.'

'Thank you, Hilda. It will be safe here.'

'I'm popping to the green room to get a sandwich. Can I get you anything?' Hilda asked, looking from Natalie to Ena.

'Just a coffee for me,' Natalie said.

'Mrs Green?'

Ena nodded. 'I'd like the same, please.'

'So,' Natalie said, when Hilda had gone, 'what the hell are we going to do? It cost more than three thousand pounds.'

Ena's eyes widened. She had no idea about the cost of these things. 'You're insured?'

'Of course, but with that amount of money at stake, there's bound to be an investigation. Even if they do agree to pay out, it won't be before opening night, and there isn't enough money in the Young Albert account to replace the system in the interim.'

'Does George know?'

'No. I haven't had time to tell her, and I don't want to, yet. You're the first person I've told.'

'You're going to have to tell her if it isn't found soon.'

Natalie sighed loudly. 'I know. It's so damn

annoying. The building work is finished. Both theatres, the Derby Bloom auditorium and the Margot Dudley Studio are ready for performances but for a few basic fixtures and fittings. The last time I was down there, the stage curtains in the auditorium were waiting to be hung, and the wall lights needed putting up.' She was close to tears.

'How many people are still working in the building?' Ena asked.

'Only a handful of men. What I don't understand is how anyone could steal something as big as a sound system without being seen.'

There was a knock on the door, and Hilda entered with three cups of coffee on a tray. She put Natalie and Ena's coffee in front of them. 'I'll write up the notes of this morning's meeting.' She put out her hand, and Natalie gave her the notepad. 'Unless you need me…'

'No, it's fine, Hilda. We're discussing the theft at the Young Albert. I'll tell you what we decide later. Thanks for the coffee.'

Hilda tutted and shook her head. 'You know where I am,' she said, leaving with her coffee and closing the door behind her.

Ena took a sip of her coffee to give Hilda time to return to her office. Except for the short time she had spent with her in Connor Wolf's progress meeting, Ena didn't know her. She knew she was Natalie's secretary, and as such, the last thing Ena wanted to do was offend her, but it was imperative that she ask the question. 'Natalie, do you trust Hilda?'

'Yes, a hundred per cent. This place would grind to a halt without her. Hilda was Anton's secretary. They worked together very closely. Hilda was with him when he had his heart attack.'

'I didn't know.'

'She blamed herself for not realising he was unwell.' Natalie shook her head slowly. 'It happened so quickly, there was nothing she or anyone else could have done. When Anton died, Hilda was heartbroken.'

'So, you kept her on?'

'It was more a case of me convincing her to stay. As you know, I was the front-of-house manager. I didn't have a secretary; I didn't need one, but taking over Anton's job as theatre manager – running the theatre, booking the shows, doing the paperwork, making sure everyone was paid on time, the tax was paid as well as staff benefits – I needed help.'

'And Hilda was the obvious choice.'

'She's an intelligent woman, and having worked so closely with Anton, she knew everything there was to know about running the theatre. So, I persuaded her to be my secretary.'

'And what does she know about the Young Albert Theatre?' Ena took a pen and notebook from her bag and began to write.

'Everything there is to know. She's been with me every step of the way. I'm not sure how much Ben Wilson, the Young Albert's works foreman, told her about the theft.' Natalie put her head in her hands and sighed. 'He had been trying to get hold of me since first thing this morning.'

'Why didn't he telephone you from the Young Albert?'

'The phones have gone missing.'

Ena made a note. 'You obviously need telephones, but they can be replaced cheaply. A sound system can't.'

'No. At best, opening night will be delayed. At

worst–'

'Don't think about the worst scenario. Artie and I will find them. Have there been other thefts?'

Natalie shook her head and sat back in her chair. 'Ben said he didn't think the telephones had been delivered, so he got in touch with the telephone company, who said they had not only been delivered, but they had also been signed for.'

'Signed for by who?'

'Ben Wilson! But it wasn't his signature. Oh, and a box of lightbulbs went missing early on, but the thefts were so far apart he put it down to petty pilfering and didn't give any more work to a couple of casual workers that were there at the time.'

'It sounds to me as if the telephones and lightbulbs were pilfered. The sound system, however, was not. We need someone we trust over there. How well do you know the foreman? Do you trust him?'

'I didn't know him at all before I interviewed him for the job to oversee the building work.'

'But you know him now?' Ena pressed. Natalie nodded. 'And you trust him?'

'Yes. He hasn't given me a reason not to trust him. Stan, the stage doorman, has known him for years, and I've got to know him while he's been working at the Young Albert. I've seen him every Friday since giving him the job. He keeps a weekly timesheet. Puts down the men's hours and how much they've earned against their names. He gives me a copy on Fridays, and I put the men's wages into wage packets. He also gives me a list of who is booked in to work the following week, which is a lot shorter now that the work is almost finished.'

'Without these delays, would work on the theatre

have finished by now?'

'As I said, a few small things still need to be done, but as soon as the sound system had been fitted and was up and running, the cleaners would be in, and the theatre could potentially open. So yes.'

'Do you think whoever is stealing could be doing it to delay the opening of the theatre?'

'I suppose they could be, but why would they?'

'I don't know yet,' Ena said, frowning thoughtfully.

'I go to the East End every month for a progress meeting with Ben. I'm impressed with the work he and the men have done. What was an old bombed-out music hall is now a modern theatre. He has done an excellent job.' Natalie looked sincere.

'That's good.' As much as Ena respected Natalie, she wouldn't take her word for it; she would go down to the Young Albert and find out for herself how trustworthy Ben Wilson was.

'You don't look convinced, Ena.'

'Sorry, Natalie, it's my suspicious mind. I'm sure you're right about Ben.'

'I hope I am. I've always found him to be decent, hardworking and honest. He told me about the telephones, the lightbulbs and the sound system as soon as the thefts happened.'

'I don't know him, but I trust your judgment. However, I don't think we should tell him any more than he needs to know.'

CHAPTER SIX

Natalie agreed that the fewer people who knew about the thefts, the less chance there was of putting the thief on alert.

'Do you mind telling me everything Ben Wilson told you about the theft of the sound system?' Ena asked her.

Natalie thought for a moment, then lifted and dropped her shoulders. 'Ben said when he arrived at work this morning, a window in the cellar was open. The decorators store their paint down there, and he thought maybe one of them had opened it at some time for ventilation because of paint fumes. The boxes the sound system arrived in hadn't been opened yet, so he thinks the thieves got in through the window, had a look around, got lucky, picked up the boxes and walked out of the theatre's main entrance with them.'

'Did someone leave the front door unlocked?'

'No, Ben keeps a spare set of keys in his desk.'

'And were they missing?'

'No, but they were in a different place. Ben keeps them hidden at the back of the drawer. He thinks one of the thieves must have used the keys to unlock the door, and another of them put the keys back before leaving the way they came in, through the cellar window.'

'In which case, they must have known where the spare keys were kept.'

'Or, as Ben said, they were lucky.'

Ena wrote "Ben Wilson" at the top of the next page in her notebook. 'Who signed for the sound system when it was delivered?'

'Ben did,' Natalie said. 'As the foreman, Ben signs for everything, unless he's out of the building, and the only time he's likely to be out is when he's up here on Fridays. On this occasion, the delivery was so late in the afternoon that most of the men had left for the day.'

'Most of the men? Do you know who was still at the theatre when the system arrived?'

'No, but I can ask Ben.'

'Okay, thanks,' Ena said. 'So, how many men have been working at the Young Albert?'

'I'm not sure. A lot are casual workers. When the work started, skilled and unskilled men were on site. Some casual workers were employed on a daily basis, others for two or three days at a time, depending on the job. Most of the skilled men were employed on a permanent basis. Some were contracted to do specific jobs. The numbers changed from week to week depending on the work needing to be done. At the beginning of the project, a demolition company, Howson Crawley, was brought in to demolish the unsafe part of the theatre. Once the building work started, there were bricklayers, roofers, plasterers and glaziers on site most days, but they've been finished for some months.'

'Can you tell me exactly when they finished?' Ena asked.

Natalie opened a drawer on the left of her desk and took out a stack of pay sheets containing the names and addresses of the employees. 'The carpenters were there recently, modernising the sound box.' She sighed heavily. 'I can't believe after all the work that's been done to rebuild and refurbish the theatre, we may not be able to open on time.'

There was nothing Ena could say to stop her friend from worrying until she had all the facts. 'Natalie. Who has been paid recently?'

'Sorry, Ena. Where was I?' she said, running her finger along the names and dates on the pay sheets. 'The final payday for the carpenters was last Friday. The glaziers two weeks before that, but the plasterers, bricklayers and roofers–' She took out another paysheet. 'It's been a couple of months since the builders were there. Ben will have details of the men employed by Howson Crawley. If he hasn't, he can tell you the dates they started work and when they finished. He keeps records of everything; I expect he has copies. There are still decorators painting the dressing rooms and offices and a couple of electricians waiting to fit the sound system.' Natalie inhaled deeply. 'We can't afford to have them sitting around drinking tea all day, but without the sound system to fit...' She shrugged her shoulders.

'Can I borrow the list of employees?'

'You can have a copy. Hilda will have one on file. She makes carbon copies of every document she types. She's nothing if she isn't thorough.'

Jumping up from her chair, Natalie left the room. Minutes later, she returned with a sheet of paper containing the names of all the men employed at the Young Albert from the first day of work to the previous Friday.

'Thank you,' Ena said. She was interested in the carpenters in the last couple of weeks and the electricians who were still there. She read down the list of names. Some had given addresses, but most had notes by their names saying, "Casual Labourer". Some were for one week, others for two. The list included Ben Wilson, site manager and foreman, who was listed as permanent.

'One of these names belongs to our thief–'

'Or thieves,' Natalie added.

Maybe, Ena thought.

'It won't be easy for them to sell something as big and expensive as a sound system down Portobello Road market,' Natalie said.

'No... which could work in our favour. Who would want a theatre sound system?'

'Besides another theatre, I don't know. Maybe a ballroom or a cinema.'

Ena thought for a second. 'I have an idea.'

Leaning her elbows on her desk, eyes wide, Natalie was eager to hear what Ena had to say. 'Go on!'

'Do you think Ben Wilson would give my colleague, Artie Mallory, a job at the Young Albert?'

'I'm sure he would. He doesn't need any more labour at the moment, but I'll get Hilda to go down there and explain who Artie is and why he will be there. I'll telephone you, let you know what Ben says.'

'It's a shame you can't telephone Ben. The fewer people who know about Artie, the better.'

Natalie leaned back in her chair. 'Ena, I trust Hilda.'

'Yes, I'm sorry, I know you do. And I'm sure you have every reason to trust her. I'm sorry, Natalie. Of course, Hilda is trustworthy. I'm overthinking. I do that when I have my suspicious hat on.' Natalie trusted her secretary, but Ena didn't trust anyone until she knew everything there was to know about them. 'The foreman will need a reason to take Artie on, so the other men don't get suspicious.' She got up to leave.

'Leave it to me, Ena. Ben knows the importance of finding the thief.'

'Good. If he agrees to give Artie a job, and Artie plays a wide-boy, a Jack-the-lad character, he might find out who's behind the thefts. And while he's at the theatre, I'll go down and meet Ben and have a look around to see where the building is vulnerable. I'll take a walk around the area, too, and see if any of the local musical instrument shops know anything about sound systems. You never know, someone might sell second-hand systems.'

'They won't sell them, Ena. Sound systems are made to order. The speakers alone are six feet tall, and the mixing desk is made to accommodate however many turntables and recorders each theatre needs.'

'How long will it take for the company to make another system?'

Natalie blew out her cheeks. 'I don't know for sure. Two weeks, three... Longer than we've got unless I can pull in a few favours – and find the money. It won't be easy to raise three thousand pounds. I'll telephone Strand Electrics, the company that made the system, and ask if they can build a replacement. If they can, I'll ask if they could build it in time for opening night.' She sighed. 'More importantly, how much will a duplicate system cost?'

'Does it have to be an exact duplicate? Wouldn't a smaller, less expensive system be good enough?'

'Maybe. I'll talk to Strand. We need loudspeakers on either side of the proscenium arch. It's a big auditorium,' she said. 'I don't think we'd get away with fewer than four speakers. Then there's the sound desk itself. We need a mixing desk with at least three recorders and turntables. There's music for the show, of course, and for the audience when they come into the auditorium and again for the intervals – and then there's front of house and the bar. I don't see how we can get away with fewer than three. I'll ask the designer at Strand. You never know, he might come up with an alternative.'

'It's worth a try.'

'It is. Leave it with me.'

'I know it's a long shot,' Ena said, 'but it can't hurt to have a look around a few music outlets, make a few enquiries. Someone might have heard of a second-hand, or, in this case, a new sound system for sale.' She glanced at her watch. 'I'd better go; I promised George and Betsy I'd catch up with them. They are going to be in the green room.'

'Give me two minutes to ask Hilda to go down to the Young Albert, and I'll come with you,' Natalie said, putting her notebook in the drawer and following Ena out of her office.

CHAPTER SEVEN

'Nancy not with you, Ena?' George asked when Ena was seated at a table in the green room with a sandwich and a cup of coffee.

'I saw her after the meeting. She said she was going to the café next door to get something to eat before going to the band rehearsal at noon.'

'She usually joins us. Oh well,' George said, 'we'll discuss anything relevant with her later. Nancy is a hard worker. Her contribution to the script of *Tribute* has been invaluable.'

Ena was delighted to hear George compliment her niece. 'From what she said, she would like to be involved in the Young Albert when it's up and running.'

'We'd like that too, wouldn't we, George?' Betsy said.

'Yes, very much. I'll talk to her after *Tribute* has opened, tell her what's on offer, ask her what she'd like to do, and take it from there.' She turned her attention to Natalie. 'You weren't at the meeting. Would you like us to fill you in?'

'No!' Natalie said, abruptly. 'Ena gave me a breakdown, and I have Hilda's notes.'

George looked at Natalie questioningly. 'There isn't a problem, is there?'

'No. Ben Wilson arrived as I was leaving the office with an update on the work at the Young Albert.

As he'd come to see me, I thought I'd better say hello.'
Smiling at Ena for confirmation, she opened Hilda's
notebook. 'I was surprised to see a date was agreed for
the costumes to be taken to the Young Albert for the
dress and technical rehearsal.'

'Eventually,' George said.

'It was a bit fraught, but at least they agreed on
something,' Betsy added.

'They haven't got on for as long I've known
them,' George said.

Betsy shook her head in agreement.

'Wolf and Rose talking to each other,' Natalie
said to Ena, 'is a first.'

'How long has Rose been the wardrobe mistress
here?' Ena asked her.

'Since Miss Lesley retired, so…' Natalie thought
for a moment, 'it's coming up for ten years.'

'And Wolf?'

It was George who answered. 'Connor Wolf was
brought in to direct *Tribute*. He hasn't worked at the
Prince Albert before.'

'I've been watching him. He's a great director,'
Natalie said. 'A little brusque sometimes…'

'Which he was today.'

'So was Rose.'

'What's the story with those two?' Ena asked,
looking from George to Natalie. 'They obviously have
history.'

'I heard, but don't quote me in case it isn't true,'
George said, 'that they worked together twelve, fifteen
years ago when Rose was a budding actress. Connor
was the director of a show she was in. It opened at
Theatr Clwyd in Mold, was there for four weeks, and
did the rounds before going to the Palace Theatre in

Manchester for two weeks. The Palace was the last venue on the tour before the show transferred to the West End.'

'Except it didn't,' Betsy put in. 'Well, it transferred, but it didn't get as far as the opening night.'

'Why?' Ena asked.

'Again, this is only what I heard, but Wolf and Rose had an affair on the tour.'

'I think it was more than an affair!' Betsy said.

George nodded. 'It often happens with leading ladies and their directors, or with actors and actresses. They spend a lot of time together, running lines and rehearsing.'

'It's because they work so closely,' Betsy added.

George nodded, and smiled at Betsy. 'They did their best to keep the affair a secret, but you know what theatres are like for gossip.'

'What happened?' Ena asked, turning to Betsy. 'You said the show came into London, but it didn't open.'

'No, it didn't. A week into rehearsals, the notice went up, and that was that. It closed before it opened. Someone working on it told one of the dancers at the Prince Albert that the show had money problems. They said the backers didn't think it was West End material and pulled out.'

'Was it? West End material?' Ena asked Natalie.

'Oh yes. It was modern and very classy. A very stylish musical revue with some hugely talented artists in it.'

'And Rose was one of them?'

'Yes, she was the leading lady, and hugely talented. Apart from Margot, she was the best dancer I have ever seen grace a stage. The show was sold out well in advance in all the provincial theatres. Producers and managers were queuing up to take it. *The Stage* gave the show a fantastic review and hinted that it was going elsewhere after six weeks in the West End. Although they couldn't print the destination because it hadn't been officially confirmed, they knew, as everyone did, that the producers were taking it to New York. It was going to open on Broadway.'

'It couldn't have closed because of lack of money if American producers were interested in it! So, what happened?'

'No one knows. There was a lot of speculation, but...' Natalie looked at George.

George shook her head and scrunched up her shoulders. 'I don't know. I heard, and again, please don't quote me, but because Rose had been predicted to be the next big name in the West End – and, possibly, on Broadway – the London producers wouldn't collaborate with American producers, and as they couldn't do it themselves, they shut the show down. The newspapers did some digging after the show closed. No one knows how they found out Rose had been seeing Wolf, but they chased her down to her parents' house in the West Country. The papers reported that a source close to Miss Allen said that Rose was told by her lover, the director of the show, that she wasn't good enough to go to Broadway and she had walked out on opening night. Total lies. Rose didn't walk out; she went home to the West Country after the closing notice went up. One of the rags said Rose had gone home to her parents to recover from a broken heart.'

'Someone must have tipped off the newspapers

about their affair,' Ena said.

'Betsy and I did wonder if someone had leaked the affair to the papers, but why make up a cruel story like Rose not being good enough to go with the show to New York?'

'Maybe someone blamed Rose for the show closing, for it not going to New York?'

'Who knows? In the end, we decided that no one could blame Rose for the show not transferring because she lost out as well as the rest of the cast. Maybe the papers had put two and two together and come up with four, for once.'

'About exhaustion and a broken heart, yes – but not that he told her she wasn't good enough to go to New York. That was a lie,' Betsy said.

'Anyway,' George continued, 'Rose didn't come back to London, and in early September, Terence Rattigan's play *The Browning Version* premiered in place of the revue, and Connor Wolf went back to Manchester to direct a Noel Coward play. I can't remember which one it was. It isn't important now anyway.'

'If it had only been the red-tops that reported on Wolf and Rose being lovers, I think Rose would have eventually resumed her career, but the Sunday after the opening night of *The Browning Version*, the *News of the World* raked up the story again with the headline "Star-crossed Lovers". I think that's what determined Rose to give up dancing and stay out of the limelight.'

'They destroyed her career.'

Ena shook her head. 'Anything to sell papers!'

'It's big news when one half of a pair of potential stars goes north and the other south. It usually means that particular song has been sung, and the show is over.'

'And now Rose is working in theatre as a wardrobe mistress,' Ena said. 'If she was as talented as you say, it's a shame she gave up her career. I suppose she's too old to dance now, but perhaps one day she'll resume her acting career.'

'I doubt it,' Natalie said. 'She's a well-respected wardrobe mistress. We design all the Prince Albert's costumes together. She's not only one of the best costume designers I know, she's also an amazing cutter. She'd be in demand in the West End if she didn't work here. I know theatre managers who would give their back teeth to have her design costumes for their shows.' She paused for a moment, then continued. 'I hope we never lose her. She's a real asset.'

'Everyone loves working with her. The dressers especially,' Betsy added.

'I hope Connor hasn't upset her,' George said. 'We can't afford to lose her if we're going to get *Tribute* on in time for the twenty-fifth anniversary of VE Day.'

CHAPTER EIGHT

'Well, hello,' Artie said as he returned from lunch, pretending to be shocked to see Ena at her desk in the investigating agency. 'And how is the dramatic world of thespians these days?'

'Dramatic!' Ena replied.

'Oo – do tell. I have been stuck in this office on my own for weeks…'

'Two days!' Ena corrected.

'Well, it feels like weeks. I'm starved of human contact. I need action and excitement! Come on, spill the beans. What's going on?'

'There have been thefts at the Young Albert Theatre. Small stuff at first – petty pilfering: a couple of telephones, a box of light bulbs – but the thief has got cocky. The sound system for the main auditorium disappeared last night.'

'That's a bit big to carry out under your arm.'

'Not if it was still in the boxes it arrived in, which it was. It hadn't been unpacked. It was delivered late in the day and stolen later in the evening or during the night. Whenever it was, it had gone by this morning.'

'It would still take more than one person,' Artie said. 'Any ideas?'

'A couple.' Ena jumped up from her desk and headed into the kitchen. 'Want a cuppa?'

Artie followed her. 'You're making *me* tea?'

'So?'

Sucking in his breath and squinting, Artie took the kettle from her and filled it with water. 'What do you want?'

'Well–'

'I knew it! You never make me tea unless you want something!' Leaning against the sink, he folded his arms. Ena pulled the tea towel from the kitchen rail, rolled it into a ball, and hurled it at him. Dodging the missile, he shouted, 'I'll have you for assault!' Then he picked up the tea towel, flicked Ena with it and ran out of the kitchen.

'I'm making the tea, so behave, or I won't make you one,' she said, taking a tin of tea from the cupboard and spooning three teaspoons of leaves into the teapot.

Ena loved working for herself. She hadn't once regretted leaving the Home Office. She hated the bureaucracy, chauvinism, one-upmanship, the rules and regulations that were written at the turn of the century, and the lies. She hated the lies more than anything else. The only good things about the HO were her colleagues, Artie and Sid, who left to work with her at Dudley Green Associates as soon as they could.

Tears pricked at the back of Ena's eyes as she remembered how horribly her friend and colleague Sid had been murdered by Helen Crowther, the personal assistant to the head of M15 – a woman beyond reproach who was also a Nazi spy. It was while investigating the mole at MI5 that Sid was killed. Ena still blamed herself for putting him in a situation that cost him his life. She exposed Crowther as a spy, but at what cost?

'Come on then, let's hear it, Ena!' Artie said,

returning to the kitchen and taking the milk from the refrigerator.

She looked up at him and smiled. 'Sorry, I was miles away.'

'You want me to do something – and I can tell by your oh-so-sweet smile that you want me to do something I am not going to like. Out with it!'

'Well… I was thinking that if the foreman will give you a job at the theatre, you could go undercover.'

'What?' Artie burst into laughter. 'Of course I could. I can carry a hod of bricks as well as the next builder. After all, I'm built like a bricky.'

'Don't be daft! The building work finished months ago. There are only a few electric wires to check and light fittings to… to fit.'

'That's a job for an electrician. Who's going to believe I'm an electrician?' Artie asked, running his fingers through his thick wavy hair.

'And telephones. The telephones aren't connected yet. You could be a telephone engineer sent to connect them, and while you're waiting you could have a cuppa with the lads.'

Artie grimaced as he poured milk into each mug. While Ena stirred the tea in the pot, he leaned against the worktop, hands on hips, and pulled a face like a defiant schoolboy.

'You got the better of some of the most experienced conmen in espionage when we worked for the Home Office,' she said. 'You were a master of disguise.'

'I wasn't bad, was I?' he replied, sticking his thumbs under imaginary lapels and smiling.

'Not bad? You were amazing.'

'In those days, it was put on the uniform, carry the

corresponding workman's bag and tell some knucklehead who opened the door that there was a fault on his telephone line, or his electricity meter needed reading. It wasn't real electrician's work.'

Ena gave Artie his drink and followed him out of the kitchen and into the office. She sat at her desk and took a sip of tea. 'If I can set it up, will you do it?'

He rolled his eyes and gave an exaggerated sigh. 'Yes... alright... It'll be good to get out of the office and get my hands dirty.' Stretching out his hands, he grimaced again. 'I suppose I shall have to cut my fingernails. I can't be a bricky with manicured nails.'

'You won't be a bricky! The building work was finished months ago.' Ena waved her hand towards her colleague, picked up the telephone and dialled the number for the theatre. 'Hello, Stan, it's Ena Green. I'd like to speak to Mrs Goldman.' She held and waited.

'I'm sorry, Mrs Green, Mrs Goldman isn't in her office. Should I ask her to telephone you when she returns?'

Ena thought about asking to speak to Hilda. As Natalie's secretary, she would probably know if Natalie had talked to Ben Wilson about giving Artie a job, but Ena wasn't sure about Hilda yet and decided against it. 'Yes, please, Stan. Later today or tomorrow, when she has time. Goodbye.'

She turned back to Artie. 'Since you've been manning the office on your own for two whole days,' she said, mockingly, 'why don't you get off? I have a ton of paperwork to do. I'll be here for another couple of hours.'

'In which case,' Artie said, taking a sheet of paper from his desk drawer and putting it on her desk, 'my expenses for last month.'

She glanced down at the list. 'I might not be able to get to the bank tomorrow, but I'll get your money as soon as I can, okay?'

'Whenever will be fine. If possible, I'd like it before the weekend. Will you be in the office in the morning?'

'I will, first thing. I must go to the theatre later. Stan, on the stage door, will get hold of me if you need me.'

'See you in the morning. Don't work too late,' Artie called, throwing his jacket over his shoulder.

Ena waved Artie's expense sheet in the air and called, 'Goodnight.' When she heard the door to the street close, she went out and locked it. It was time to get to grips with the bills and Artie's wages and expenses. Artie was right; they needed paying clients. And they would have, soon. She decided to place an ad in *The Times*, as soon as the stolen sound system was found and Natalie had paid for her and Artie's time. She didn't want to charge Natalie, but she couldn't keep asking Henry to bail the agency out. However willing her husband was to help financially, he was only a sleeping partner.

Ena looked at Artie's expense sheet again and groaned. She would have to bury her pride. The only way she was going to pay Artie this week was to ask her husband to loan the agency the money.

CHAPTER NINE

Ena filled the kettle and switched it on. Adding a teaspoon of Nescafé instant coffee to her mug and then Artie's, she heard the telephone ringing. Leaving the kitchen and crossing to her desk, she picked up the receiver. 'Dudley Green Associates, Ena Dudley speaking.'

'Hello, Ena?'

'Natalie, thanks for ringing back,' Ena said, recognising Natalie Goldman's voice.

'I have good news. Ben Wilson has agreed to give Artie a job as an electrician.'

Ena laughed. 'Artie will be happy,' she said, tongue in cheek. 'Did Ben take much persuading?' She was still not convinced the foreman hadn't had anything to do with the theft of the sound system. But then, Ena assumed everyone was guilty until she had proven them innocent. In this case, everyone who worked at the Young Albert Theatre was a suspect until she met them, which she needed to do sooner rather than later.

'Not at all. He welcomed the idea.'

'That's good. When does he want Artie to start?'

'Tomorrow, if it's okay with Artie.'

'I'm sure it will be. There's nothing he needs to do here that I can't do.'

'Ah! Sorry, Ena, but I had a message from Connor Wolf. He wants you in tomorrow. He's had a scene of the show rewritten and wants you to watch the rehearsal mid-morning.'

Ena heard the street door open and then slam shut. 'Thank you, Natalie,' she said. 'Here's Artie now. I'll give him the good news. Thanks for ringing. See you tomorrow morning.' Putting down the telephone, she returned to the kitchen, poured hot water onto the coffee granules and added milk.

'Good morning!' Artie called, entering the office.

'Morning. I've made you a coffee.'

'You're making the drinks two days running,' he said, flopping into his chair. 'That's a bad sign. However, if you're still trying to bribe me, make it black and strong.'

'Would you like to wear it or drink it?' Ena asked her colleague. Then she took a closer look. 'Oh dear, I think you had better drink it,' she said, putting a mug of steaming hot coffee on his desk. 'You look as if you had a heavy night.'

'Seriously heavy,' Artie replied, picking up his coffee, taking a drink and spluttering. 'Ah! It's bloody hot!'

'That could have something to do with the fact that I have just made it,' Ena said.

'Dare I ask if Natalie Goldman phoned last night?'

'You dare, and she did not.'

'Reprieve!' Artie said, leaning back in his chair and folding his arms across his chest.

'She phoned this morning,' Ena said, laughing. 'The foreman at the Young Albert has put you down as an electrician.'

'I can hardly change a light bulb!'

'Well, you are the best we've got–'

'I'm the *only* one we've got!' Artie snapped. 'How about *you* donning a pair of overalls and changing light bulbs?'

'I've changed plenty of light bulbs in my time. But don't change the subject. Put on your best cockney accent and don't clean your fingernails.' Artie stretched out his hands, feigned shock and sighed loudly. 'Cheer up! No one will know you're not an electrician until the stolen sound system is found. By then, it won't matter.'

'What if we don't find the system? Will it be replaced?' he asked.

'I doubt it. There isn't any money left. Anyway, until we know one way or another, you'll be sitting on your bum playing cards and drinking tea with the other chaps down there. It'll give you time to get to know them and hopefully find out who might be light-fingered. If anyone asks you to help with other jobs, play willing.'

'What if it's thieving more equipment?'

'Go along with it. It might lead us to the stolen sound equipment.'

Artie grinned. 'I can see it now: your pet policeman hauling me into Bow Street nick and you having to come and bail me out.'

'Remind me, what was it you said yesterday? Oh, yes, "I'm starved of human contact. I need action and excitement!"'

'All right, you win.' Artie blew on his coffee and took a sip. 'And while I'm sitting on my bum, playing cards and drinking tea, will I get paid?'

Ena hated making excuses to Artie; he deserved to be paid on time without having to ask her. 'Maybe not as an electrician, but you'll be paid as an investigator when we catch the thief. I'm sure Natalie will…'

'Ena!' Artie shook his head. 'You're not sure? So, a fee hasn't been agreed? We can't afford to keep working pro bono.'

'And we won't, but first, let's catch this damn thief.' She took the sheet of names out of her handbag and waved it at Artie. 'This is a list of Young Albert employees before, during, and after the sound system was stolen.'

Leaving his seat, Artie crossed to Ena's desk and read down the list. The names meant nothing to him. Giving it back to Ena, he said, 'Hopefully, I'll get the measure of some of these blokes tomorrow.'

Ena nodded. 'I'll come into the office first thing and check the post. Then I'm going to the Prince Albert. Connor Wolf has made some changes to the show. He wants me to see the rehearsal and there'll be a production meeting afterwards. God knows why he wants me there; I'm hardly a theatre aficionado. So, if you need me, telephone the stage door and I'll let Stan know where I'll be.'

'Okay, if you'll be here in the morning, it makes sense that I go to the Young Albert Theatre from home. I'll get there early, hopefully before the other workers.' Artie drummed his fingers on his desk. 'Can we trust the foreman?'

'Natalie thinks so. She has told him who you are, and he seemed eager to have you down there. If he is trustworthy, by telling him why you're there, he'll be onside. If he isn't trustworthy, to keep suspicion away from himself, he'll be too helpful and hopefully slip up.'

Ena folded the list of names and returned it to her

handbag. 'But now I'm going to Bow Street police station to see Dan Powell,' she said, getting up and leaving her desk.

CHAPTER TEN

Detective Chief Inspector Dan Powell beamed a welcoming smile as he jumped up from his chair and crossed the room, arms outstretched. 'Ena! It's been too long. How are you?'

'I'm well, thank you.'

'Sit down,' he said, pulling out a chair from beneath his desk. Walking around to his seat, he picked up the telephone before sitting down. 'Tea?'

Ena nodded. 'Thank you, that would be lovely.'

'Two teas, Janet,' he said, when the telephone was answered. 'And have we got any of those chocolate biscuits you're so keen on?' Janet must have said yes, because Dan Powell continued with, 'And two plates. Thank you, Janet.' He put down the phone with a smile. 'Now, Ena, what can I do for you?'

'Do you remember my friends, Natalie Goldman and George Derby Bloom? Natalie's husband and George's father were involved in getting young Jewish students out of Germany during the war. The students lived with the Goldmans and worked at the theatre, in the chorus and backstage, while they waited for new identity papers and passports before being taken to Liverpool, and then by ship to New York.'

Dan Powell nodded. 'I also remember when Mr Derby Bloom was murdered,' he said, shaking his head. 'Such a terrible thing to happen to a man who had saved so many lives.' Before Ena had time to reply, there was a knock on the door. 'Come in,' he shouted.

A young WPC entered carrying a tray with cups, saucers, a teapot, milk and a plate of chocolate biscuits. She put the tray on the DCI's desk. 'Mrs Green, do you have sugar?'

'No, Janet. I'm happy without it.'

The WPC looked at Dan Powell. 'And you're still going without, aren't you, sir?'

Dan patted his stomach. 'I am, Janet.'

Smiling, Janet poured the tea and put one cup in front of Ena and one in front of her boss, along with the plate of chocolate biscuits. 'Enjoy your tea and biscuits, sir,' she said. Still smiling, she turned to the door, nodded at Ena and said, 'Mrs Green.'

'So,' Ena said, 'you've given up sugar?'

'I'm watching my weight,' Dan replied, taking a bite out of a digestive.

Ena took a biscuit. 'It's a good thing I'm not!' she said, and the two old friends laughed at the irony of refusing sugar but eating chocolate biscuits.

Ena liked Dan Powell. She had known him since he was a DI and considered him a friend. No matter how many times she had turned up at Bow Street police station asking for his help, he had never been too busy for her.

'So, Ena, what can I do for you?' the inspector asked.

Ena couldn't help but smile. Again, her friend had offered to help. She showed him the list of employees who had worked at the Young Albert. 'Do you recognise any of these names, Dan? I'm trying to find out if anyone on this list is known to the police.'

The inspector read down the list and shook his head. 'No, I don't recognise anyone here.' He read the names again. 'I can find out if anyone on the list has a record or if they've ever been called in for questioning. The front desk keeps a visitors' log. I'll get Janet – WPC Harmon – to check the names against the log.' Picking up the list, the inspector crossed the room to the door. 'Won't be a minute,' he said, leaving the room.

Ena looked around the familiar office. The old safe in the corner brought back memories, some happy and some sad. Ena remembered how Dan, a detective inspector back then, had kept all manner of documents safely locked in his safe for her, including at the time when her friend and associate, Sid Parfitt, was murdered. He had left clues for Ena to find his briefcase, which contained not only newspaper cuttings, photographs and a journal recording events during the 1936 Olympics in Berlin, but also information that helped her find his killer. The most important document was a letter addressed to her, stating evidence that she was able to use to expose Helen Crowther, the woman who killed Sid and also tried to kill Ena. Eventually, when the net was closing in on her and she was about to be exposed as the mole at MI5, she killed herself, made it look as if she'd been murdered, and set up Henry.

Inspector Powell had let Ena use the Met's resources more than once. He had also introduced her to the Met's pathologist at St. Thomas' Hospital. It was an autopsy at St. Thomas's that proved a glass of lemon cordial that Ena had taken from Mr Derby Bloom's room was laced with poison. The inspector had also given her information on two Italian brothers who ran an extortion racket and were threatening her neighbour and friend, Emilio Bellucci, at Café

Romano.

Some of the cases she had worked on since becoming a private investigator would not have been solved without Detective Inspector Powell's help. Ena wondered if he would or could help her now he was a Detective Chief Inspector.

The door opened, shaking Ena from her reverie. Dan Powell entered and sat back down at his desk. 'WPC Harmon is going to check the list against the station's arrest records.' He took a sip of his tea. 'So, what are you investigating, Ena?'

'The theft of a theatre sound system from the Young Albert,' she said, adding, 'George Derby Bloom's father left money to build a theatre for young underprivileged men and women in the East End to help them fulfil their potential in music and drama.'

'That's a wonderful idea. Such a tragedy that he was murdered.'

Ena nodded. 'He was an incredible man.'

'So, when does the theatre open?'

'It is due to open in less than a month. The show to launch the opening is a tribute to my sister Margot. During the war, Mr Derby Bloom's daughter George was in the same theatre company at the Prince Albert as Margot. George, her friend Betsy, and Margot joined ENSA and toured in concert parties entertaining troops all over the country. But now the sound system has been stolen, and they don't know if they can open after all.'

'Can the sound system be replaced?' Dan said.

'No. The money George's father left was spent on demolishing part of an old music hall and building the new theatre. There is no cash left.'

CHAPTER ELEVEN

'Do you think it was an inside job?' Dan asked Ena.

'Yes, I do.'

'Looks to me like the thief is someone who has worked at the theatre.'

'It's also possible that he is still working there,' she said. 'Things have been going missing for some time. Small things at first – telephones, light bulbs, that sort of thing – but at the end of last week the entire sound system went.'

Dan Powell sucked in his breath. 'That's a bit of a leap. From petty thieving and pilfering to make a few bob on the side to stealing something the size of a theatre sound system. It would be big, wouldn't it?'

'Yes, the soundboard alone is huge. It fits into a sound box. The box also houses the controls for the stage and auditorium lights. Lights and sound are controlled from the box.'

'Has the light system gone too?'

'No, that had already been fitted; it's only the sound system that's missing. It arrived late one afternoon and went during that night. The different components hadn't even been taken out of their boxes.'

'Easy to get your mates round and carry it out if it was still in boxes.'

'You'd need a couple of strong mates though. The speakers are over six feet tall and weigh a ton. Well, not literally a ton, but...' Ena shrugged. 'And there's the soundboard.'

'What about security? Wasn't there anyone on the premises?'

'Presumably not. Though I expect there will be in future.'

'How did the thieves get in?'

'Ben Harris, the foreman, said a window in the cellar had been left open accidentally. The painters and decorators are in, and he thinks it was probably left open to air the place and get rid of paint fumes. He thinks the thieves got lucky, saw the open window, picked up the boxes and walked out of the front door.'

'Keys?'

'He keeps a spare set in his desk drawer. They are still there but in a slightly different place.'

'What do you think about the window being left open, Ena?'

'If it was left open – and I don't think it was – I don't think it was by accident. Any of the men working at the theatre could have opened that window at any time. Especially the decorators, who work on their own. They are the only ones still actively employed. Most of the men sit around drinking tea. It would be easy for any of them to say they were going to the toilet and open the window. But whether the window was left open by accident or on purpose, I don't think it was how the thieves got into the theatre. I think it was left open to make us think it was the point of entry and stop us from looking further. I'd put money on someone having had a key cut and walking in off the street. How they got boxes out of the building, I've yet to find out.'

'Making their getaway via the front door carrying large boxes would be risky,' Dan Powell said. 'The street isn't a main road, but there would be every chance of them being seen. Men carrying boxes out of a theatre at night would look suspicious.'

Ena nodded her agreement. 'I intend to go down to the Young Albert and look around. I'll have a better idea of what's what then.'

'Who reported the theft, and when?'

Ena had dreaded Dan asking her that question. 'It hasn't been reported yet.'

The DCI's eyes widened in disbelief. 'Ena, you of all people should know that every hour a crime goes unreported is an hour lost. The sound system could be halfway across the Continent by now.'

'It wasn't my theft to report.'

'Okay, I'll let you off, but someone should have reported it.'

'I agree. However, I don't think it will be halfway to anywhere.'

'Explain?'

'I can't be sure, it's just a gut feeling, but I don't think the pilfering and the theft of the sound system are connected. I think they're separate incidents. I don't think a window was left open by accident. It wasn't a spur-of-the-moment thing, where a thief got lucky.' Ena shook her head. 'It feels personal. I think someone is trying to delay the opening of the theatre.'

Dan frowned. 'Who would gain by stopping the theatre from opening?'

'That's what I don't know, and what I need to find out.'

They were interrupted by three taps on the door. 'Come in, Janet,' Dan called out.

'Thank you, sir.' WPC Harman walked to the side of the inspector's desk and placed the list of names Ena had given her in front of him. 'None of these people have a record, not at this station,' she said, 'but Ben Wilson was brought in and questioned about a burglary some years ago.'

'The foreman? That's a turn-up for the books. Who remembered him, Janet?'

'Front desk, sir. Sergeant Ackland. He said it was ten years ago.'

'The sergeant's got a hell of a good memory. Is he sure?' DCI Powell questioned.

'Yes, sir. Sarge said he knew him when they were kids. They were in the same youth club.'

'Thank you, Constable.'

'Sir!' The young WPC collected the empty cups and put them on the tray with the teapot and milk. Ena saw her eyes twinkle in a slight smile as she picked up the biscuits.

'Just because he was brought in for questioning in connection with a robbery ten years ago doesn't mean he's connected to the theft at the theatre, does it?' Ena said. 'If he did steal before, he'd be stupid to start stealing again when there are so few men working in the building, wouldn't he?' She stood up to leave. 'Thank you for your help, Dan,' she said, worry lines etched on her forehead.

'Ena, there are a lot of nicks in London. Just because no one on the theatre's wage list is known to us–'

'Except Ben Wilson.'

The DCI got up and walked around his desk. 'Come on, I'll see you out.'

As they approached the door leading to the public entrance hall of Bow Street police station, Dan took hold of her elbow. 'Hang on, Ena, I'm going to ask the desk sergeant about Wilson.' He opened the door to the front desk area, and when Sergeant Ackland had finished speaking to a member of the public, he beckoned him over. 'Sergeant, what can you tell Mrs Green and me about Ben Harris?'

'Not a great deal, sir. I haven't seen Ben for seven or eight years. When I knew him, he was what you'd call a straight arrow. We met when we were kids – well, teenagers. We were members of the same youth club. Some rum-uns went to that club, but Ben wasn't one of them. I was surprised when he was brought in for questioning about a theft where he was working. Hotwiring the boss's Jag and taking it for a joyride until it ran out of petrol wasn't Ben's style at all.'

'Did they find out who took the car?'

'A casual worker that Ben had sacked. I can't remember what for, but the lad tried to frame Ben. He took his gloves and left them on the front seat of the car when he dumped it.' The desk sergeant shook his head.

'Thank you, Sergeant.' The Chief Inspector turned to Ena. 'Does that make you feel any better?'

'Yes, it does. Thank you, Dan.'

The DCI opened the pass door and stood to the side to let Ena through. 'Anything else happens, you'll let me know?'

'Of course. Thank you.' Crossing the entrance hall, Ena turned, mouthed 'Thank you' to the desk sergeant, and then left.

CHAPTER TWELVE

'Hello, Stan,' Ena said to the Prince Albert doorman. 'Could I ask a favour?'

'Of course, Mrs Green,' he said, in his usual kind manner.

'My assistant Artie Mallory may telephone to speak to me. I'm going to Natalie's office now. I don't know how long I'll be there, so if he rings and I'm not in the office with Natalie, would you take a message, please?'

The ever-amenable Stan said it would be a pleasure, and Ena pushed open the door leading backstage. Arriving at Natalie's office, she knocked on the door, but there was no answer. Natalie must already be at the rehearsal.

Before opening the door leading to the public areas, Ena heard Hilda's voice. Turning back, she saw a man holding open the door for Hilda to enter the office. The secretary stopped before going in and looked up at the man, who leaned forward and whispered something in her ear. Hilda laughed. Turning back, she looked at Ena and waved.

Smiling, Ena waved back. 'I'm late. I should be in the rehearsal with Natalie.'

The man almost skipped along the corridor and pushed open the door to the theatre's public area. It was all Ena could do not to laugh. Seeing Hilda with a man reminded her of when she was a child and, looking out of her bedroom window, had seen her eldest sister Bess kissing a boy at the gate.

Thanking the man, Ena walked the short distance to the door that would take her into the stalls. Still smiling, she opened the door and stood behind the blackout curtain. Once she had closed the door, she parted the curtains and snuck into the dark auditorium. As the lights came up, she spotted Natalie next to the centre aisle, half a dozen rows back, and she took a seat next to her.

'Opening positions!' Connor Wolf shouted. 'We're going from curtain up. Everyone in place, please!'

Joe Singer strode across the front of the stage and was met by his ASM, Lilian, who was entering from the wings. 'I've checked the green room, dressing rooms and toilets. Everyone's here,' she said.

'Thank you,' Joe replied.

A couple of stagehands ambled in from the wings on the other side of the stage, sparking a chorus of chatter from the assembled cast. Connor Wolf, arms open wide, palms up, looked at Joe. 'Get them to be quiet, Joe.'

'Quiet, please!' the stage manager shouted. He clapped his hands. 'Qui-et!' Seeing Joe's red face, the excited dancers and singers stopped talking one by one until there was absolute silence. 'Thank you!' he said.

Joe walked upstage, turned left to the prompt corner and took his seat. He had remained visible during the early rehearsals but, sometime before the show opened, he would get one of the carpenters to screw his high-backed stool and wooden stand onto a flat metal plate that they would then screw to the floor in the wings. He placed his script on top of the stand, opened it at scene one and put on his headphones. The script was marked with different coloured symbols to cue the technical changes, sound and lights, not only from the control box at the back of the stalls but from the fly tower high above the stage. From where he sat, he could call for scenery and furniture to be flown in, should it be needed.

During the first couple of weeks of rehearsal, Joe often gave line prompts. He didn't enjoy that part of the job, but it was necessary because pauses in dialogue disturbed the thought process of many actors. A quick prompt meant the show had continuity and ran smoothly. During the technical and dress rehearsals, fewer prompts were needed. Almost everyone was off the book, and an artist forgetting his or her lines was rare in a performance. Nonetheless, Joe was ready if a prompt was needed. He took his job seriously and was respected by theatre owners and managers, not only in the West End of London but in the repertory theatres and touring venues in the provinces.

'OK, people!' Wolf shouted. 'From the top, again! Act one, scene one. Margot on her way to the Prince Albert Theatre to be interviewed for the job of usherette. Opening positions, please!'

The curtains closed and, while the artists found their places, Connor Wolf pushed his way through the opening in the middle. Taking the steps at the side of the orchestra pit from the stage to the stalls, he settled himself into his seat next to Charlotte.

As the lights in the auditorium went down, the curtains opened, and lights on the stage came up to reveal flats painted like shop fronts, a café and the Prince Albert Theatre stage door beneath a street sign that said "Maiden Lane". Ena's niece, Natalie, playing young Margot – or Margaret, as she was still called then – danced along Maiden Lane, twirling around and swinging her handbag. She stopped and looked at her reflection in the window of a café, smiling at what she saw before dancing on.

She stopped again and, swaying from side to side, put a hand up to her mouth in surprise when she saw the stage door of the Prince Albert Theatre. At that moment, an air raid siren began to wail and there was the sound of bombs falling and exploding. People ran along the street from every direction shouting to each other to take shelter in Aldwych underground station. Two women beckoned to Margaret. Another took her by the hand. Margaret began to follow them but then broke away. She turned and looked again at the stage door.

The sound of more bombs exploding was deafening and she put her hands over her ears. Several men and women ran past her. Someone shouted: 'The underground is this way. Come on, it's too dangerous to stay on the street!' Margaret halted her step. Torn between safety or risking her life and carrying on to the theatre, she turned this way and that before running to the stage door. The sound of falling masonry was heard and she was caught in the beam of a searchlight as it crossed the stage. She put up one hand to shield her eyes; with the other, she pushed open the door. With a frightened expression on her face, she looked up at the sky. Caught again in the beam of a searchlight that stayed on her, Margaret shrugged her shoulders, turned to face the audience and, smiling broadly, danced through the Prince Albert Theatre's stage door.

As the stage door slowly closed, the sound of bombs and air raid sirens began to fade. The artists on stage started to leave, and lights in the make-believe windows of the shops went out one by one, leaving only the searchlight beams roaming over a darkening stage. Eventually, a solitary search light crisscrossed the blacked-out empty stage until the heavy velvet curtains were fully drawn.

'Scene change!' Joe shouted. 'Curtains open, please.'

Ena watched as the curtains opened. Members of stage management entered from the back of the stage carrying chairs, which they lined up diagonally across the bottom right of the stage. Girl dancers, dressed in coats and hats and portraying members of the audience, took their seats, and boy dancers stood behind the chairs, ready to clear them when the dance proper began.

'Dancers sitting on the first row of chairs, remain seated. React as if you're watching a show,' Connor Wolf shouted. 'Dancers on the second row, stand up when the music starts, and throw your coats and hats into the wings. And boys? Drag the chairs backwards, leaving a big enough area for the girls to dance – and then join them. Okay, let's do it!'

The house lights dimmed and the stage lights faded, leaving a spotlight on Natalie, as Margot. She pulled the curtains across a door with a fluorescent light above saying "EXIT", and ran downstage, stopping as if she was behind the audience. When the orchestra struck up and the artists began to dance and sing, Margot copied their dance steps and sang the songs. As Margot sang louder, the chorus sang quieter. The lights on the chorus began to fade, and a spotlight came up on Margot, who was singing on her own, beautifully.

She danced back to her usherette's seat, pulled back the exit curtain, and sang, 'Grab your coat and get your hat, leave your worries on the doorstep, just direct your feet to the sunny side of the street.' Margot shone her torch on the floor to guide the singers and dancers playing the audience out. When the last of them had left, Margot looked out into the audience and bowed before turning on her heels and following the chorus through the exit curtain and into the wings.

Connor Wolf leapt out of his seat. 'Everyone on stage, please.'

Natalie nudged Ena. 'Shall we go?'

'What about the production meeting?' Ena asked.

'I've cancelled it. I need to meet with Wolf and Singer, and the company, to tell them about the theft of the sound system.' Natalie had a determined look in her eyes. 'By hook or by damn crook – if you'll excuse the pun – the Young Albert Theatre *will* open on time.'

Eva nodded. 'I want to talk to you about that.'

'And I want to talk to you about an idea I've had for a fundraiser, which is another reason I need to speak to Wolf and Singer,' Natalie said. 'I've already spoken to some members of the company. They think a fundraiser is a great idea, and they are willing to help with it. I now have to persuade Wolf to let them off rehearsals early on the day, so they can get to the Young Albert to help with it.'

'I see. How long do you think you'll be in the meeting?'

'Unfortunately, it isn't the only meeting I have scheduled. I'll be tied up in meetings most of today.'

'What about lunchtime? Will you be free then?' Ena asked.

'You can try me at around one o'clock, but I doubt I'll be able to stop for long.'

'If you're busy at lunchtime, how about we meet up later? Henry and I, and Artie and his partner Rupert, are going to the Lamb and Flag tonight. We're meeting at eight. Why don't you join us?'

'I'd love to,' Natalie said. 'I'll need a drink by the end of today! How about we meet earlier, around six-thirty? Then we'll have time to talk about the fundraiser before the men arrive.'

'Good idea. I should be finished at the office by then.'

'And, you never know, Artie might have news about the theft at the Young Albert.'

'It's a bit too soon, I suspect,' Ena said. 'With him only starting there today, I doubt he'll have had time to find out much about the men he's working with, but you never know.'

As the lights dimmed and the band struck up to rehearse the scene again, Ena and Natalie made their way to the back of the stalls and out of the auditorium.

'I've got a few errands to run. I'll see you tonight,' Ena said. She followed Natalie to her office and continued along the corridor. There had been no message from Artie so, after saying goodbye to Stan, Ena made her exit by the stage door.

CHAPTER THIRTEEN

A cab was pulling away from the curb after dropping off a fare outside the café on Maiden Lane. Ena ran into the road and flagged it down. 'The Young Albert Theatre, please, Chapel Park Road, Whitechapel.'

The Strand, as always, was bumper to bumper with traffic, but it wasn't long before Arundel Street, Temple Place, and the spring flowers of Victoria Embankment Gardens were behind them. The taxi turned onto the Embankment, where there were noticeably fewer cars. The Thames, on the other hand, was bustling with activity. Ena opened the window and, cooled by the breeze coming off the river, watched the barges and tugs, laden with timber, bricks and other building materials, sail along the river destined for the docks, which were undergoing redevelopment.

Sitting back in her seat, Ena marvelled at the Tower of London. Once the gateway to the city, it had gone from being a royal palace to a political prison and a place of execution. She shuddered at the thought. After passing Tower Bridge, with its majestic towers and distinctive design, she wound up the window and looked at her watch. The journey to Whitechapel from Maiden Lane had taken twenty-five minutes. She would soon be at the Young Albert Theatre.

The area famously known for the serial murderer Jack the Ripper in 1888 had been heavily bombed during the war, and although the shops on the High Street had been repaired and others rebuilt, some areas remained untouched.

As they turned from the shops and market along Whitechapel Road onto Chapel Park Road, the Young Albert Theatre came into view. She was impressed with the building. Although the front, where she assumed the foyer, box office and cloakroom would be, looked new, it had been restored to resemble the front of the original music hall.

Paying the cabbie, Ena walked down the wide steps to the theatre's main entrance and rapped hard on the door. She didn't have to wait long before the door was opened.

'Mr Wilson?' Ena said, shaking the foreman's hand. 'My name is Ena Green. I'm Margot Dudley's sister and a friend of Natalie Goldman.'

'Hello, Mrs Green. We met earlier – not formally, of course. At the Prince Albert Theatre, when my friend Hilda and I were coming from the stage door to her office.'

'Of course we did. Hello again,' Ena said, avoiding Ben Wilson's eyes for fear she'd giggle. 'I've just come from a rehearsal of *Tribute*,' she went on, 'and I thought, as I'd seen that part of the show before, I'd come down and have a look at this fabulous new theatre. Oh!' She put her hand to her mouth. 'If you have time, of course?' she said, pretending to be carried away with the excitement of it all.

'It would be a pleasure, Mrs Green,' Ben said. 'We'll start with the Derby Bloom Theatre, the Young Albert's main auditorium.' He guided her into the main theatre. 'As you can see, the Derby Bloom is a traditional pros arch theatre. The auditorium seats six hundred people.' He led Ena down the side aisle to the front of the stalls. 'It has a traditional stage, although not as deep as most West End stages. The tall doors at the back of the stage lead to the scenery dock. It's used for building and storing flats and other scenery. It's big enough to store a dozen sets. There's also storage underneath the stage in the trap room.'

'A trap room!' Ena said. 'That sounds ominous.'

Ben laughed. 'It isn't in use, but the trap room allows access to the stage from a room below. Once upon a time, stagehands brought equipment up to the stage via lifts. And in the days of the music hall, entertainers would suddenly appear or disappear. During magic acts, magicians would help their assistants into boxes, which stayed on stage while the assistant was lowered into the trap room by a winch. The next time she appeared, it would be at the back of the stalls.

'We don't have hydraulics to allow such entrances, but one day,' Ben said, crossing his fingers, 'artists might appear from beneath this stage. The Theatre Royal on Drury Lane has a wonderful system of hydraulic stage lifts. It was installed in the late 1890s and restored in 1919. Best in the world, they say… but ignore me, hydraulics cost a fortune. Oh, but there's something we do have that I think is better than the Royal: magnificent maroon stage curtains. They are waiting to be hung, along with the exit lights above the doors in this and the Margot Dudley Studio.'

'It's amazing what you've done, Mr Wilson,' Ena said.

'Thank you, Mrs Green,' replied the Young Albert's foreman, rocking backwards and forward on the balls of his feet.

'Mr Wilson, I understand a sound box has already been built and only the sound system itself was stolen?'

'The sound box was built long ago and refurbished six months ago,' Ben said, striding up the centre aisle and out through a door marked "Foyer". 'It's up here.'

Ena followed Ben up a short set of stairs to a landing on what was a mezzanine floor, halfway between the ground and first floors. 'To our right is the balcony. A little further along this passage are the boxes,' he said, 'They weren't damaged in the Blitz, but they are filthy. A good clean and a touch of paint, they'll be as good as new.'

Ena opened the door of the first box and marvelled at the rich cream walls and gilt swirls. 'It's like something out of an old movie,' she said. 'What beautiful maroon velvet seats … and all the gilt on the cornices.'

'There are three boxes on either side. There isn't a royal box, but these boxes would have been used by dignitaries in the days of the music hall.'

'There are only six seats. Are there bigger boxes?'

'No. Usually, only five. Six seats are unusual for theatres of this size.'

'And the gallery.' Ena looked to her right. 'It's small.'

'It is. It can't be used until the seating has been replaced. Mr Wolf and his assistant will watch the show from the gallery, but there won't be any audience up here.' Ben left the box first and led the way back along the passage. 'The sound box,' he said, opening the door to what Ena could see immediately had been a cinema projection room. 'It's a permanent fixture.

Has been since it was a cinema. It's ideal for sound, lights, and all visuals. This glass,' he tapped the large square window, 'gives a perfect view of the stage.' Trailing his hand along the lighting board, he said, 'The lighting system was fitted some time ago, the sound system... Well, you know about that. I hope you can find the thief, Mrs Green. Our work over the last six months will have been for nothing if the theatre doesn't open.' He sounded genuinely concerned.

'My associate and I are doing everything we can, Mr Wilson.'

'Yes, of course, I'm sorry. So,' he said, brightening, 'now to the Margot Dudley Studio. After you,' he said, closing the door to the sound box and following Ena to the ground floor and the foyer.

On the left of the foyer were tall black double doors with a wooden sign that read "The Margot Dudley Studio". Ena pushed open the doors.

'The studio is very modern,' Ben told her. 'It's what the Americans call a theatre-in-the-round, or an arena theatre. The stage is in the middle, and the audience, instead of sitting in front of the stage to watch the show, sits on all sides. Theatre-in-the-round was common in ancient times, particularly in Greece and Rome. There are theatres-in-the-round in America, but it wasn't until a director called Stephen Joseph came to England and founded the Stephen Joseph Theatre in Scarborough, North Yorkshire, that theatre-in-the-round came to Britain.

'I believe the Young Vic, in The Cut, will have a main theatre and a refurbished studio space. The foreman there reckons it'll be ready to open in the autumn. It's what they call a breezeblock building. It was a butcher's shop until it became a bombsite.'

'So, the Young Albert will open first?' Ena said.

'It will if we can replace the sound box. There's no chance of it opening until we get another.'

'Or if we find the thief and where it's being kept.' If he or they haven't already sold it, Ena thought. 'Do you have any idea who could have stolen it, or where they might have sold it?'

Ben stopped in his tracks. 'No idea. If I knew who'd taken it, I'd ring the bugger's neck!' He looked out of the only window in the corridor. 'Got a lot of history, this site. They say there was a monastery here until the sixteenth century. And you know it was also a music hall. Very popular too, I heard.'

'So many wonderful buildings were destroyed in the war.'

'More than in most places. The East End was turned to rubble in a flash. At least the music hall was closed when the Luftwaffe got it.'

'My niece told me that part of the original music hall survived the bombing,' Ena said.

'It did, and we've done our best to preserve what we could. Miss Derby Bloom was most particular. The other buildings along the road weren't so lucky. Most of the neighbouring shops were hit at night after the workers had gone home, but fifty-four people who lived here were sheltering in the cellar of a bakery when it was hit. They were all killed.'

CHAPTER FOUTEEN

They walked past several offices along a corridor between front of house and the dressing rooms, and arrived at the stage door. 'This looks like it's part of the original building,' Ena said.

'It is,' Ben replied. 'The offices and dressing rooms, too. But not the front of house.' Soon they were back at the main entrance, which Ena could see was newly built, along with the box office. 'And we're back where we started.' Ben opened the double doors leading to the main road and showed Ena out.

'Thank you, Ben,' she said, shaking his hand. As she walked up the steps to the pavement, she heard him shut and lock the doors behind her.

Ena noticed a slabbed footpath alongside a mud driveway that ran down the side of the theatre. She walked to the end of the building, turned and walked around the back. The path, which led to the stage door and the scenery dock doors, had been newly laid and was level; the rest, a huge expanse of wasteland, was a jungle of building materials and rubble. At the bottom of what Ena could only describe as a wilderness were trees choked with ivy, gangly shrubs and a carpet of weeds. It had probably been someone's garden. Outside the dock doors, the ground was compacted mud, flattened by heavy lorries delivering bricks and building materials.

She looked around. The trees concealed the exits

at the back of the theatre, the dock doors, and the stage door. Part of the waste ground on the left was also overgrown with trees. To her right, assorted vehicles were parked behind neighbouring buildings that were being built or restored. Lorries and vans would be coming and going all day along Chapel Street. A van turning off the main road, pulling up in front of the dock doors and being loaded with boxes wouldn't attract attention. It would just be another workman taking excess material away. Easy for a thief. Ena had a feeling that the Young Albert's sound system wasn't going to be found easily, or quickly.

Chapel Street, off the main Whitechapel Road, was half a mile long – and it was busy. There were a lot of record shops, which, if she had more time, she'd have enjoyed browsing. A board on the corner of Whitechapel Road and Chapel Mews proclaimed "Music Maestro! If you want it, we can get it!" It was hardly Tin Pan Alley, but it looked interesting. Ena turned into the narrow cobbled passageway and walked the short distance to the bottom, where she found a double-fronted music shop.

The peeling paint on the door and window frames and greasy smeared windows belied the gaiety of the name Music Maestro; nor would the fading sign saying "Studio For Hire" encourage pop groups or singers from the popular cafés in the West End to record their singles here, Ena thought.

She peered through the grimy window, which was dressed with percussion and brass instruments, a guitar at its centre. It was too dark to see anything inside other than the ivory and ebony keys of an upright piano next to the window. Spotting a large handwritten sign that said "We Buy and Sell – nothing too big or too small", Ena pushed open the door and went in.

The interior of the shop was as run down as the exterior. It was so dusty Ena wanted to sneeze. 'Hello?' she called. There was a beaded curtain at the back of the counter. She assumed it hid a door leading to another room, a storeroom perhaps, or living quarters. A glass-fronted cabinet on her right was full of wind instruments. Next to that, a deep open shelf displayed brass instruments. In front of the window was the piano she'd seen from outside. At the far end of the room was a row of guitars on stands and, behind them, a double bass and two sets of drums. It was hardly Sound City, the famous music shop on Shaftesbury Avenue. Then again, this area wasn't exactly the West End.

'Hello?' she called again. 'Anyone there?'

'I am sorry to keep you waiting.' A man sporting a straggly beard and grey hair in need of a cut appeared through the curtain, the beads making rhythmic clinks and tinkles as it swung behind him. 'I didn't hear the bell.' He stared at the wooden panel above the door.

Ena followed his gaze. There was no bell.

'Oh dear, silly me! It came off the frame a while ago. I must put it back up.' The man laughed. 'And I shall, just as soon as I remember where I put it. It *is* somewhere safe.' He put up his hand to assure her. 'I always put things in safe places.' He laughed again. 'It's simply a matter of remembering where the safe places are. Now, my dear,' he said, standing to attention behind the shop's counter, 'how can I help you?'

'I'm looking for a sound system.'

'Right…' the man said, rubbing his hands together. 'I have a lovely walnut cabinet with a record player and AM/FM built-in radio. I also have one with a drinks cabinet on one end and a cupboard to store your records in on the other. Both are beautiful pieces of furniture. Either would enhance the most modern of sitting rooms.'

'It isn't for a home,' Ena said. 'It's for a theatre.'

'A theatre? Oh, I see.' As he peered at her over the top of his glasses, Ena wondered if he did see. He pulled on his beard and looked around the room. 'No, no, no. I don't have anything like that. I could possibly get one for you?'

'Would you be able to get a second-hand system?' she asked, enthusiastically. 'It's just that I don't have a lot of money.'

The old man's brow furrowed. 'Oh, dear, I'm not sure. I could make enquiries. Would a cinema system suit you? I have seen cinema and dance hall sound systems for sale in my industry magazines. Now, when was it? And which…' He scratched his head. 'I can't say I've seen any recently, though.'

'Thank you,' Ena said. 'I won't ask you to make enquiries. I just thought, as I was passing, I'd pop in on the off-chance and ask. I'll buy some music magazines and have a look through them. Thank you for your time.' As she opened the door, she looked up. There was no bell housing. She suspected there hadn't been a bell for many years. 'Thanks again,' she called over her shoulder. 'Goodbye.'

CHAPTER FIFTEEN

It was approaching lunchtime, so Ena thought she would check with Stan at the stage door to see whether Natalie was in her office and if she was free.

As her taxi turned into Maiden Lane, another cab pulled up directly in front of it. 'Looks like the Lane's congested, Miss,' the driver said. 'I can drive you down when it clears, but it might be quicker for you to walk the rest of the way.'

'I will, thanks.' Ena grabbed her handbag and jumped out of the taxi. 'Keep the change,' she said, handing the driver five shillings.

Seeing a familiar figure ahead of her, Ena ran along Maiden Lane and caught up with the Prince Albert's wardrobe mistress. 'Rose!' she said, relieving her of a large Army and Navy carrier bag.

'Thank you, Ena. So many cars were parked along the lane that the taxi couldn't get down and had to drop me off on Southampton Street.'

Ena pushed open the stage door and waved to Stan, who was peering out from behind the glass hatch of his office. Then she followed Rose through the door leading backstage, along the rabbit warren of passages and up two flights of stairs to Wardrobe. 'How do you manage to climb those stairs every day?' Ena said, out of breath. 'You must be fit.'

'I climb them several times, more some days,' Rose said, laughing. 'I suppose I'm used to it. Thank you for your help, Ena. I'll hang those uniforms up when I've sorted through this lot.' She tipped a variety of scarves, cravats, gloves, hats and other paraphernalia onto a long table running down the side of the room.

'I'll put these on coat hangers,' Ena said, noticing a portable clothes rack. 'I'm in no hurry to get back to the office. There isn't anything I need to do that can't be done by my associate.' She crossed her fingers behind her back to counter the lie; although she hadn't seen Artie at the Young Albert, she knew he was working there today.

While Rose neatly paired the accessories – gloves by each matching glove, socks by the colour of each military uniform – side by side on the long table, Ena hung up army, navy and air force uniforms. It was noon by the time they had emptied the bags and put them all in order.

'Is that everything?' Ena asked.

'For the time being.' Rose took her jacket from the end of the row of clothes. 'I think it's time for a break.'

'I'm getting hungry,' Ena said, checking her watch. 'Good Lord, it's almost one. Why don't we get something to eat? Do you have the time?'

'I'll make time – though there won't be a table free in the café on Maiden Lane at this time of day.'

'We could go to Dooley's on the Strand.'

Rose's eyes widened in surprise at Ena's suggestion. 'I was thinking more of having a snack than a meal!'

'We can have a sandwich in the green room then.'

'No!' Rose snapped. 'Sorry, it's just that the green room will be packed.'

Ena tried not to show her shock at Rose's sharp reaction. She wondered if she was trying to avoid Connor Wolf. Did she feel embarrassed because of how she'd responded to what Wolf said in the meeting the day before?

Rose looked around the room. 'Well, I've done as much as I can do until the wardrobe maintenance girls come in later this afternoon so, yes, let's go to Dooley's. It'll make a nice change.'

As they crossed The Strand, on what looked to Ena like a clear road, a black car driving at speed appeared out of nowhere. 'Look out!' she shouted, pushing Rose and then dragging her by the sleeve of her coat to the safety of the pavement in front of Dooley's.

Rose gasped. 'What on earth! Where did that car come from?'

Turning on her heels, Ena saw a woman staring at her from the passenger seat. The driver had been reckless, and, by the look of shock on the passenger's face, she knew it. The car stopped for a second. Ena leaned forward and looked the woman in the eye. The woman turned away, and the car pulled away at speed.

'Are you okay, Rose?'

'I think so. Are you?'

'Yes. Come on, let's get inside.'

A waiter offered the women a table for two in the window. Simultaneously, they said no, and laughed. Unaware of what had taken place outside, the waiter looked from one to the other and led them to a corner table on the far side of the room.

Seated with menus, Ena and Rose discussed what they would eat. Ena, who had missed breakfast and was ravenous, chose lasagna; Rose, a chicken salad.

Neither wanted a starter but they asked for a pot of tea. While they waited for their food, Ena said, 'Did you recognise the woman driving the car that almost ran us down?'

'No, I didn't see her.'

'What about the car?'

Rose shook her head. 'It was black, but that is all I noticed.'

'Well, the woman recognised us. At least, I think she recognised me. I leaned forward, and when she saw me, she looked surprised.'

'Probably surprised that the car hadn't hit us.'

'It must have been going at a hell of a pace to appear out of the blue like that.'

A second later, the waiter arrived with their lunch. Ena heard Rose take a breath. It sounded like relief.

When they had finished eating, Ena ordered coffee and Rose another pot of tea. Adding milk to her coffee, Ena said, 'Everything seems to be going to plan with the play. I don't know much about theatre productions, especially not musicals, but I was impressed with the opening scenes. The singers and dancers were amazing, and the music was wonderful.' Then she laughed. 'As for the sound effects... The first time I walked into the auditorium, I thought I was back in the early forties, with air raid sirens wailing, and bombs going off. It was loud for the space, but then that's how it was in the war. The atmosphere was spot on. Natalie, my niece, acted as determined as I'm sure my sister Margot was to get to the theatre amid the chaos and danger. She was excellent. If the rest of the show is as good as the opening, it's going to be a hit.'

Rose looked up from stirring her tea. 'Connor Wolf knows his stuff. He is one of the best directors that–' She stopped suddenly and took a sip of tea.

Seeing the hint of a blush on Rose's cheeks, Ena changed the subject. 'I hope the Young Albert Theatre will be ready for opening night.'

CHAPTER SIXTEEN

'The Young Albert will be ready all right, if Michael Brookes, the great entrepreneur, has anything to do with it,' Rose said. 'He is one of the theatre's main sponsors. I don't suppose any of his wealthy pals got away without contributing. Brookes can be very persuasive.'

Ena heard the sarcasm in her voice as she talked about Michael Brookes and wondered what he had done or said to make Rose so bitter. She decided that a woman as experienced in theatre as Rose Allen would have a good reason for reacting as she did about Brookes. And, if she wanted to tell her about the man, she would do so in her own time.

For now, Ena decided not to pursue it. Instead, she said, 'George has worked hard to make her father's dream of building a theatre for underprivileged youngsters come true. They'll be able to learn and express themselves through music and dance in the East End, and you never know, some might go on to be professional singers and dancers in the West End.'

Rose sighed. 'It is so close to opening night, and the theatre isn't finished. Did you know there has been a delay? It doesn't matter how good the artists, music, set, director–'

'And costumes,' Ena added.

Rose smiled. 'Thank you, and costumes. But if the theatre isn't finished on time, it is academic how good each department is.'

'Wolf is confident it will be.'

'Wolf!' Rose scoffed.

Ena realised she'd hit a nerve by mentioning Connor Wolf. 'I'm sorry, I didn't mean to go on about him.'

'No, it's fine. You might have gathered that Wolf and I are not each other's biggest fans,' Rose said. 'By *the performance* at the meeting, you have probably guessed that Connor and I have history?' Without giving Ena time to reply, she dropped her voice to a whisper. 'The way I reacted to him was very unprofessional. I can't speak for him, but for my part, I apologise.'

'There's no need to apologise. As for professional, you're extremely professional.'

Rose turned to Ena, 'But–'

'And human. It's good to know you're a normal human being with feelings. I did sense that there might have been a falling-out between the two of you at the meeting, yes, but that's life.'

Rose buried her face in her hands.

'Oh, Rose, I'm sorry…' Ena reached across the table and laid her hand on Rose's arm. 'I didn't mean to stir up the past, make you feel unhappy.'

'You haven't, not really. I need to pull myself together. It was a long time ago that I knew Connor. I should be over him by now.'

Ena waited for Rose to tell her more. She didn't have to wait long.

'I need to find a way of working with Connor for the duration of *Tribute*,' she said. 'He'll move on a couple of weeks into the run, when any wrinkles have been ironed out.' She inhaled deeply. 'Once he has gone – and he will, he's an ambitious man – there will be no reason for me to ever see him again.' She looked at Ena. Tears filled her eyes and, falling onto her cheeks, she brushed them away with the back of her hand.

After several seconds had passed, Ena said, 'Do you want to talk about it? I'm a good listener.' Seeing indecision in Rose's eyes, she added, 'I understand if it would be too painful, but it might help.'

Rose took a deep breath. 'Connor and I were once in love.' A smile mixed with sadness washed over her face as more tears fell. She took a handkerchief from her handbag and wiped her face. 'However hard you try, you can't switch off the feelings you have for someone, can you?'

Ena reached across the table again to take her hand, but Rose shook her head.

'I'm alright, Ena. It's time I got over Connor.' She twisted the tear-stained handkerchief around her fingers. 'It's just that I remember how happy we once were.' Rose dabbed at her eyes. 'Recalling those days, you know, the love we had for one another and the life we had planned together reminds me of what I've lost. What we had was special.' She took a deep breath. 'Then, one day, everything changed. I haven't been happy since, but I've been trying. I go out, I see friends. I've even been out with a couple of nice men. I had a relationship with one guy. It was nothing serious and didn't last, but I was getting on with my life.

'And now Connor is working at the Prince Albert Theatre!' she snapped, 'I see him every day, and because we are working on the same show, I have to speak to him. I try to be civil, but every time I look at him, it brings back the heartbreak and pain. After all this time, it is still so raw, Ena. I wish the damn man had never accepted the job as artistic director of *Tribute*. I'm sorry. I'm bitter, and it's not like me.'

At that moment, the waiter arrived to clear the table of the tea and coffee pots. Balancing the tray on his left palm, he said, 'Can I get you anything else?'

'Yes,' Rose said. 'I'm not ready to go back to work yet.' She looked at Ena.

Ena nodded. 'Nor am I.' She looked at her watch. 'I have time for another coffee if you have?'

'I'd like a glass of white wine, please,' Rose said.

'I'll bring you the wine list.' The waiter turned to leave.

'That won't be necessary. I'll have a glass of whatever you recommend.' She looked questioningly at Ena.

'I'll have the same.'

Sipping a glass of chilled white wine, Rose began. 'I met Connor on the set of a show called *West End Nights*. It was a review, a collection of love songs and dance routines.' Her eyes sparkled at the memory. 'When we first started seeing each other, we knew the risks to our working relationship. We were worried that if the rest of the company knew, especially my fellow cast members, they might think Connor would show me favouritism. But we couldn't stop seeing each other, so we agreed not to make our relationship public. With hindsight, perhaps we should have been open about it,' Rose mused, 'but at the time, for the sake of work, we thought it best to keep our affair under wraps. We saw each other when we could, grabbing an hour here and half an hour there.

'We were young. We had our lives and careers in front of us. Connor was a few years older than me, but not many. He was good-looking and confident – and a wonderful director. He knew how to bring out the best in the artists he worked with. The first time he gave me one-to-one notes, he looked into my eyes, and he reached a place that no director, no man had ever reached in me, before or since. He made me believe I was capable of anything.'

'Natalie told me that you were a hugely talented singer and dancer,' Ena said.

'She's very kind. People said I had talent, but...' Rose gave a cynical laugh. 'Showbusiness is fickle. One week, you're the leading lady, the toast of London; the next, you can't get a part in the chorus. I was lucky that I had a strong voice and a wide vocal range. I was lucky too that dancing came easy to me.' She smiled. 'I was spotted by an American producer called Lou Kingman. He wanted to take me and the show to Broadway when its run in the West End had finished. It was such an exciting time. When Lou Kingman asked Connor if he'd direct the show on Broadway, which was rare in those days, because Broadway was a closed shop where British directors were concerned – and actors, for that matter – we couldn't have been happier.' She blew out her cheeks, and her smile faded.

'What is it, Rose?'

'Scarlet Brookes. Connor's wife.'

CHAPTER SEVENTEEN

Ena's eyes widened with shock. 'Connor was married when you met him?'

'No. Scarlet wasn't his wife then; she was his ex-girlfriend. They met when they worked together the year before. By the time I met Connor, their relationship had been over for at least six months.'

'I see. So, what was the problem?' Ena asked.

'Scarlet was the problem. The minute she heard about Broadway, she wanted to be with Connor. Her father, Michael Brookes, was the show's West End producer and when Scarlet told him she still loved Connor and she wanted him back, he did everything in his power to make it happen. He badgered Connor and blackmailed him into taking Scarlet out again.'

'How? By threatening Connor's future as the director of *West End Nights*?' Ena asked.

'No. Connor said he would have walked away from the show and taken his chances. No, Scarlet's father threatened *everyone's* future. He said he would pull the show and put the cast, crew, stage management, and anyone else involved with the show out of work.'

'Michael Brookes didn't give Connor much choice.'

'He didn't give him any choice at all. Although Connor hadn't dated Scarlet for six months, he didn't want to be the reason so many people were suddenly unemployed, many of whom were his friends, artists he'd worked with on projects in the past.'

'That's a hell of a situation to be in,' Ena said.

'The business could be like that in those days. It seemed everyone – producers, backers, agents – all wanted something from someone. Except for Connor. Connor just wanted to direct shows.'

'And keep people in work.'

'Yes.' Rose laughed. 'I'm making him sound like a saint. He was far from that, but he was fiercely loyal to those who worked for him. So, he became *friends* with Scarlet to keep her happy, and he agreed to stop seeing me to keep her father happy.'

Rose's eyes glistened. Ena thought she was about to cry again. 'What is it, Rose?'

'Connor and I didn't stop seeing each other.'

'And Scarlet found out?'

'Not for some time. We were very careful. We only realised she knew about us when she went from accepting Connor as a friend to becoming obsessed with him.' Rose rolled her eyes and shook her head. 'She became nasty. She told Connor she was glad to be free of him. She said she'd had several offers from more handsome, more prosperous men, and as far as directors went, Connor was the worst director she'd worked with. Hah!' Rose said. 'Then she started to play the heartbroken, last-to-know girlfriend. And she kept it up until she had divided the company. In the end, working with some cast members became so difficult that, for the sake of the show, Connor and I stopped seeing each other completely.'

Rose shook her head in despair. 'Again, Connor tried to do the right thing, for the sake of the show and the company. Eventually he told Scarlet that he liked and respected her, but he didn't feel about her the way she felt about him. She had known from the beginning that he didn't want a serious relationship with her.'

'But she did.'

'Yes. She wanted both, a career and Connor.'

'A case of "If I can't have him, no one can!"'

'Yes, I'm sure of it. I don't think she cared one way or another about Connor until he was with me. To Scarlet, being Connor's ex-girlfriend wouldn't do. She was used to being the centre of attention, and if she couldn't be the leading lady – because I was – she wanted to be the artistic director's lady. That Connor preferred me was a massive blow to Scarlet's ego. She had a nasty streak, and she could be intimidating. Don't think I'm being unkind, but Scarlet was not the best dancer I've worked with. She used her father's name to get work. She also used his name as a threat. Some of the backstage staff, particularly the dressers, hated working with her. They did because of the persuasive power she had over her father, who they knew was able to influence other directors and producers.'

'So people kept on Scarlet's good side because they were frightened of losing their jobs?' Ena said, shocked.

'Or worse. Theatre is a small world, and bad news spreads quickly. Reputations can be ruined overnight.'

'I'm surprised that no one complained about her.'

'Who would they complain to? The company manager? Connor? There was nothing either of them could do because she'd have gone straight to her father. He made sure she got whatever she wanted – by fair means or foul.'

'Was Michael Brookes unscrupulous?'

'There were rumours, but I honestly don't know. What I do know is that what Scarlet wanted, Scarlet got, and to hell with the consequences.'

'And what about New York? Did the show go to Broadway?' Ena asked.

'No. Towards the end of the West End run, the gossip columnists mysteriously got hold of photographs of Scarlet and Connor from the year before and plastered them all over the newspapers. There were photographs of them on tour chatting, leaving a restaurant, getting into a taxi, and articles about the beautiful dancer, Scarlet Brookes, and her lover, director Connor Wolf. They called me the "other woman" and took photographs of me coming out of the theatre by the stage door, looking unhappy. In one, I was frowning because the sun was in my eyes, but the readers of the red tops were told that I was the bitter other woman who had tried to break up their relationship. But there *was* no relationship between them to break up, except in Scarlet's head. Most people in the business knew the truth, especially those who Connor and I had worked with, but it was all very messy. It must have been embarrassing for Lou Kingman. Michael Brookes kept Kingman's name out of the newspapers, hoping that the Broadway transfer would still happen, but the American was one person Brookes couldn't manipulate, blackmail or buy. Lou dropped *West End Nights* like a hot potato and went back to New York, and who could blame him?'

'What I don't understand is, Connor loved you,' Ena said. 'Why did he marry Scarlet?'

Rose took a deep breath. 'I found out some months later that Connor and Scarlet had been in an accident. Connor had been invited to an end-of-season party, and Scarlet and her parents were there. It was in the countryside, somewhere in Surrey, I think; near where the Brookes' lived. Scarlet didn't feel well, and although Michael Brookes knew Connor wasn't in a relationship with her, he asked him to take her home. He said he had business to discuss with the host, so he and Scarlet's mother couldn't leave the party early. Connor agreed, reluctantly. I don't know the details, but on the way the car left the road and plunged into a ditch.'

'Good God!' Ena gasped. 'Were they injured?'

'Connor was, more than Scarlet at the time, although he recovered quickly, while Scarlet's injuries are long-lasting. Luckily, her parents saw the car when they were driving home an hour later and stopped. They were first on the scene and, as no other vehicles were involved, Michael Brookes had the accident hushed up.'

Ena frowned. 'Why hush it up? Anyone can have an accident.'

'To avoid a scandal. Except for Scarlet's mother, they had all been drinking heavily. Scarlet's mother drove to the nearest telephone box, phoned 999, and her father stayed with Scarlet. When the ambulance arrived, they found Connor unconscious behind the steering wheel. When he eventually came round, he had no recollection of the accident.'

'And Scarlet?'

'She was in the passenger seat. She was in shock, but she was conscious throughout the ordeal and told the police exactly what had happened.'

'She was lucky,' Ena said.

Rose nodded in agreement. 'Lucky to get out alive because the car's passenger side sustained the most damage.' She sighed. 'But Scarlet was not as lucky as she might have been because, after the accident, she wasn't able to dance. Her career was over. It has been fifteen years, and she still can't walk without a stick.'

'After all this time?' Ena asked.

'Yes. It's something to do with nerve damage.' Rose grimaced. 'She is still very glamorous, though, even with a walking stick.'

'And Connor was definitely driving?' Ena asked.

'Yes. It was Scarlet's car, but she was too ill to drive. As I said, Connor was unconscious at the wheel. There was blood on the dashboard on the passenger side from a cut on Scarlet's forehead. The accident led to Scarlet playing the forgiving girlfriend who had to give up her dancing career.'

Ena shook her head. 'How unfair fate can be. They weren't together. They didn't even go to the party together!'

Rose nodded. 'It was only that Scarlet felt ill, and her father had some deal or other going on and asked Connor to take her home, that they left the party together.'

'Do you think Scarlet was ill, or was it a ploy to get Connor on his own?'

'Who knows?' Rose said. 'Scarlet was always devious. She always got what she wanted, one way or the other. Though I don't think she planned on being crippled for the rest of her life to get her man.'

'Wolf landed himself a wife doing her father a favour,' Ena said. 'Call me suspicious, which I admit I am, but getting Wolf to take her home could be construed as entrapment.'

CHAPTER EIGHTEEN

Ena took off her jacket and hung it up behind the office door.

'A working lunch?' Artie teased.

'You could call it that.'

'Good-oh. I hope good old-fashioned money was involved. We could do with some.'

'It wasn't, sorry.' Ena leaned back in her chair and expelled a lungful of air. As she took her desk diary from the drawer, she noticed an envelope with Artie's name on the front, written in Henry's handwriting. 'Oh,' she said, giving it to Artie.

'What this?'

'Your expenses. I promised you'd have them before the weekend.'

'Thank you, Ena.' Without checking its contents, Artie put the envelope in his jacket pocket. 'How was the meeting with Natalie?'

'There wasn't one. She cancelled because she was going to tell Connor Wolf and the company about the theft of the sound system. I had lunch with Rose Allen, the wardrobe mistress, instead.'

'And?'

'There's something dodgy about Wolf's wife. But I'll tell you about the devious Mrs Wolf later. Before lunch, I went to the Young Albert and Ben Wilson gave me the grand tour. The main auditorium is very impressive, and I loved the boxes. They're the same as they were in the old music hall days. I loved the Margot Dudley Studio, too. Margot is going to be in her element when she sees it, don't you think?' Before Artie could answer, Ena added, 'I didn't see you there. Where were you when you should have been hard at work playing cards and drinking tea?'

'Very funny.' Artie screwed up his face in an exaggerated grin. 'We were sent home almost as soon as we arrived. Ben said he had to go to the Strand and pick something up from the Prince Albert, and he gave us the rest of the day off.'

'With pay?'

'Your guess is as good as mine.' He sighed. 'What did your favourite copper, the handsome Detective Chief Inspector Dan Powell, have to say about Wilson?'

'It's a long story, but the short version is, I gave him the list of men who had worked or were still working at the Young Albert, his WPC checked the names against the custody logging-in book – and one flagged up. Ben Wilson was taken to Bow Street for questioning in connection with a burglary some years ago but was never charged.'

'No smoke without fire?' Artie asked.

'Not sure. The desk sergeant at Bow Street called him a "straight arrow". He'd known him since they were teenagers; they went to the same youth club. He said he was surprised when Ben was brought in for questioning because the Ben Wilson he had known would rather give money away than steal it.'

'What does Natalie think?'

'I haven't had time to tell her yet, but anyway, she said she trusts him a hundred per cent.'

Artie raised his eyebrows. 'What did you make of

him?'

'The first time I met him, or the second?' Ena laughed. 'The first time I met him was this morning when I was going to the rehearsal. He was opening the office door for Natalie's secretary, Hilda. She was giggling. They looked very cosy. I don't think he had to pick up something, but somebody. I think he and Hilda might be a little more than friendly.'

'Sly old fox.'

'The second time was when he gave me the grand tour of the Young Albert.'

'So,' Artie said, 'do you think he's involved in the thefts?'

'I wasn't with him long enough to be absolutely sure, but my gut tells me no. If you think about it, he has been on the project from the beginning. He is genuinely proud of the work that's been done. I can't think of a motive, so no, I don't think he is involved. When I left, I had a look around. I walked down the side of the theatre to the stage door and the back of the building. The scene dock has huge doors. They're ten or more feet high – and together they are probably as wide.'

'I saw a lorry unloading flats and scenery for *Tribute* into the dock,' Artie said. 'A sound system could be taken out as easily as scenery is brought in.'

'My thoughts exactly,' Ena agreed. 'The theatre's main doors open onto Chapel Park Road, which was busy when I was there. Not only a lot of cars but pedestrians too. But the dock doors open onto a huge expanse of waste ground, so a van wouldn't be seen.'

'Chapel Park Road is close to the shops on Whitechapel Road. It might be busy in the daytime, but it wouldn't be busy at night.'

'Maybe not, but it would still be quicker and safer to drive a van to the back of the theatre and load it from the scene dock. No one is likely to walk or drive down there at night unless they are up to no good. And the area isn't overlooked. Some properties are still under construction, and the office building on the right of the theatre would have been in darkness by six-thirty at the latest. Office workers usually go home at five-thirty, and I'm guessing the cleaners would have been done by six.'

'The row of shops on the left of the theatre is empty,' Artie said. 'They have "To Let" signs in their windows, so there wouldn't have been anyone on either side of the theatre to see anything.' Getting up and going to the kitchen, he added, 'Want a drink?'

'Coffee, please.' Ena followed him and stood in the doorway. 'I walked up to the shops. There are a lot of record shops on Whitechapel Road.'

'Buy anything?'

'No. I'd have liked to have had a browse around, but there wasn't time. There was one shop that appealed to my imagination.' She grinned. 'Music Maestro! It advertised the sale of new and second-hand music equipment. From the outside, it looked Dickensian, and inside, apart from musical instruments, it was so dusty I expected to see Lady Faversham appear. Instead, the guy who ran the place looked like the Nutty Professor, but older. He talked about the bell above the door,' Ena laughed, 'but there was no bell.'

Artie passed her a cup of coffee and she returned to her desk. 'What about you?' she said, when he came into the office with his drink. 'Have you found out anything interesting in the short time you've been at the Young Albert?'

'No. I got to know a bit about a couple of the chaps. There's Harry, he's about fifty. He's friendly enough, but he doesn't say much. He's more interested in the racing results in the *Daily Mirror* than he is in talking.'

'If he's a gambler, he might have lost money on the horses. Do you think it possible that he owes his bookie and stole the sound system to pay off his debt?'

Artie thought for a few seconds. 'No. He is a couple-of-bob-each-way type of gambler. I can't see him as a high roller.'

'I'm wishful thinking. Go on!'

'There's Doug. He's a bit younger than Harry. He's probably mid to late forties. He talks about his kids and grandkids all the time. Nice chap. He strikes me as the kind of guy who, if he found a shilling on the floor of the local shop, would hand it over the counter to the assistant.

'And then there's David. At a guess, David is in his late-twenties to early-thirties. He's a bit moody and doesn't say a lot, but he's probably the most interesting of the three. I'll find out more about him and the other chaps tomorrow. I wasn't there long enough today to get to know them.'

CHAPTER NINETEEN

'Anyway, what have you been up to since you left the Young Albert?' Ena asked Artie while they drank their coffee.

'I haven't been idle, if that's what you think!' he responded. 'I met up with a couple of pals who have worked in the West End for years. I asked them about the producer, Michael Brookes.' Artie picked up his notebook and read from it. 'He is loaded with money. He was an impresario and is now an entrepreneur – don't ask me what the difference is. Suffice it to say he has fingers in a lot of pies. As far as theatre goes, he began life as a stagehand, worked his way up to being a stage manager, and from there to company manager. He started putting on plays in the fringe and, almost overnight, put plays and musicals on in the provinces before taking them on tour and bringing them to the West End.'

'How long has he been promoting and producing shows in London?' Ena asked.

'Since the mid-fifties. Maybe longer.'

'He must have come into some serious money. Taking shows into the West End costs a fortune.'

Artie scanned the page. 'The first production was 1955 or 56.'

'What business was he in before going into theatre?'

'No idea. That is the interesting thing. Before

becoming a stagehand in 1950, there is no record of him.'

'There must be some record of him somewhere!' Ena said. 'Even if he was brought up in another country, born there even, there would be a record of him somewhere when he came to England. Keep looking, will you? And see what you can find out about his wife.'

'Elsbeth Brookes.'

'Find out when they got married and if she came from money. I bet you a fiver she did.'

'You haven't got a fiver!'

Ena laughed. 'True.'

'Moving on… What about their daughter, Connor Wolf's wife?' Artie said. 'You said you thought there was something dodgy about her.'

'Scarlet. Not dodgy in the criminal sense, but there's something that doesn't sit right with me. She's a daddy's girl, she's spoilt, and she's used to getting her own way.'

'There's nothing sinister about that.'

'Not in itself, no, but my gut tells me that something isn't right. Wolf married her after they'd been in a car crash. They were both injured and although Wolf came off worse initially, Scarlet's legs were so badly injured she had to give up dancing.'

'Who was driving?'

'Wolf. I expect he married her out of guilt.'

'Or pity?'

'It's more likely that he was blackmailed into marrying her by her father,' Ena said, darkly.

'Nice!' Artie said, scribbling "Blackmail?" on his notepad.

'Scarlet still uses a stick. The accident left her

with damaged nerves in her legs, apparently.'

'It must have been hard for her to give up her career at such a young age,' Artie said. 'I presume she was young. Do you know what she looks like?'

Ena shook her head. 'I've no idea how old she was when she stopped dancing, and I've never seen her.'

'With a name like Scarlet, I imagine she's tall and willowy with raven black hair and big green eyes. I expect she will wear designer clothes. As money is no object, she'll have the best of everything.'

Ena laughed. 'She may be as you describe her. We'll soon know. She's bound to be at the Young Albert on the opening night of *Tribute*.'

'In the meantime, I'll go to the Spotlight offices and get some background on her,' Artie said. 'They'll have photos and a CV from her time as a hoofer.'

'Good idea. I'm meeting Natalie when rehearsals finish.' Ena flicked open the notepad on her desk. 'Did anything else happen while I was out?'

'Three letters came in the afternoon post.' Artie jumped up, grabbed the envelopes from the top of the filing cabinet and dropped them on Ena's desk.

'Ah, lovely.' She turned the first envelope over and read the return address on the back. 'A letter from Jeanie McKinley. And two bills. Ugh! Not so lovely. They can wait.' Slipping the brass letter opener under the flap of Jeanie's letter, Ena sliced it open and read the enclosed card. 'Great! Jeanie and Gerry are coming to the opening night. And Jeanie is coming up to London next week. She wonders if we can meet her. I'll give her a ring and arrange a day and time. It will be lovely to see her.'

Ena sat back in her chair. 'Without Jeanie's help

when she worked at the Willows nursing home, we would never have known George's father had been murdered.' A wave of sadness washed over Ena as she recalled how Andrea Thornton, the granddaughter of a resident recuperating from an operation at the Willows, had tried to poison her grandmother for her inheritance and poisoned George's father instead.

'What are you thinking about?' Artie asked.

'How unfair it was that George's father died because he drank someone else's cordial by mistake.'

'I still get the feeling that someone has walked over my grave when I think that the mad granddaughter almost killed you, Ena.'

Ena blew out her cheeks and shivered. 'And her young brother. My God, how Andrea abused that boy. I still don't understand why she felt it necessary to torture him. Mrs Thornton had enough money for them both.'

'But she would have to wait for the old lady to die before they inherited.'

'Mrs Thornton had already given Andrea money. The only reason she refused to give her any more was because she was taking drugs.'

'I expect she was desperate for a fix and wasn't in her right mind.'

'You're probably right. She was mentally unstable. I wonder if she's still in the Hibbert Hospital for the Mentally Ill, or if she's been moved.'

'She might have been released,' Artie said.

Ena's mouth dropped open. 'I hope that isn't why Jeanie wants to meet me. On the bright side,' she added, 'through intense physiotherapy, Jeanie's partner Gerry has not only given Mrs Thornton's grandson Rory the mobility he needed to walk again, but Jeanie has given him the confidence to get on with his life. I wonder if Rory is still working with Gerry?' Pondering the question, Ena got up and went into the kitchen. 'Jeanie and I have a lot to talk about when we meet next week. I'll ring her first thing tomorrow.'

*

'Ena?'

'Hello, darling. I'm putting my warpaint on,' Ena shouted from the bathroom. 'You're home early,' she said, as her husband Henry poked his head around the bathroom door.

'I came home to get a file I read over the weekend. I need it for a briefing this evening.'

'You're not going back to Cheltenham, are you?'

'No, it's in town.'

'Good. I'm meeting Natalie at six-thirty, so I'll see you at eight.'

'Highsmith will be in the meeting, so I'll grab a cab now and get a lift with him to the Lamb. We'll have a bite to eat later.'

'Good idea,' Ena said, 'save me cooking.' She laughed as she checked her reflection in the mirror. Henry was more than capable of cooking their evening meal and often did. Making a show of squeezing past him in the bathroom doorway, she stopped and kissed him. 'I'd better get a move on, or I'll be late,' she added, going into the bedroom and putting on clean clothes.

'I'll see you later,' Henry shouted, picking up the file and heading downstairs. 'I'll be at the Lamb around 8 o'clock.'

'Try not to be late, darling,' Ena called, hearing Henry open and then close the door to the street.

CHAPTER TWENTY

Natalie was waiting for Ena when she arrived. 'The fundraiser is arranged for next weekend,' she said, excitement sparkling in her eyes. 'I can't believe it is going to happen! Hilda and I have already taken two dozen replies by telephone since the invitations were sent out, which is marvellous considering it's such short notice. That's probably all the people we'll have at the event. I'm just hoping the money we need to replace the sound system and complete the rest of the work at the Young Albert will be raised in time for the dress rehearsal, or there'll be no opening night. Tomorrow, I'll telephone the people I haven't heard from, and then we'll have a clearer picture of how many to cater for.'

'And how many investors will be there?' Ena said.

'Exactly. "Friends of the Young Albert". The cleaners are in now, and I have caterers on standby, and if everything goes to plan...' She raised her hand and crossed her fingers. 'It should be a good evening.' Natalie looked across the table at Ena. 'What do you think?'

'I think it's a great idea. What time will the fundraiser start?'

'I thought seven-thirty.'

Ena nodded. 'Most people will have eaten by then and won't want a sit-down meal.'

'I thought a light but quality finger buffet? Nothing too elaborate: cold meats, cheeses, a selection of savoury canapés?'

'And a few bottles of wine.'

'Satisfy their stomachs and their thirst, and hopefully, they'll put their hands in their pockets! I don't know whether Margot told you, but when she, George and Betsy toured with ENSA, Tommy Trinder was one of the stars of the concert parties.' Ena nodded. 'Well, I got in touch with his agent, and although Tommy can't be at the fundraiser because he has a prior engagement, he's going to try to get to *Tribute's* opening night. If he does get to it, his agent said he is sure Tommy would say a few words about when he and Margot were in ENSA. Apparently, for a time, they were all on the same bill. What do you think, Ena?'

'I think it would be wonderful.'

Natalie bit her lip. 'I pray he'll be at the first night. Margot would be over the moon. She talked about Tommy Trinder a lot when she stopped touring with ENSA. He was good to Margot, to George and Betsy too. Now,' Natalie said, after taking a drink of her wine, 'what did you want to tell me this morning at the theatre?'

Ena didn't want to dampen Natalie's enthusiasm, but she needed her to know what she'd learned about Ben Wilson. 'I showed the list of Young Albert workers to DCI Powell at Bow Street station, and he told me that Ben was once interviewed in connection with a burglary.' Natalie's smile faded. 'It was only an interview; he wasn't charged,' Ena went on. 'The desk sergeant knew him when they were young, and he called Ben a straight arrow. He said he was surprised when Ben was brought in for questioning because the boy he knew was a generous chap.'

'I did know, Ena,' Natalie said. 'Ben told me when he was first interviewed for the job of foreman. He said he was framed, and I believed him.'

'I'm pleased Ben told you that because I went to the Young Albert, he showed me around, and I liked him. I don't think he had anything to do with the thefts.' Ena paused, wondering if she should tell Natalie that Ben had sent the men home.

'What is it, Ena?'

'It's probably nothing, but Artie was in the office when I got back from lunch. Ben had sent the men home almost as soon as they arrived. He said he had to go somewhere. He didn't say where. Artie and I thought it was a bit odd, that's all.'

Natalie gasped. 'Oh, Ena, I was going to telephone you after I'd spoken to Ben. I am sorry, it went clear out of my head! I telephoned him at home last night and asked him to come into the theatre and speak to the company about the theft of the sound system. I am a coward, but in my defence, I thought it would be better coming from him.'

Ena laughed. 'You told me you had called a meeting to tell the company.'

'I did call a meeting, and I had every intention of telling them, but they were all so excited about the show I didn't have the heart. They were so happy. All they could talk about was how great rehearsals were going and how wonderful it was to be part of a tribute show for Margot Dudley. "A legend" was what one young dancer called her. Margot's daughter and nieces were embarrassed, I think. They are happy to hear good things about Margot, but I could tell they felt self-conscious. Of course, they have known George and Betsy for a while. They have been around since the beginning. They were part of the auditioning process.'

'It's lovely that Margot is still remembered after all this time,' Ena said.

'Goodness knows how the artists will react when they finally meet her. Your sister is still talked about in musical theatre. She really is a legend in the theatre world.'

'Artie?' Ena jumped up and waved to her colleague. 'Over here.'

'I'll get a beer,' Artie said. 'Do you ladies want another?'

'No, I'm fine.'

'Natalie?'

'Not for me, thank you, Artie.'

'Just me then. Oh,' he said, digging into his pocket, 'this is for you, Ena. Not much, I'm afraid, but I have other lines of enquiry, as they say.' He handed her an envelope.

Taking out the contents, Ena put three head-and-shoulders shots of Scarlet Wolf in three different poses on the table.

Natalie looked surprised. 'Are you investigating Scarlet?'

'No, not investigating her. I just find her early career interesting.'

'You suspect, as we all do, that she trapped Connor Wolf into marrying her?'

Before Ena could make up a suitable excuse for having the photographs, Artie appeared with his pint of beer. 'She seems to have been a devious woman,' he said, sitting down.

'I believe she still is.' Natalie picked up a photograph to take a closer look. 'Good photographer. He used a soft light,' she said, putting it back on the table.

'Who's for another drink?' Henry said from behind Ena.

'Henry! I almost jumped out of my skin.' Ena stood up and welcomed her husband with a hug. Then she turned her attention to the man next to him. 'Hello, Rupert. It's good to see you. Natalie, you know Rupert Highsmith, don't you? Rupert works at GCHQ with Henry.'

After kissing Henry on both cheeks, Natalie shook Rupert Highsmith's hand. 'Yes, we met at your flat warming party.'

Rupert squeezed Artie's shoulder and sat down next to him.

'Same again?' Henry asked, looking at Ena and then Natalie.

'I'll have my usual, darling.'

'Not for me, Henry, thank you, I need to get back to the theatre,' Natalie said. 'Good to see you again, Rupert. Good night, Artie.' She took her jacket from the back of her chair and put it on. 'I'll see you tomorrow, Ena?'

'Yes. And I'll bring you up to speed with any progress we've made at the Young Albert.' Ena looked at Artie.

'Not much to tell yet, I'm afraid, but I'll soon get to know my fellow brickies.'

'Brickies indeed.' Slapping Artie on the shoulder, Ena left her seat. 'Natalie, I'll walk out with you.'

Once they were outside, Ena said: 'Brickie is a

private joke between Artie and me. He thought I was going to send him in as a bricklayer. With his boyish looks and slender figure, he doesn't look as if he could get away with being a labourer, but he could. Artie was the best undercover operative I worked with at the Home Office. He still is. He's like a chameleon: he can change personality and facial expression in a second, and there isn't an accent he can't do convincingly.'

'Perhaps he should be an actor.'

Ena burst into laughter. 'For goodness' sake, don't tell him that. I'll never hear the end of it!'

'Thank you for investigating the thefts at the Young Albert,' Natalie said. Ena lifted her hand to wave the thanks away. 'And,' she continued, smiling, 'I think I know why you're looking into Scarlet Wolf's past. I'd be interested to hear what you find out about the devious madam.'

Ena grinned. 'I'll let you know what I find out about her – if there is anything, of course. There's no client confidentiality involved; I'm just curious.'

After hugging Natalie goodbye, Ena watched her friend walk the short distance along Rose Street and turn into Floral Street. A flush of heat and a sudden feeling of anxiety washed over her. Grateful to be outside in the cool evening air, she leaned on the wall at the side of the pub door and took several slow, calming breaths.

CHAPTER TWENTY-ONE

'What are you eating?' Ena asked Henry as she returned to the table.

It's the latest thing in pub cuisine,' he said, laughing. 'It's called "chicken in a basket". It's a breast of chicken in batter, sitting on top of a pile of thin chips,' he explained.

'Chicken in a basket?' Ena said. 'What on earth will they do with food next?'

'It's all the trend in your part of the world, Ena,' Rupert said.

'Where, in Covent Garden?'

Artie looked up at the ceiling and chuckled. 'The Midlands! The landlord said it was invented in a pub in the Cotswolds.'

'Food in a basket? It'll never catch on.' Before taking her seat, Ena looked around the room. Several couples were eating out of plastic baskets. 'Oh, well, in for a penny,' she said, picking up a fork and prodding the chicken. 'It's a bit rubbery.' She sliced a slither from the small breast of chicken and put it in her mouth. 'Quite tasty though.'

'Ketchup?' Artie held up a bottle of tomato sauce.

Ena shook her head. 'You watch too many American films.'

'What do you think of the chicken?' Artie asked.

Ena put one hand up to her mouth, waving the question away with the other while she chewed.

'Rupert, Henry, what's your verdict on this new culinary delight from the north?' Artie asked.

'Better than fish and chips!' Rupert said, to which everyone jeered.

'What's wrong with a plate of good old fish and chips?' Henry asked.

'How long have you got?' Rupert replied.

'What about you, Henry? What do you think?'

'Tasty, but not as tasty as fish and chips,' he said.

Artie laughed. 'Ena, what about you?'

'I didn't have to cook it, and I don't have to wash up,' Ena said, 'so, it's ten out of ten.'

Henry made an O of his mouth and feigned surprise, and everyone laughed. They all knew Henry did more than his share of cooking and washing up in the Green household.

At that moment, the landlord called time, and they finished their drinks.

'It has been a lovely evening,' Ena said, kissing Rupert on the cheek. 'Thank you for the culinary experience, Artie,' she said, hugging her colleague. 'Don't be late for work tomorrow,' she added, laughing. 'A brickie's work and all that.'

'I'm nothing if I am not punctual!' Artie said, flicking his hair with his fingertips.

Shaking hands, the men said goodnight and followed Ena out of the pub.

'Can we give you a lift?' Rupert asked. 'The car's round the corner in Floral Street.'

Ena linked her arm through Henry's and cuddled up to him. 'It only takes five minutes to walk home from here, and it's such a lovely night,' she said, looking up at Henry and hoping he would agree. 'Darling?'

'We're fine, thanks. We'll be home before you've turned the car around. Thanks anyway. Good night, Artie,' he said, and to Rupert, 'See you tomorrow in Cheltenham, Highsmith.'

As they walked home, Ena told Henry about Natalie's fundraising evening and her visit to the Young Albert. 'The thieves could easily have driven a van to the back of the theatre, opened the dock doors and filled the van with boxes,' she said. 'It wouldn't have taken any time at all. There's building work going on at the back of the neighbouring shops and offices, but there are no workmen there at night, and the buildings at the front of the theatre, on either side of the main entrance, are in darkness by six-thirty.'

'Do you think it's an inside job?' Henry asked.

'Dan Powell asked me the same question. Yes, I do,' she replied. 'It's either a workman who works or has worked at the theatre, or it's someone who works for the company that built the sound system. I think it's more likely to be someone connected with the theatre. I can't see anyone working for the manufacturer stealing it, not on the day it was delivered; it would be too obvious. Also, engineers are paid a good wage, whereas the casual labourers at the theatre are not. Artie's getting to know the chaps at the Young Albert, but if he draws a blank, I might have to go down to the company that made the system.'

They turned into Mercer Street and past Café Romano. 'That reminds me,' Ena said, 'I had a letter from Jeanie McKinley. She and Gerry will be at *Tribute's* opening night. She's coming up to town next week, and we're going to Café Romano for lunch.'

CHAPTER TWENTY-TWO

The next morning, Ena was walking along Maiden Lane towards the Prince Albert when she saw Rose standing by the stage door, waving frantically. She put up her hand in a greeting and walked briskly to her.

'This was on my cutting table when I arrived at work today,' Rose said, handing Ena an envelope.

'Rose, you're shaking! You need a cup of hot sweet tea.' Ena pushed open the door to the café next to the theatre and took Rose by the arm. 'A table for two, please.' The young waitress turned to a table in the window. 'No,' Ena said, 'if you don't mind, we'd rather have a table away from the window.'

'Of course.' The waitress led the way to the back of the café, to a table in the alcove furthest from the door.

'Thank you,' Ena said. 'And we'd like a pot of tea for two.'

When the waitress left, Ena opened the envelope and took out a sheet of paper. Words cut from newspapers read: KEEP YOUR FILTHY HANDS ON YOUR JOB AND OFF OTHER PEOPLE'S HUSBANDS OR ELSE!

Ena turned it over. There was nothing on the back. 'Is this the first threatening letter you've received, or have there been others?'

'I've had two before this, but I destroyed them,' Rose said.

Ena put the letter back in the envelope and put it in her shoulder bag. 'Is it okay if I show this to my colleague? He might recognise the newspaper the words have been taken from to create this piece of garbage.' Taking Rose's hand, she added, 'Were the other letters handwritten, or were they the same as this?'

'The same. The first one said I should get another job and the second said I should be careful crossing the road.' Rose took a shaky breath.

The waitress brought a pot of tea and two cups. Ena poured and added a spoon of sugar to Rose's tea. 'Drink this,' she said.

'It's silly letting something like an anonymous letter get to me,' said Rose, 'but not only does it upset me, it has made me bloody angry.'

'My advice, for what it's worth, is don't let it upset you. Stay angry.'

While they drank their tea, the words "Be careful crossing the road" rolled around Ena's mind, reminding her of the day she and Rose were almost knocked down by a car crossing the Strand outside Dooley's restaurant. She looked at Rose, who was deep in thought, probably thinking the same.

'I must get back to the theatre,' Rose said, drinking the last of her tea and putting the cup in the saucer.

'And I must go down to Soho. Leave this with me,' said Ena, patting her shoulder bag. 'I shall do my damnedest to find out who sent this rubbish. In the meantime, try not to worry. Easier said than done, I know, but the kind of people who send threatening letters rarely act on their threats. They are cowards.' Ena knew that to be true. She also knew it would not be much comfort to Rose.

*

On Shaftesbury Avenue, bright with marquee lights and giant photographs of actors and actresses, people were queuing up to see matinees or buy tickets for evening shows. The streets of Soho bustled with shopgirls and boys, hippies, tourists, performers, and street vendors selling T-shirts with slogans like "Ban The Bomb" and "Make Love Not War". With its vibrant young people, diverse crowds and artistic flair, the energy was palpable.

As Ena turned into Wardour Street, rock songs by Led Zeppelin, The Who, The Rolling Stones and Dusty Springfield spilled onto the streets from cafés, bistros, shoe shops and boutiques selling trendy clothes and records. Rock, pop, soul and Motown music filled the air, but it was *Let It Be* by The Beatles that Ena could hear the most.

In Denmark Street, shop windows advertised fuzzboxes and strings for guitars. Ena stopped outside a music shop called Regent Sound. In the window, posters showed Shel Talmy in rehearsal with The Who and wished The Rolling Stones success with their new record, *You Can't Always Get What You Want*.

As she ventured in, a man welcomed her. 'Tex Cooper at your service, madam. I am the manager of Regent Sound. How can I help you?'

'I'm looking for a sound system. I hope I've come to the right place,' she said.

'Denmark Street is the centre of all things music,' the manager told her. 'Every part of the music industry is represented down here in Tin Pan Alley. There isn't a musical instrument you can't buy on this street! And there are not only shops but studios and publishers too. You'll laugh, but you see this record?' The man took a 45 from the shelf behind him. 'This is *Come Back Baby*. Reggie Dwight recorded it in the studios upstairs,' he said, looking up at the shop's ceiling, 'and it became a hit single. He signed it for me when he came in with his band, Bluesology. See? "To Tex at Regent Sound, keep playing the blues, Elton John".'

'Why did he sign it Elton John?' Ena asked.

'Ah, well, he calls himself that now, but when he made this record, he was Reggie Dwight. That's his real name, you see.' Running his finger along the shelf to remove any dust that might be present, the manager put the disc back in its place reverently. 'Before Reggie recorded *Come Back Baby*, he worked for Mills Music. He was the tea boy. He was only sixteen or seventeen then but look at him now – gone from making tea to making records!' He laughed. 'Who'd have believed it, eh? Course, it was a while ago now. The lad was a wonderful pianist, you know.'

Before the manager had time to tell Ena more anecdotes about Elton John, aka Reggie Dwight, she asked if it was all right to have a look around.

'Of course. And if you need any help, just ask.'

Ena was overwhelmed by the variety of musical instruments on display and was so entertained by the manager's stories of artists who had recorded songs in the studios above the shop, she almost forgot why she had come into Regent Sound. Eventually, she said, 'There is something you could help me with.'

'Of course. When you came in, you said you were looking for a sound system, and here's me rattling on.'

'Don't apologise,' Ena said. 'I found the stories

fascinating. But yes, I am looking for a sound system, the kind that is installed in theatres, and I wondered if you had any in stock.'

The manager sucked in a sharp breath. 'No, love, the sound systems you're talking about are way too big and too expensive to keep in stock.'

Ena felt like a fool. She was so far behind the times that she didn't even know the correct terminology. Still, however interesting her morning in Soho had been, she had come on business, and she needed to ask the question. 'Do you know of anyone, or have you heard of anyone, selling such a system? New or second-hand?'

'No one along here sells the big systems for theatres or cinemas. They're bespoke, see. Each system is made to fit a specific space and the kind of sound that is needed. And the requirements of a picture house would be different to a theatre.'

'Yes, I see that.'

'I could get in touch with a couple of companies for you. Get someone to come–'

'No! No, that's very kind of you but I don't want to put you to any trouble,' Ena said. 'I'll go back to the theatre, and I'll make a few calls.'

'They're expensive,' the man said. 'They're not your everyday item. As I said, it's not the sort of thing we can afford to stock. Shops like ours cater for rock bands, singers and musicians – we sell all their sound equipment… Hang on,' he said, 'having said that, I'm not sure what Top Gear sells besides musical instruments. They've not long been open. I was told they hold a lot of stock in warehouses, so you never know.' He pointed to the left of the door. 'They're at number five. They might be able to help you. Point you in the right direction, if nothing else.'

The manager looked over at the guitar section, where several thin, pasty-faced youths with long hair and wispy beards were discussing the various makes. 'I'd better see what my customers want,' he said, as a young girl approached the counter.

'I heard you talking about *Come Back Baby* by Reggie Dwight. Do you know where I can get a copy?'

The shop owner smiled. 'I told you, my young friend, the tea boy is still in demand!' he called to Ena as she opened the door to leave.

Ena walked down Denmark Street to Top Gear. The windows were dressed much the same as those at Regent Sound and the interior was similar, although it was brighter; it looked as if it had been recently painted and the walls were not as smoke-stained. A young man was discussing a guitar with a young woman wearing a long dusky pink and brown paisley-patterned coat, brown and white loons, a matching pink crocheted top, and a pink floppy-brimmed hat.

'Can I help you?' a young woman behind the counter asked. She had Twiggy's androgynous look, a pixie haircut and black eye makeup that framed big round eyes.

'I'm looking for a sound system. The kind used in a theatre,' Ena said. The girl looked blank. 'It's to direct sound – and the lights too – onto a stage?' she explained.

The Twiggy-lookalike shook her head slowly. 'I don't suppose you know the make of the system?'

Mesmerised by the young woman's appearance, it was Ena's turn to shake her head. 'I'm sorry, I should have found that out before I started looking, shouldn't I?'

The girl nodded. 'Yeah! Would'a been best.'

'Thank you,' Ena said. 'I'll find out what the company's name is and come back.'

'We're open Monday to Saturday,' the girl said, parrot fashion and without emotion, as if she'd already said it a hundred times that day. She probably had.

CHAPTER TWENTY-THREE

'Dudley Green Associates, can I help you?'

'Ena, it's me,' Artie said. 'How much longer will you be in the office? I have something rather interesting to tell you.'

'Another hour.'

'I'll be there in half an hour.' The line went dead.

Ena was hungry. She hadn't eaten since breakfast. After she left Soho, she had returned to the office, picked up the car and driven to Connor and Scarlet Wolf's address in the hope of catching a glimpse of Scarlet. Something had been niggling at her since she and Rose had lunched at Dooley's. She'd slowed down as she approached the house, but there were no cars in the drive and no signs of life, so she returned to the office. Seeing Scarlet Wolf would have to wait.

She ran upstairs to the flat and made two ham and two cheese sandwiches. Henry was working in Cheltenham and wouldn't be home for dinner, so she didn't need to cook. She was happier with a couple of sandwiches and a cup of coffee than she was with a hot meal, anyway.

Returning to the office, Ena put the sandwiches on the conference table, put a tea towel over them to keep them fresh, and went into the kitchen to make coffee. Before she had time to return, she heard Artie calling her. 'Sit down at the table and help yourself to something to eat,' she called back. Carrying two mugs of coffee, she walked into the office just in time to see Artie throw his coat onto the hook on the back of the door. 'I hate it when you do that!' she said. 'I can never get my coat to stay on the bloody hook without placing it just right, however hard I try.'

'It's just one of my many talents,' Artie said, tucking into a sandwich.

'So, tell me,' Ena said, 'what's so interesting that you had to come to the office from the Young Albert instead of going home and telephoning me?'

'I had a thought.' Artie took a gulp of his coffee. 'Most actors and singers have theatrical agents, right?' Ena nodded. 'So, I telephoned the Spotlight offices and got through to the guy I talked to yesterday. He gave me the name and address of Scarlet Brookes' old agent, Jim Bonner. His office is in Battersea.'

'You went to see him?'

'I did, and he was most helpful. He was a talkative old guy, chatted a lot of rubbish about how he had made this actor and that actress stars, if it wasn't for him, and so forth, which I suspect is a load of tosh. However,' Artie pulled his put-out face, 'after I'd removed his hand from my thigh several times, he got out some old photographs of Scarlet that had been taken at Theatre Clwyd in North Wales.'

'I know the show toured for several weeks after opening at Theatre Clwyd,' Ena said.

'Ah, but you don't know about Scarlet's best friend, a dancer called Sylvia August. They were inseparable. Scarlet and Sylvia told each other everything.'

'And how do you know this?'

'Because not only did Jim Bonner tell me, but he gave me this photograph.' Artie pulled out a grainy

117

picture of two young women. 'I asked him who the blonde girl was, and he gave me her name and address.' He pushed a piece of paper across the table to Ena.

'Did you go to see her?'

'I did, but I didn't get a reply. I waited for half an hour, then decided to come here and give you this lot.' Artie gestured to the collection of photographs as he picked up another sandwich.

'Good work! But weren't you supposed to be at the Young Albert today?'

'Ah, that's where my acting skills come in. One of the blokes had the runs, and the foreman sent him home. So, after lunch, I went to the gents' a couple of times, and when I told the foreman I also had the runs, he told me to go home.'

'And that's when you went to Battersea?' Ena picked up the scrap of paper with Sylvia August's address on it. 'Five Marley Street, Brixton. I know it; it's a five-minute walk from Brixton station.'

'Correct. I'm just peeved that I didn't get to talk to her. I'll try again tomorrow.'

'I think you should go to the Young Albert tomorrow. Tell Ben Wilson it must have been something you ate that upset your stomach.'

'Will you have time to see Sylvia August? I think one of us should.'

'Yes, plenty of time. I'm meeting Jeanie McKinlay at Café Romano for lunch. I'll see Sylvia first, if she's in. Oh,' Ena said, 'I almost forgot. I saw Rose Allen today and she gave me this.' Taking the threatening letter from her shoulder bag, she handed it to Artie.

'That's not nice. Not nice at all. Can I borrow it?'

he said.

'Why?'

'Well, if I must go to the Young Albert tomorrow, I'll check the print style on this letter against the stack of newspapers the lads have been reading. They're mostly rags, *the Sun* and *the Daily Mirror*, but you never know, there might be a match.'

CHAPTER TWENTY-FOUR

Ena read the name cards above the three bells outside number five, Marley Street, Brixton. Sylvia August had the top flat. She rang the bell. Ten o'clock was early for a dancer if she had been working in a West End show. Ena knew from Margot that the curtain usually came down at ten-thirty so, by the time Sylvia got home and had something to eat, it would have been getting on for midnight. Later if she'd been out after the show. The life of a dancer was late nights and late mornings, Margot used to say.

Ena rang the bell again, stepped back and looked up at the windows. The curtains on the top floor were drawn, as were the curtains on the first and ground floors. A house of theatricals, or bohemians? She waited another five minutes. It would take a while to walk down two flights of stairs, but this long? She didn't think so and decided to leave.

As she turned to walk away, the door opened and a bleary-eyed blonde woman, who Ena recognised from the photograph, squinted in the daylight. 'Do you know what time it is?' she said, coughing.

'Yes. I'm sorry to call so early, but I hoped to catch you before you go off to rehearsal, or… Sorry, are you the dancer, Sylvia August?'

'Yes,' Sylvia said, hesitantly. 'And you are?'

'Ena Green.' She took a card from her handbag and gave it to Sylvia.

'A private investigator? What do you want with me?' Sylvia said. Before Ena could reply, she added, 'Unless a distant relative of mine has died and left me a fortune, I'm not interested.'

'It's about Scarlet Wolf,' Ena said quickly, before Sylvia had time to retreat. She had a vacant look on her face. 'Scarlet Brookes?' Ena said. 'You worked with her some years ago.'

Recognition spread across Sylvia's face and she looked less worried. 'Oh!' She put her hand in her dressing gown pocket and pulled out a pack of cigarettes and a box of matches. Taking a cigarette from the pack, she lit it. 'Want one?'

'No, thank you.'

'What do you want to know about Scarlet?' Sylvia asked, exhaling a stream of cigarette smoke.

'I wonder, could I come in? It's damp out here. Not good for your throat. I wouldn't want you to catch a chill... I know from my sister that singers need to protect their voices.'

'We do, you're right,' Sylvia said, taking a drag of her cigarette. 'Come in.'

Ena stepped into the building's grubby hallway. Through a frosted glass door on her left, she could see stairs leading to the upper floors.

'This was a Victorian terrace before it was converted,' Sylvia said. 'I'm on the top floor. There isn't a lift.'

They walked up two flights of stairs and Sylvia pushed open the door to her room. 'Excuse the mess,' she said, moving a woolly jumper to make space for Ena to sit on an old settee. 'Sit down. I'll make a drink. Coffee alright?'

'Thank you, that would be lovely.' As Sylvia

crossed to a small galley kitchen, Ena moved an ashtray overflowing with cigarette butts to the end of a small coffee table to make space.

'Yuk! The milk's off,' Sylvia said, sniffing an almost empty bottle that looked more like clotted cream than milk. 'Will black coffee be okay?'

'Yes, fine.'

Sylvia put the coffees down in front of Ena and then took a quarter bottle of whisky from her dressing gown pocket. 'As we don't have any milk, we'll have to make do with this,' she said, pouring a glug into her mug.

'Not for me,' Ena said. 'I have to work this afternoon.'

'Suit yourself!'

Ena picked up her coffee and took a sip. 'Thank you, this is just what I need.'

'This damn place is like a fridge,' Sylvia said, looking annoyed. 'I have a nip of Scotch now and again to keep the cold from getting to my bones.' She lit another cigarette but didn't offer one to Ena. 'So, who gave you my name and address?'

'Your ex-theatrical agent, Jim Bonner. He said you and Scarlet Wolf – Brookes – were inseparable at one time.'

'That old letch! I'm surprised he remembers me, but then I did kick him in his pride and joy. I don't suppose he told you about that, though.'

'No, he didn't.'

'He tried it on with all his new clients. His office was once where he lived.' Sylvia laughed. 'Where he crawled back to when his wives caught him having affairs.'

'Wives?'

'He's on his third. He lives in Kent, and has two little kids, but he stays in London when he goes to see his artists in shows. He's not a bad agent, he gets his clients work, but he's a creep.'

'Did he try it on with Scarlet?'

'Good God, no. He wouldn't have dared. Her father was powerful even then. No, it was only artists like me who didn't have anyone to stand up for them that he tried to bed. I thought about reporting him to the union, but he'd only have to say I wanted an agent and it was me who tried to seduce him. I was a nobody, and he was well-known. No one would have believed me.'

Ena didn't know how these things worked, but she was beginning to realise that showbusiness was a different world to the one she lived in.

'So, what do you want to know about Miss World?' Sylvia said, her face set in a frosty frown that not even the whisky-laced coffee could thaw.

Keen to get her talking freely, Ena shivered noticeably. 'It *is* a bit cold in here. Could I have that tot of whisky after all?'

Sylvia's face lit up. 'Of course,' she said, unscrewing the lid and pouring a measure into Ena's mug. 'Cheers,' she said, raising her drink.

'Cheers!' Ena did the same, then took a sip. 'Oh, that's better,' she said, holding the mug with both hands.

Sylvia leaned back on the settee and closed her eyes. Ena could see she had once been beautiful, and still was, in a faded sort of way. Tall and slender, with long limbs, high cheekbones, a straight nose and sparkling almond-shaped eyes, hazel with flecks of gold, she had a wit and sparkle that would once have turned heads. She wasn't traditionally pretty, but she was beautiful.

'We were best friends,' Sylvia said, eventually. 'We told each other everything, shared everything. Well, we did until she took my fella off me. A two-timing bugger, he was. But that's not the point. Scarlet could have had any bloke she wanted, but she had to have mine.' Sylvia reached for the whisky and poured another shot into her mug, which was now empty of coffee. 'You?'

'No thanks,' Ena said, 'I've still got half a mug.'

Sylvia continued. 'Yes, the two-timing, double-crossing... And my so-called best friend was no better.'

'Did they stay together long?' Ena asked.

'Until he saw what she was really like.' Sylvia shook her head. 'Scarlet gets what Scarlet wants and Scarlet made bloody sure she got Connor alright.'

Ena could hardly believe what she was hearing. So, Sylvia was with Connor Wolf before Scarlet, and way before Connor and Rose were together. 'Scarlet sounds like a devious person.'

'Ha! You don't know the half of it. She's married to Connor now, the scheming bitch.'

'Perhaps Connor married her on the rebound from you.'

'No, it wasn't like that. Between him leaving me and becoming a victim of Ma and Pa Brookes, he met a dancer called Rose something. He fell hook, line, and sinker for her – and she for him.'

CHAPTER TWENTY-FIVE

'Rose was in his show. She and Connor tried to keep their relationship a secret from the rest of the company, but everyone knew. Real love, it was,' Sylvia said, smiling. Deep in thought, she looked into the mid-distance. 'I was pleased he'd found someone like Rose. She was a genuine person; she was very nice. He did the dirty on me, but it was way before he knew Rose... Allen. That's right, Rose Allen was her name. No idea where she is now.' She took a swig of her whisky.

'Rose is the wardrobe mistress at the Prince Albert Theatre on the Strand,' Ena said.

'What? I knew she'd given up dancing, but I didn't know she was working in theatre again. What a shame. She was a beautiful dancer. Well, she was more than that. She was the main dancer. It was sad how her and Connor's relationship ended.' Sylvia picked up the whisky bottle. 'Here,' she said, 'we'll share the last drop.'

Ena held out her mug, and Sylvia poured an equal measure into both mugs. 'Now,' she said, looking squarely into Ena's face, 'what is it you really want to know about Scarlet Wolf?'

Ena laughed. 'You're a canny lady, Sylvia.'

'I've had to be,' she said, her voice full of cynicism. She put down her mug with a thump. 'Where do I start? Shall I tell you how Scarlet came round here one night begging me to forgive her, telling me that I was her best friend, and how she regretted hurting me, and that she'd do anything to put things right? Or shall I tell you how she lied and manipulated me, and how she hated Rose Allen so much she threatened to make her pay for taking Connor from her?'

'She didn't see the irony in someone taking Connor from her when she'd taken him from you?' Ena asked.

'No. Scarlet is too self-centred to even consider that.'

'I thought Connor and Scarlet's relationship was over by the time he met Rose,' Ena said.

'Their relationship *was* over. It had been over for months. She told me herself she didn't want Connor. She told me outright that she didn't love him.'

'Then why did she marry him? Was it because she didn't want anyone else to have him?'

'Partly, yes, but the thing is, if he hadn't been an up-and-coming West End director, she wouldn't have looked at him twice. I doubt her mother would have let her. No, Scarlet hung onto him because she couldn't bear the thought of him being with someone else, especially a dancer as brilliant as Rose.' Sylvia put her head in her hands. 'I'm sorry, Ena. I've been drinking too much lately. Sometimes I feel so lost, so used by the Brookes.'

'Would you like a cup of coffee?'

Sylvia wiped her tears with the back of her hand. 'I'll make it,' she said, getting up.

'No, let me.' Ena picked up the mugs and went into the small galley kitchen. She put the kettle on and, while it boiled, poured the dregs of coffee left in each mug into the sink and turned on the tap. After rinsing both mugs, she put in a heaped teaspoon of coffee from a jar on the worktop. 'Do you have sugar, Sylvia?'

'Yes, please, it's in the cupboard above the sink.'

As Ena came back with the fresh coffee, she spotted a photograph of Sylvia in a medieval costume. She was right; Sylvia had been beautiful. 'I hope it's strong enough for you,' she said, handing the still tearful woman a mug.

'It'll be fine. Thank you.'

'Are you okay to go on?' Ena asked. 'I could call another day if talking about Connor is too painful.'

Sylvia shook her head. 'I got over Connor a long time ago, and life's too short to hold grudges.' Taking a deep breath, she pushed a curl of hair from her face and, with a warm smile, said, 'What else would you like to know?'

'You said you felt used by the Brookes.'

'Yes, and I did. You know I said Scarlet came here begging me to forgive her?' Ena nodded. 'Well, she didn't really come here for forgiveness. She and Connor had an accident and she needed to get something off her chest.'

'But why come to you?'

'She had no one else to go to. Everyone knows how nasty she can be, how two-faced and manipulative she is. She was even able to manipulate her father. Some people she worked with were frightened of her, scared of losing their jobs. Apart from that, Scarlet was a user; she used people, and when they had served their purpose, she dropped them.'

'She must have known what she was doing?'

'No, she has no idea how she uses people; that's

her problem. I couldn't believe it when she wondered why people were avoiding her. She put it down to her father being a rich producer, said her so-called friends were jealous.'

'She was her own worst enemy.'

'She was, but she didn't know it. Probably still doesn't. By the end of the tour, everyone knew she'd lied about Connor having an affair with Rose while she was still with him. They knew she didn't want Connor, that she just didn't want Rose to have him. She was jealous of Rose and did her utmost to make everyone believe Rose was the scheming other woman so they'd feel sorry for her, but when the company learned the truth, no one wanted to know her. They didn't trust her after that. If they didn't have to work with her on stage, they steered clear of her. She was a sociopath! She had little or no compassion and felt no shame. She'd used up all her friends by the time she and Connor had the accident. She told me that there was only me she could turn to. And I was stupid enough to let her back into my life.'

'I know about the accident,' Ena said. 'I know Connor was conned into taking Scarlet home. Her father had business to do with the host of the party they were at. He didn't bank on Conner ditching the car and Scarlet badly injuring her legs.'

'Ah, yes, the accident!' Sylvia said, sarcastically. She reached for her cigarettes and offered the packet to Ena, who took one this time. Sylvia struck a match and lit Ena's cigarette before lighting her own. 'Connor didn't ditch the car. He wasn't driving. Scarlet was.'

Ena had suspected as much. 'Are you sure?' she asked.

'Oh, yes. Scarlet was driving, all right. It was her car. She told me she was driving. It was why she came here that night. She lost control of the car going round a bend and ended up going off the road into a ditch. Connor was in the passenger seat; he was thrown clear of the car and was unconscious. Scarlet's left leg was trapped between the driver's seat and the handbrake. When her parents arrived, they freed her and got her out of the car. She wasn't as badly injured as she claims. She'd bumped her head on the steering wheel, but it was nothing. They helped her into the passenger seat. Then they carried Connor round to the driver's side of the car and laid him down on the ground with the door open. It was a mirror image of what had happened. Michael Brookes stayed at the scene and his wife, Scarlet's mother, drove to the nearest village and telephoned for an ambulance.'

'I was told Scarlet's head injury happened when she hit her head on the dashboard on the passenger side of the car.'

Sylvia shrugged. 'Couldn't have happened. She wasn't in the passenger seat until after the crash.'

'And Connor has no memory of Scarlet driving the car, or how the accident happened?'

'Not at the time, he didn't.'

'So, Brookes paid to have the accident hushed up, and Connor felt it was his duty to marry Scarlet?'

'Yes. As you said, he married her out of guilt! She told me she didn't want to marry Connor. She didn't love him.'

'I'm confused,' Ena said. 'Why did she marry him if she didn't want him?'

'She said if Connor's memory returned and he remembered she had been driving on the night of the accident, her parents would go to prison for perverting the course of justice.'

'Scarlet would have done too. She was complicit in covering up the accident,' Ena said.

'It was the first time in her life she didn't get what she wanted. She felt she had no choice but to marry Connor.'

'And, as Connor's wife, Scarlet wouldn't be called to testify against him if the truth came out.' Ena said.

'Rich people like the Brookes think they can buy anyone and anything, even husbands and dancing careers for their spoilt daughters.' Sylvia exhaled loudly and shook her head. 'Scarlet had a decent voice, but she wasn't a good dancer.'

CHAPTER TWENTY-SIX

'Have you always been a dancer?' Ena asked Sylvia.

'No, I was an actress. I trained at the London Academy of Music and Dramatic Art. I had some success at the beginning of my career but then I suddenly found myself out of work. In the fifties, it seemed every show in the West End was a musical, and they all wanted chorus girls who could understudy the main and lead dancers, so I auditioned for the chorus of *Can-Can* when it came to the Coliseum from Broadway, and I got the job.'

'And did you dance the can-can?'

Sylvia laughed. 'Believe it or not, I did! I needed a lot of training to get it right. It was a large cast and a large chorus – and it was hard work, but it was fun.'

'Did you understudy a leading role?'

'Yes, but I never got to go on. Some artists would throw up in the wings before going on stage, but they'd never give the understudy a chance. There was no such thing as understudy rehearsals, but I was ready. I could have gone on for any of the dancers I covered. I had a good voice too. With hindsight, I should have held out for an acting role, but I needed a job, so when I was offered the back row of the chorus, I took it. I think it had more to do with my height and the fact that I had long legs than my dancing ability. I went from one chorus job to another. LAMDA had trained me to sing, and I could hold my own as a dancer by the time I met

Connor.'

'Did you want to work with him, or was it that you fell for him?'

'I wanted to work with him. He was the talk of the theatre world at the time. An up-and-coming star.' Smiling, she added, 'He was the best young director in town.'

'He still is,' Ena said. 'Not so young now, but he has a great reputation.'

Looking defeated, Sylvia shrugged her shoulders. 'Eventually, I stopped putting actress on my CV, gave up acting and concentrated on a singing and dancing career.' She took another drink. 'I wish I'd got an out-of-work job as a waitress in a café instead of a spot in the chorus. I might still be acting.'

'Which show are you in now?'

'I'm not in a show.' Sylvia pressed her lips together tightly and stubbed out her cigarette. 'I'm a hostess at Danbury's. It's a private club in Mayfair. From nine in the evening until three o'clock in the morning, I entertain lonely men. Businessmen, mostly. They could be in town for a night or a week – and some of them come back. So, I listen to them. They often have wives who don't listen and children who are too busy with their own lives to care. Sometimes they are put under pressure by their bosses to perform better.' She laughed. 'If you need to know about business growth and progress reports, the best insurance policy to buy, or stocks and shares, I could probably advise you.'

'I'll bear that in mind.'

'I know it sounds grubby, but I genuinely try to make their lives happier for the time they are in the club. I laugh at their jokes, congratulate them when they've had a good week and sympathise if they've had a bad one. I know they buy overpriced bottles of champagne, but they know it's overpriced. And before you ask, no, I don't drink it; I drink lemonade with just enough ginger wine in it to make it look like champagne. It may look sleazy, and I suppose it is, but I never let the old boys pay more than they can afford.'

'Are all the customers elderly?' Ena asked.

'No, there are as many middle-aged men, and some younger, but they go for the younger women, who *do* drink champagne. Not too much, but enough to crank up the bar bill, dull their senses and take away their inhibitions.'

'I see.'

'Yes. It's up to each girl what they do after their shift ends. I come home.'

'I'd have thought it was dangerous travelling from Mayfair in the early hours of the morning,' Ena said.

'It would be, but the Danbury supplies taxis to take the hostesses home. It makes up for them not paying us a decent wage. The money isn't bad, but we earn every penny. It isn't easy spending five or six hours a night in the company of strangers, having to entertain them.'

'Are you working tonight?'

'Yes, I work Monday to Saturday.' Sylvia shrugged her shoulders. 'It pays the rent and I've been putting a bit of money by each week to pay for acting classes. I should have stayed an actress.'

'Surely you can go back to it?'

'You'd think so, wouldn't you?' Sylvia lit her last cigarette and looked at Ena, embarrassed. 'It won't be easy for me to get acting work. I've been out of the business for such a long time, but it's what I trained for. I don't want to end up old and lonely like the men at Danbury's, but I need new headshots and a new CV. That'll be a challenge with a ten-year gap. I can't see an agent taking me on these days; I've been out of the business too long. And television companies can't afford to deal with twenty or thirty actors; they would rather negotiate contracts with four or five agents.' She took a drag of her cigarette and blew out a stream of smoke. 'So, I shall spend the money I've earned at Danbury's on acting classes and a professional photographer. I've got a plan.' She winked at Ena.

'Good for you. I was looking at the photograph of you on the bookcase. You're wearing a Jacobean costume. When was that taken?'

'My final year at LAMDA. I played Lady Macbeth. I was a good actress! I'm too old to be a dancer now, but you never know, if I take some classes, have new publicity photographs taken and fudge my CV, I might try my luck at getting another agent.'

'I think you should. Will you keep me posted?'

'I will, Ena. I'd like to.'

Ena looked at her wristwatch. 'I must go. I'm meeting an old friend in Covent Garden.' She pushed herself off the settee and took her jacket from the arm of the chair. 'Thank you for the coffee and–'

'Whisky?'

Ena laughed. 'I was going to say your time, but yes, thank you for the whisky. I owe you a drink. If you're ever in Covent Garden…'

'I've got your card; I'll look you up.'

'I'd like that.' Buttoning up her jacket and grabbing her handbag, Ena crossed the bare floorboards of Sylvia's living room to the door. 'No need to see me out,' she said.

'Thanks. Still in my nightclothes at midday. What would the neighbours say?'

'Lucky you, probably!' Both women laughed. 'Goodbye, Sylvia,' Ena said. 'And don't forget, if you ever need to talk to someone, give me a ring.'

CHAPTER TWENTY-SEVEN

On the corner of Marley Street and Stockwell Road was a grocery shop. Ena nipped across the road and popped in. 'A pint of milk and a packet of cigarettes, please.'

'What brand?' the shopkeeper asked.

Ena laughed. 'The kind that comes from a cow.'

The shopkeeper rolled his eyes. Then he took a bottle of milk from a glass cabinet and plopped it on the counter. 'What brand of cigarettes?'

Ena burst out laughing. 'I'm sorry. Of course, cigarettes. I have no idea. They had filters. The box was green.' She looked along the shelf behind him. 'I think they were Players Number Six.'

'Ten or twenty, miss?'

'Twenty.'

The man put the cigarettes next to the milk. 'Anything else?'

'I don't suppose you sell whisky?' He shook his head slowly. 'I'll have a loaf of bread, then.'

As if in slow motion, the shopkeeper backed along the counter and picked up a sliced loaf.

Ena took her purse from her bag. 'How much do I owe you?'

'Five and six,' he said, putting Ena's purchases in a brown paper bag.

Ena gave him the correct money. 'Thank you,' she said, slipping past another customer as they entered the shop.

'Excuse me!' Ena shouted to a young man about to close the street door to number five. 'Please don't close the door. I'd like to leave this bag in the hall for Miss August.'

He looked from Ena to the row of bells. 'You could ring her bell. She's up. I heard her singing. Paper thin, these walls,' he said, pressing Sylvia's bell before jogging down the steps.

A short while later, Sylvia appeared at the door, still in her dressing gown. 'Hello! Did you forget something?'

Ena handed Sylvia the paper bag. 'No, but because I was partly responsible for finishing your whisky, I wanted to replace it. Unfortunately, the shop at the end of the road doesn't sell alcohol, so I bought milk instead.'

Sylvia looked in the bag. 'You shouldn't have bought me ciggies as well,' she said.

'I wanted to replace the ones I smoked. Besides, I want to invite you to the opening night of *Tribute* at the Young Albert.'

'It's kind of you, but if Scarlet and Connor are going to be there…'

'Connor will be there; he's the show's director. I don't know about Scarlet, but I expect she'll be there too. I thought you could do a bit of mingling afterwards. You might meet people you used to know or, better still, become acquainted with someone who could help you get back into acting. Also, a few of us are going to the Prince Albert Club afterwards. You'd be very welcome to join my husband and me – and my family.'

Sylvia looked unsure. 'Scarlet's bound to be at the party if she's at the show. I'm not sure I'm strong enough to meet her again.'

'I'm sorry you feel that way. I'm hoping Rose will be there.' Ena began to walk away and then turned back to Sylvia. 'Give me your telephone number and I'll give you mine.'

'I already have yours. You gave me your card…'

'Oh, yes.' They both laughed. Delving into her bag, Ena took out a notebook and pen and handed them to Sylvia. 'Give me your number, and I'll give you a ring before opening night. You never know, I might persuade you to join us.'

'You mean to check up on me? Make sure I haven't drunk myself to death?'

'Should I check up on you?' Ena asked, concerned.

'No! I'm joking. I am going to stop drinking,' Sylvia said with determination. She wrote her number in the notebook, closed it and gave it back. 'Meeting you has been special, Ena. Thank you for the invitation. I'll let you know.'

'Thanks again for your hospitality.' Ena looked at her watch. 'Oh, I didn't realise the time. I'd better get going. Take care of yourself.'

'And you. And thank you,' Sylvia called after her.

Ena smiled. She liked Sylvia August.

CHAPTER TWENTY-EIGHT

Ena spotted Jeanie McKinlay walking down Mercer Street towards Dudley Green Associates. 'Jeanie?' she called out. 'Jeanie?' The woman heard her and turned around. 'I'm so sorry I'm late,' Ena said. 'Do you still have time for some lunch?'

'Of course!' Jeanie replied.

The two friends walked back up Mercer Street to Café Romano, where Ena was greeted warmly by the proprietor, Emilio Bellucci, who showed them to a table in the restaurant's window. 'Madam Ena,' he said, placing menus in front of them, 'would you like the wine list?'

'Not for me, Emilio. Would you like wine with your meal, Jeanie?'

Jeanie shook her head. 'It's too early for me, but I'd like a coffee.'

'Ah, good. I make you fresh Italian coffee while you decide what you eat?'

'That would be good, thank you,' Jeanie said.

'Cappuccino, Signora Ena?'

'Maybe after I've eaten. At the moment, I need something stronger. I'll have a strong Americano. What about you, Jeanie?'

'I'll have an Americano too, but not strong.'

The proprietor nodded and left the women to peruse the menu. Looking down the list of pasta dishes, Ena said, 'I don't know about you, but I am ravenous!'

Within seconds, Emilio arrived with a basket of bread and two small dipping dishes of olive oil with balsamic vinegar. 'One moment, signora,' he said, returning in no time with the coffee. 'Sorry to keep you waiting. One Americano, strong, and one regular. Are you ready to order?'

'Spaghetti with prawns for me,' Ena said.

'And I'll have spaghetti carbonara, please,' added Jeanie.

Emilio collected the menus and, with a broad grin, said, 'A good choice. The prawns, she is fresh today and the pecorino Romano is the best in London.'

While the two old friends waited for their main courses, they ate the bread and drank their coffee. 'What brings you up to London, Jeanie?' Ena asked.

'Gerry is at St. Thomas's Hospital with Rory. He's having his annual check-up, so I thought I'd hitch a lift with them and catch up with you and your news while they were at the hospital.'

'My news? Gosh! Henry's well, I'm well. At least I think I am,' Ena said, touching her head. 'I'm still as impatient as ever!' She laughed. 'Artie and I have work on at the agency, so on balance, life is good. I told you about the show that's being put on as a tribute to my sister Margot, didn't I?'

'Yes, you sent us an invitation to the first night – on the anniversary of Victory in Europe Day, May 8th.'

'That's right. It's also the opening night of the new theatre, The Young Prince Albert.'

'We're looking forward to it. I'm also looking forward to seeing Miss Derby Bloom again.'

'It was George's father's wish that a theatre be

140

built in the East End so young people from poor families could learn to sing and dance; young people who don't have the same opportunities as wealthy or educated kids,' Ena said. 'The building is finished; it's just the interior that needs a few final touches. Well, it isn't that. Someone has stolen the sound system and, if it can't be found, another will have to be bought. And that's a lot of money.' She paused. 'But I'm waffling. The theft of the sound system is not your problem.'

'It's a problem for you and Mr Mallory, I expect!' Jeanie said.

'It is.' Ena laughed. 'Artie is working undercover as an electrician at the theatre. He's getting to know the men and trying to find out who might have stolen the system.'

'I hope he does. It would be terrible for Miss Derby Bloom if the show can't open.' Jeanie shook her head. 'Why would someone do such a thing? Stealing is bad enough but to steal something so important is terrible.'

'Not only that, but it will have a knock-on effect,' Ena said. 'If the show doesn't open and the theatre stays closed there won't be any box office takings, in which case there's no money to go forward with the plans for young people's workshops.' Talking to Jeanie about the reality of the situation brought it home to Ena just how important it was to find the sound system. 'It will have a devastating impact on the young people looking forward to joining the theatre. Some have small parts in the show and others are dancing in the chorus,' she said, brightening, 'and they love it. Sadly, their chance to express themselves through the arts could be short-lived.'

'It's pure greed, Ena.'

'It is. But enough of my problems. How are you?'

'I'm fine. I'm kept busy with my work, which I love.'

'And how's Mrs Thornton?'

'She is doing really well, though she has aged since the trouble with her granddaughter. She's quite frail, but she still potters around in her garden, and she's quite an artist. Her watercolours are beautiful.'

'Do you still work with Rory?'

'Yes, but less than I did. He still has regular physio sessions with Gerry. He's a miracle, he really is. He only uses one stick most of the time. His progress is amazing. Watching him when he's walking on level ground, you'd never know he'd been badly injured in a car crash as a child.'

Ena wondered if Jeanie would be able to tell whether Scarlet Wolf's injuries were real if she described them. Maybe the accident she and Connor had was so long ago now that her legs, like Rory's, were almost better. 'Are you still working in physical injuries and pain management?'

'Yes. I do a day at each of our local hospitals, St. Mark's and St. Jude's. The rest of the time I'm kept busy helping Gerry – and Mrs Thornton, of course.'

They were interrupted by Emilio. 'Spaghetti ai gamberi for Signora Ena,' he said, placing the prawn pasta in front of her. 'And spaghetti carbonara for you, signora.' He reached for the pepper mill and twisted it several times over each dish. 'Buon appetito,' he said, bowing before he left the women to enjoy their food.

CHAPTER TWENTY-NINE

After the meal, the women ordered cappuccinos. 'Jeanie,' Ena asked, 'when Rory broke his legs, did he also damage the nerves?'

Jeanie nodded. 'He still gets nerve pain, but now it's manageable.'

Ena nodded. 'Can you tell if someone has nerve damage by the way they walk?'

Jeanie gave her a puzzled look. 'Not always. The symptoms of nerve damage are pins and needles, sensitivity to the cold, and pain, which can be severe, but with medication, these things aren't always obvious. If someone walks with a limp or needs a stick for balance, it could be for one of a dozen medical conditions; even the high blood sugar levels of diabetes can lead to nerve damage. It would be best for them to be medically examined, which I'm not qualified to do. But Gerry is. Do you know someone who needs help?'

'Not exactly, but I'd like your advice about something.'

'Anything, Ena. If I can help, I will.'

'I know someone who walks with a stick. She was involved in a car accident years ago. The guy driving – or rather, the guy who was told he was driving – was thrown clear of the car and badly concussed. He had no recollection of the accident and as far as I know he still doesn't. He ended up leaving the girl he loved and marrying the girl he thought he had injured in the accident because the crash ended her dancing career.'

'He married her out of guilt?'

Ena nodded. 'It looks that way.'

'But you don't think this girl, this woman, was as badly injured as she made out?'

'No, I don't. I'm sure she was at the time, but I think she's okay now. I suspect she's been okay for some years. She's very bitter. I suppose that's because she gave up her career.'

'Yes,' Jeanie said, absentmindedly.

'Jeanie, what is it?'

'Sorry, Ena, I was listening. It's just that I'm worried about Mrs Thornton and Rory. It's my turn to ask your advice.' Jeanie's forehead was lined with concern.

'What is it, love?'

'There's a girl, her name is Orla. She has befriended Mrs Thornton and since she's been coming to the house to visit her, Rory has grown fond of her.'

'And you're not.'

'It isn't that she isn't a nice girl…'

'But you're suspicious of her?'

'Yes. I can't put my finger on it, there's just something about her that doesn't ring true. Oh, I don't know!' Jeanie blew out her cheeks. 'There isn't one specific thing. It just seems that every time I turn around, Orla is there. Don't misunderstand me,' she said, looking at her friend, 'it's good that Rory has someone of his own age to talk to. Gerry and I would like nothing more than for him to find a girlfriend, and it would be a natural progression now he's walking better and has more confidence. But the friendship between him and Orla has happened too quickly. I feel she forced the relationship in the way she did with Mrs Thornton.'

'What do you mean? When did Mrs Thornton meet this girl?'

'The first time was in the supermarket. I take her to the local shopping centre every Tuesday. We visit the post office and bank, have a cup of tea in a little café that Mrs Thornton likes, and then do the food shopping.'

'And you do this at the same time every Tuesday?' Ena asked.

'Yes.' Ena nodded for Jeanie to go on. 'The first time we met, Orla was at the counter, waiting to pay for her groceries. She was in front of us, and when she put her shopping into her bag, it split, and several items fell out. I helped her pick them up, and the shop assistant gave her another bag. She thanked me for helping her, and off she went. A couple of weeks after that, she was crossing the supermarket car park as I was putting the shopping in the boot of my car.'

'And she stopped and said hello?'

'Yes. I didn't think anything of it at the time, but she was in the supermarket the following week, and the week after that. I became suspicious when, one week, I popped to the back of the shop for something I'd forgotten, and when I returned, Mrs Thornton wasn't where I'd left her. I wasn't worried; I thought she'd probably gone outside. There are a couple of benches and a small garden on the way to the car park and she waited for me there once before. So, I paid for the shopping and left. Thankfully, she was where I thought she would be, but she wasn't on her own. Orla was with her. Apparently, it was Orla's idea to go outside and get some fresh air. And,' Jeanie said, 'since that day, Orla has become a part of Mrs Thornton's life. I didn't like leaving them together this morning.'

'Why?'

'I don't know. I just have a feeling that something's wrong.'

'What's her surname?' Ena asked.

'Tyler.'

Ena took out her notebook and wrote down the name. 'Orla's an Irish name, but Tyler isn't,' she said. 'Does she have an Irish accent?'

'Yes. She has a soft Irish lilt to her voice. I think her accent is part of her charm.'

Ena wrote "Irish", underlined it, and closed the notebook.

Jeanie nodded to Emilio, and he brought the bill. 'Today is my treat,' she said, picking it up before Ena could look at it. 'You paid for lunch the last time we met.' She put two pounds and ten shillings on top of the bill, and picked up her coat. 'I suppose I had better get down to Westminster Bridge. I'm meeting Gerry and Rory opposite St. Thomas's in a café on Royal Street.'

Outside the restaurant, Ena promised Jeanie she would find out all she could about Orla Tyler. After hugging each other and saying goodbye, Ena watched her friend walk up Mercer Street to Long Acre before going to her office.

CHAPTER THIRTY

Artie was at his desk writing up notes when Ena returned from lunch. 'How was Jeanie?'

'She's fine... It's always nice to catch up with her.'

'The frown you're wearing doesn't say fine.'

'Sorry. Jeanie's well, and so is Gerry. He was at St. Thomas's. Rory is having his annual checkup. Jeanie said he's doing brilliantly...'

'But?' Artie said.

'But,' Ena sighed, 'Jeanie is concerned about a girl named Orla Tyler who has befriended the Thorntons. Within a few weeks of meeting Mrs Thornton, the girl had made herself indispensable. I promised Jeanie I'd find out as much as I can about her.'

'I could go to Somerset House,' Artie said.

'I think you'll be better off at the Young Albert. Jeanie's perceptive, but she could be worrying about nothing. I'll drive down to Brickham and check Orla out for myself – it's only fifteen minutes to Mrs Thornton's house. What have you been up to today?'

'Well, while I've been sitting around at the Young Albert, drinking tea and reading newspapers, I've been checking the fonts against Rose's anonymous letter. Once I realised the words didn't match the *News of the World*, the *Mirror* or *The Sun*, which the lads at work read, I went to the local newsagent and bought half a dozen other papers.' Artie took a page from the inside of *The Times* newspaper from his holdall and laid it on the table. Then he placed Rose Allen's anonymous letter next to it and stood back. 'What do you see?'

Ena looked closely at the typeface of the words pasted on the threatening letter. 'The Times is the paper used to create this letter,' she said. 'At least most of it is. "OR ELSE", which was probably an afterthought, is glossy. Could it be from *The Sunday Times Magazine?*'

'Correct! The same newsprint, same size and style, but glossy.'

'Well done, Artie.'

'I'm afraid I can't take all the credit. I spotted the similarities but I wasn't certain, so I asked the foreman at the Young Albert if I could have an extended lunch break. There wasn't anything to do, so he gave me a couple of hours off. I went down to Times House in Printing House Square, Blackfriars and spoke to the print production manager. He told me that since the early thirties, the font they use is Times New Roman. He said its compact letterforms allow more text to fit into a given space, making it a practical choice for columns of newsprint – and it was designed especially for *The Times*. None of the other papers use it. I showed him Rose's letter, and he pointed out the words that were cut from *The Times* and the ones from *The Sunday Times Magazine*. They're the ones with the glossy finish. He went on for a while about the fonts of other newspapers and the differences between them, and how *The Times* has the most iconic fonts. Much of what he said wasn't relevant, so I didn't commit it to memory. He had told me all I needed to know.'

'So, it's possible that a reader of *The Times* is married to a reader of *The Sunday Times,*' Ena said.

'Because…?'

'Because *The Sunday Times* has social and cultural sections and a glossy magazine, which is popular with society ladies.'

'Like the wives of theatre producers and impresarios?' Artie said.

'Exactly. So, if both papers were used, who do we know that might take *The Times* and is likely to have a wife who reads *The Sunday Times Magazine.*'

'And use letters and words from them to threaten Rose and warn her off Connor Wolf. Are you thinking Scarlet?' Artie asked.

'I doubt Connor Wolf reads *The Times,*' Ena said, 'and Scarlet is more likely to read a fashion magazine like *Vogue* than a newspaper.'

'But you're forgetting there's the supplement! The print manager said a lot of ladies read it for the fashion and gossip.'

'True,' Ena said, 'but I'd put money on Connor Wolf reading *The Stage* and Scarlet *Vogue*. But what if the Brookes' house takes both newspapers? It could be Elsbeth Brookes who sent the anonymous letters.' She paused, deep in thought. 'Let's change tack for a moment. What kind of woman would go to that much trouble if it wasn't for her own benefit?'

Artie thought for a few seconds and then said, 'A mother who wants to secure her daughter's happiness?'

'Or a mother making sure her daughter doesn't lose her place in theatre society to a better dancer.'

CHAPTER THIRTY-ONE

As Ena turned onto the road leading to Mrs Thornton's house, a cold shiver ran through her. She would never forget where Mrs Thornton lived, nor how her granddaughter Andrea had tried to kill her – and instead killed George Derby Bloom's father, Hugo.

She parked a short distance away from the house and pulled on the handbrake. Jumping out of the car and locking it, she walked through the open gate and across the half-moon-shaped drive. On either side, the familiar fir trees and shrubs that gave the house privacy had grown much taller, blocking out what little sunlight there was. Ena felt cold. A red Mini was parked at the side of the steps leading to the front door. She hoped it meant the indispensable Orla was visiting the Thorntons today.

The grand three-storey red brick Victorian house looked much the same as the last time she and Henry were there. Holding the metal rail leading to the front door, she mounted the steps and rang the bell, which was new. She was about to ring it again when the door opened.

It was opened by a slender young woman with dark hair and green eyes. 'Hello,' she said, smiling. 'Can I help you?'

'Hello,' Ena said, returning the smile. 'My name's Ena Green. I had a business meeting in the area and, as I was near, I thought I'd call in and say hello to my friend, Mrs Thornton.'

'Come in, Mrs Green. I'm Orla, a friend of the family.'

'What a lovely name!' Ena said. 'Are you from Ireland?'

'Originally, but I haven't been back for some years.'

'That's a shame.' They walked into the large entrance hall. 'You must miss your home?'

'I've made my home in England now,' Orla said, her voice sharper and less friendly than it had been.

'I'm sorry. I didn't mean to pry.'

'It's all right,' she said, smiling again, the soft lilt back in her voice. 'Thinking about home makes me sad sometimes.' She sighed.

The hall was bright and airy, the doors on either side open, allowing the sparkle of spring sunlight to flood through tall bay windows into rooms decorated in shades of cream, with traditional furniture that looked comfortable. It was a complete contrast to the first time Ena had visited the house. Then, thick blinds were drawn across the windows, the rooms were dark and damp, and the furniture was covered with white sheets. On that occasion, Ena had entered the house by the back door, but she had left by the front.

'You've got a visitor, Mrs Thornton!' Orla called into the sitting room to an old lady.

Seeing Ena, her face broke into a broad smile. 'Ena, come in, come in. It has been so long. Let me look at you.' Mrs Thornton held Ena at arm's length and looked up at her. 'You look wonderful. This new job of yours must be suiting you.' Sitting on the settee, she patted the cushion next to her. 'Come and sit by me and tell me all about your job and your lovely husband. Harry, isn't it?'

'Henry,' Ena said. 'He's very well. He works all hours, but he seems to thrive on it. Sometimes we're so busy we're like ships that pass in the night. But what about you? How are you? How's Rory? Is he here today?'

'Yes, he's just back from London. He's in his workroom. Did you know he's studying to be a physiotherapist? He hopes to work with Gerry when he has passed his exams. It'll be a few years before he qualifies, but he will. He's determined. Who'd have thought it?' Rory's grandmother said proudly. 'After all he went through. We didn't think he'd walk again, let alone have the confidence to study and take exams. And he'll pass,' she said. 'He's very clever.'

Ena agreed with Mrs Thornton, but didn't say so. No one would have thought Rory could have survived the abuse from Andrea. What kind of sister does that to her brother? Ena swallowed hard as she remembered how shocked and distressed she had been by what she saw that day. She had looked through the window to see the boy with a makeshift gag of white cloth in his mouth. He was shaking his head; his eyes were wide and staring, and he rocked from side to side. It was clear to Ena that he was terrified, and the memory of seeing him in soiled clothes, tied to a wheelchair in a cold and sparsely furnished kitchen, had stayed with her. He was in trouble and she needed to help him. Without thinking of the danger to herself, she had smashed the glass door and run to the boy. Before she had time to untie him, Andrea had hit her over the head and knocked her out. When she came round, she, too, was tied to a chair.

'You've just missed Jeanie and Gerry,' Mrs

Thornton said, bringing Ena out of her nightmare to the present. 'They took Rory to St. Thomas's this morning for a checkup, and now they're seeing a patient at St. Mark's. They'll be so sorry they've missed you.'

'I'll call again. I have a client in Brickham. I shall be coming to meetings, so I'll be over this way again soon.'

Ena hadn't noticed Orla had left the room until she returned carrying a tea tray with four cups. She placed the tray on the occasional table in front of Mrs Thornton, poured two cups of tea and added milk and sugar to Mrs Thornton's. 'Mrs Green?' she asked.

'Just milk, please.' Orla hadn't been asked to make tea, but it was clear to Ena that she was used to making domestic decisions and carrying them out under her own volition. 'Thank you.'

'Orla dear, would you tell Rory that Ena's here?' Mrs Thornton said.

Ena waited until they were alone. 'Does Orla live locally?' she asked.

'Yes, a couple of miles away, I think,' Mrs Thornton said. 'She's been very kind to me and a great help to Rory. You won't recognise him, Ena! He has turned into a lovely young man. Gerry has worked with him so much that he now walks without a stick in the house. And Jeanie,' she looked to the heavens and shook her head, 'Jeanie has given him back his confidence. Sometimes I see the carefree little boy with the cheeky grin that Rory was before... before the accident, smiling back at me.' She took a handkerchief from her sleeve and wiped her eyes. 'It's a joy to watch him and Orla together,' she said, clearing her throat. 'The two of them are always teasing each other and laughing. I hate saying it, but I wish Orla had been Rory's sister rather than Andrea.'

'After what Andrea put you all through, it doesn't surprise me that you say that!' said Ena. 'Is Orla the same age as Andrea?'

'No, she's a few years younger. Why do you ask?'

'No reason. I just wondered if they had known each other at some time. As Orla lives locally, they might have gone to the same youth club or dances.' Mrs Thornton looked puzzled by Ena's suggestion. Thankfully, she was saved from having to explain by Rory's arrival.

'Ena?' he called, as he entered the sitting room, followed by Orla. As Ena stood to greet him, he threw his arms around her. 'How lovely to see you!'

Orla refreshed the teacups and poured a cup of tea for herself and Rory. 'Tea, Rory?' she said.

'Yes, thank you.' He let go of Ena and sat in the armchair next to her. 'Have you caught any art thieves or spies lately?' he said, laughing. Then, turning to Orla, he added, 'Ena's a private detective. Come on, then, which one of us is under suspicion?'

Ena laughed. 'It's my day off if you don't mind, Mr Thornton! Unless you've done something illegal that you wish to tell me about?' She stared into Rory's eyes and did her best to look menacing. 'No? Okay, in that case, I'll finish my tea. Thank you, Orla,' she said, raising her cup.

Ena looked at her wristwatch. 'Goodness, the time has gone by quickly! I'd better get going.' She put her cup on the tray and stood up. 'Thanks for that,' she said to Orla.

'Do you have to go back to work, Ena?' Mrs Thornton asked.

'No. Henry and I are going to a fundraising party tonight.' She looked at Rory. 'I am working on a case,' she said 'A theft. Hopefully, tonight we'll raise enough money to replace what was stolen.'

'What?' Rory said. 'Are you telling me you haven't cracked the case?'

'Not yet, but I will!' She winked at Mrs Thornton.

'I'll walk you out,' he said, heaving himself out of the armchair.

Ena accepted. 'Goodbye, Mrs Thornton,' she said.

'Don't leave it so long before you come and see us again.'

'I won't. I shall see my client in Brickham in a week or two. I'll pop in if that's okay?'

Calls of 'Of course it is,' and 'We'd love to see you!' followed Ena along the hall to the front door.

Rory opened it and hugged her again. 'Give Henry and Artie my best wishes, will you? And don't forget your promise to Nan to come and see us again soon.'

'I won't,' Ena said, taking the steps down to the drive. Before turning into the road, she looked back. Rory was leaning against the doorframe, waving. Ena waved back, hoping with all her heart she wouldn't discover anything about Orla that would hurt him or his grandmother.

Once he'd stepped inside the house and closed the door, she walked along the road to her car. Full of foreboding, she drove back to London.

CHAPTER THIRTY-TWO

With money Henry had given her for her birthday, Ena had bought what the shop assistant called a "stylish cocktail dress", a black knee-length dress with a classic empire line design and sequins around the cuffs. The assistant had showed her several dresses that fell above the knee, but Ena knew what she looked best in.

Before dressing, she had styled her hair in a sleek, fashionable bob. Now sitting at her dressing table, she applied black eyeliner and pale pink lipstick and put on a pair of dangling earrings and a gold chain with a diamond drop.

She decided on an evening shawl instead of a jacket. Slipping her feet into black high-heeled shoes, she threw the shawl around her shoulders, picked up her clutch bag and joined Henry in the living room.

'You look beautiful, darling,' he said.

'Thank you,' she replied, straightening his tie. 'You don't look so bad yourself.'

'Then let's get going to this fundraiser. Shall we take the car or get a cab?'

'Cab,' she said, heading down the stairs.

*

'Good Lord, if it isn't Highsmith! Rupert, old chap, fancy seeing you here.' Michael Brookes shook

Rupert's hand vigorously before turning to Henry.

'Henry Green,' Rupert said. 'Henry, meet Michael Brookes, an old colleague of mine. Or should I say, sparring partner.' Rupert and Michael giggled like schoolboys peeping into the girls' changing room. 'Henry works at Cheltenham – for his sins.' They laughed again.

'How do you do, Henry?' Michael said, shaking Henry's hand in the same manner. Then he turned his attention back to Rupert. 'What are you doing here, old man?' Before Rupert could reply, he added, 'Don't tell me you two are the late-night cabaret?'

Ena turned at the sound of raucous laughter. Catching Artie's eye, she mouthed, 'What's going on?' Artie shook his head and beckoned her over.

As she arrived at Henry's side, he put an arm around her shoulders. 'This is my wife, Ena,' he said. 'Darling, this is an old chum of Highsmith's, Michael Brookes.'

'How do you do, Michael?'

'Very well, Ena, thank you,' Michael replied. Suddenly, an attractive woman appeared at his side. She slipped her hand through his arm and his face lit up. 'Hello darling,' he said, tenderly, before turning to a younger woman who had arrived with her. 'Scarlet, I'm pleased you decided to come after all.' He looked over towards the door. 'Connor not with you?'

'He and his stage manager were having an animated discussion about the blocking of one of the scenes,' Scarlet said, with a throwaway flick of her hand. 'Charlotte, his assistant, said something about the rehearsal finishing late. James was parked outside so, as Mum was in the car waiting for me, I gave his assistant his suit and told her to tell him to get a cab. I expect he'll be here soon.' She lifted an ornate black and gold walking stick and waved it vaguely in the air.

Turning back to the group, Michael said, 'Henry, Ena – this is my wife Elsbeth, and my daughter, Scarlet.'

Neither of the women offered Ena their hands. 'Hello,' she said, smiling.

'Pleased to meet you,' Henry said.

'And this,' Michael said, ignoring Henry, 'is the famous Rupert Highsmith. We worked together in the good old, bad old days. And this is…?'

'Artie,' Rupert said.

Elsbeth Brookes, older than Ena by ten or more years, was dressed in a classic green silk cocktail dress with a high neckline, nipped-in waistline and a straight skirt that brushed her knees. Her daughter looked glamorous in a figure-hugging black satin dress that was similar in design but had a shorter skirt. With her piercing green eyes, blood-red lips, and dark hair pulled back in a ballerina bun, Scarlet Wolf was striking to look at.

After a round of polite greetings and smiles, Ena turned to see Artie, wide-eyed, staring at Scarlet, and she kicked his foot. He grimaced and opened his mouth to complain but, realising why Ena had kicked him, hid his shock with a fit of coughing.

Ena took a sip of her whisky. 'I'm going to the bar to get some ice,' she said, raising her almost empty glass. 'Would you like me to bring some water for your cough, Artie?'

'I'll come with you.' Artie put his hand up to his mouth and coughed again for good measure. 'Would anyone like a drink while I'm at the bar?' he croaked. Only Rupert took him up on the offer, so he followed

Ena through the throng of wealthy businessmen and theatre people.

'As we were leaving the group, I heard Michael Brookes ask Henry if you and I worked together, although I don't know what business it is of his,' Ena said when they were far enough away from the Brookes clan that they wouldn't be overheard.

'He's a man who likes to know everything about the people in his company,' Artie said. 'When I told Rupert I couldn't find any record of Brookes, he laughed and said there *was* no record of him before he started working in theatre because he was a spook. He worked for Five and GCHQ.'

'That doesn't surprise me. What did you make of his daughter, Scarlet?'

Artie screwed up his face. 'The way she talked about her husband was a bit off. She didn't sound like a devoted wife.'

'I don't think she is,' Ena said, absentmindedly. 'Did you notice the way she was standing? I thought she was dependent on a walking stick. Except when she lifted it while she was complaining about Wolf and the stage manager, she hardly used it.'

'I wonder if she uses it on Wolf!' Artie laughed. 'I know bold patterns are in, but that stick was a bit brassy for a woman who thinks she's a cut above.'

'She certainly doesn't try to hide it.'

'Perhaps she sees it as a fashion accessory.'

'Mm...' Ena agreed. Seeing an approaching waiter, she drank the last of her whisky, put the empty glass on his tray and took a flute of champagne. She put the glass to her lips but didn't drink.

Artie took a glass for himself and one for Rupert. 'You're miles away,' he said. 'What are you thinking?'

'What? Oh, I was thinking about Scarlet. I know her from somewhere. I might not have met her formally until tonight, but I've seen her before. I recognise that haughty look and her eyes... There's something about those piercing green eyes and that jet black hair...'

'She's a bit too old to wear her hair scraped back off her face like that,' Artie said. 'It's too severe. Doesn't do her any favours. She looks like an ageing ballet dancer.'

'I suppose it's why she wears it in that style. She's probably trying to look like Margot Fonteyn.'

'Not in a million years could she look like Dame Margot!'

'I agree. Come on,' Ena said, 'let's get back to Rupert and Henry.'

As she turned, she heard a familiar voice behind her say: 'Who couldn't look like Dame Margot?'

CHAPTER THIRTY-THREE

'Priscilla?' Ena squealed. She put her half-empty glass on the bar and threw her arms around her friend. 'And dear Charles,' she said, kissing the man on both cheeks. 'It has been ages. You both look well.' She turned to Artie. 'You remember my friends, Priscilla and Charles Galbraith?'

'I do indeed,' Artie said, warily, lifting both glasses and looking from one to the other.

'It was Priscilla who introduced me to fine cuisine at the Savoy,' Ena said.

Priscilla hooted with laughter. 'And fine art!'

'We first met at an art gallery.'

'The art theft investigation,' Artie said. 'I remember. It's lovely to see you again, Priscilla. I'd shake your hand, except–'

They all laughed. 'Come here.' Ena took one of the glasses from her colleague.

Artie clasped Priscilla and then Charles's hand enthusiastically. 'Pleased to see you both.'

'And you, Artie,' Priscilla said.

'So, Priscilla, what have you been up to?'

'Charles is supposed to be retired.' She rolled her eyes.

Charles chuckled. 'She doesn't approve of me keeping an eye on things at the office from home.'

'I see less of him now than when he went into the city every day!'

'That isn't true,' Charles said jovially, taking his wife's hand. 'We spend much more time together. She brings me tea and biscuits every half hour.'

Artie laughed. 'Don't knock it, Charles; I am rarely offered tea and never biscuits – unless I go out and buy them.'

Ena stepped back and feigned shock. 'I made the tea twice this week!'

'Only because you wanted something,' Artie joked.

'True!' Ena agreed, laughing. 'I promise to make the tea more often from now on. And I'll buy the biscuits.'

'I'll drink to that.' Artie raised his glass, and Ena and the Galbraiths did the same.

'I hope you make time to enjoy your retirement, Charles,' Ena said. 'From experience, working at home must be as bad as living above the shop. No one tells you it's time to stop.'

'I don't mind Charles working from home, but it would be nice to go out occasionally,' Priscilla said. 'I worry that he's working too hard,' she whispered to Ena.

'I heard that!' Charles said. 'My dear, if you had to put up with me under your feet all day, you'd soon send me back to the city. This way, I'm in the next room.' He looked lovingly into his wife's eyes. 'And being at home, I can keep an eye on you,' he said, lifting her hand and kissing it.

'If you'll excuse me,' Artie said, 'I had better take Rupert his champagne.'

'Sorry!' Ena laughed as she handed Artie the glass. 'I forgot that was Rupert's bubbly.'

'It's been lovely meeting you both again,' Artie

said. 'Will you be at the first night of *Tribute*?'

Priscilla nodded. 'Oh, yes, we already have our tickets.'

'And are you going to the first night party at the Prince Albert Club?' Ena asked.

'We've been invited, so, all being well–'

'Then I shall see you there,' Artie said.

'I had better get back to Henry,' Ena said. 'You will join us? Henry would love to see you both.'

'We will, thank you. Oh, Ena?' Charles said. 'Before I forget…'

'What is it, Charles?'

'There's something I'd like you and Artie to investigate. It's a family matter. I'd like you to find a relative. I won't go into it now – tonight is neither the time nor the place – but perhaps in a couple of weeks when you're free…'

'Of course!' Artie and Ena said in unison.

'We'll help in any way we can. You only have to ask,' Ena added. 'Come into the office when it's convenient.'

'I have a better idea,' Priscilla said. 'Why don't you and Henry, Artie and Rupert come to dinner with us one night? After we've eaten, Charles, you can take Ena and Artie into your study and tell them what you've found out so far.'

'That's the perfect solution,' he said. 'Now, Artie, go and take your friend his drink! I've delayed you long enough.'

'I'll take you over to Henry and then find a table,' Ena said. 'I don't know about you, but I'm ravenous.'

Henry was as happy to see the Galbraiths as Ena had been. She left Priscilla chatting to Artie and Rupert, while Henry and Charles put the world to rights.

Michael and Elsbeth Brookes, along with Scarlet, had begun networking. Ena watched how Michael worked the room, pointing at everyone he approached, his eyes wide with surprise, vigorously shaking their hands as if they were the only people he was interested in. Elsbeth was as vacuous as her husband. Her smile never changed, as if it had been painted on.

Most people stood around in small groups admiring the work that had been done at the theatre. From the snippets of conversation Ena overheard, the patrons who had invested their hard-earned cash approved of the way their money had been spent. Some people were talking about a tour of the building they had taken earlier in the evening. It had been suggested by Ben Wilson, and Ena knew from the day he showed her around it was something he took delight in. It was a good way to get those attending the fundraiser to put their hands in their pockets again. The more she learned about the Young Albert's foreman, the more she liked him.

A few people were discussing the cost of a new sound system, and it seemed to Ena that while they were appalled by the theft, each of them considered supporting the Young Albert Theatre to be important both for their standing in the business community and the young people of the East End. It sounded to Ena that they were all willing to help financially to ensure the theatre opened on time. While money could do harm in the wrong hands, it could also do good, and she hoped that would be the case tonight.

Finding a table to seat six, Ena draped her shawl across the back of one chair, and dropped her clutch on another. She smiled to herself. Looking around the assembled crowd, she knew this was one place in the East End where she could leave her bag in the certain knowledge that it would be safe.

Returning to her friends, she suggested they move to the table she'd secured, if not to sit down, then to be there when they were ready to eat. Everyone thought it a good idea and, still talking, made their way slowly across the room.

By the time they were seated, Natalie was going from table to table, asking her guests to help themselves to food. A long table with a starched white tablecloth was laid with cheese, ham, salmon and coronation chicken sandwiches. Bowls of Twiglets, nuts and crisps were placed between dishes of breaded prawns, a variety of dips, a cheese fondue with Melba toast, mushroom and prawn vol-au-vents, devilled eggs, and sausage rolls. There were pineapple hedgehogs of cubes of cheddar cheese and silverskin onions, mozzarella balls, and olives, figs and Parma ham on cocktail sticks at either end of the table; alongside were glass dishes of prawn cocktails and, at the centre, a whole poached salmon with cucumber scales.

On the approach to the buffet table was a small side table holding crockery and cutlery. At the far end, a sweet trolley with Black Forest gateau and a trifle. And all the time, waiters and waitresses walked among the guests with trays of canapés, bottles of white wine and jugs of red wine.

Artie caught up with Ena at the buffet table. 'How did it go at the Thorntons today? Are Jeanie's concerns about the girl justified?'

'I'm not sure,' Ena said. 'She has an Irish accent, and when I asked her if she was missing Ireland, she became defensive. She recovered and seemed okay until Rory joked about me being an investigator and asked if I was on a case. She didn't say anything, but I could see she was uncomfortable.'

'Suspicious of you?'

'Or worried. Anyway, there was little I could do today. I'll do a bit of digging, see if anything comes up.'

With their plates loaded with delicious food, Ena and Artie returned to the table in time to hear Natalie Goldman announce the first of the evening's events from the apron in front of the stage curtains.

'Ladies and gentlemen, would you please put your hands together for the Prince Albert Theatre Company?' Singers and dancers appeared from stage left and right to join Natalie. Smiling, they took a bow. 'Our beautiful dancers will be walking among you selling raffle tickets,' Natalie said, applauding the female artists as they left the stage. 'And while you dig deep for the chance to win one of the wonderful prizes, you will be entertained by four of our singers with a Bing Crosby and Andrews Sisters song from 1945, *Ac-Cent-Tchu-Ate the Positive.*'

Five shillings for a strip of raffle tickets was expensive, but Ena didn't care. It was for a good cause. As a dancer approached her, she mouthed that she would like a pound's worth and smiled sweetly at Henry, who paid for them. She didn't know what the prizes were; she hadn't looked, and she didn't care.

The song ended to rapturous applause, and the Young Albert singers took a bow.

CHAPTER THIRTY-FOUR

When there was quiet, Natalie Goldman thanked the artists and said, 'Ladies and gentlemen, you wouldn't be here tonight unless you felt as passionate as I do about this new venture to help underprivileged young people. This venue, the Young Albert Theatre, could only be built because of the compassion and generosity of one man, a true humanitarian, Hugo Derby Bloom. Ladies and gentlemen, please welcome his daughter, George Derby Bloom.'

George took to the stage and waited for the applause to die down. 'In the 1930s, my father was an entrepreneur. Long before the war, he and other businessmen in our town knew what was happening to Jewish people – innocent men, women and children. While many chose to ignore what was going on, my father did not. He helped dozens of young people, mostly students, to escape Nazi Germany. They were young people who, without my father and the late Anton Goldman,' she looked at Natalie and smiled, 'would not have survived. Hugo Derby Bloom and Anton Goldman not only saved the lives of many young people, they also gave them the opportunity to do something worthwhile in the world, which,' she said, 'from the dozens of letters my father received, many of them have.'

Applause cut into George's speech. When it ended, she added, 'Now, through Natalie and me, they are still helping young people. The Young Albert Theatre will give youngsters of all faiths and none, and of all colours, the opportunity to learn and develop, to express themselves not through crime and aggression, not through hatred of people who may not look or think the same as them, but through theatre, drama, song and dance. Thank you.'

Ena forced back her tears as she remembered the evening when Natalie told her the story of Hugo Derby Bloom and how he had financed the escape of dozens of students across the English Channel to London. 'Hidden in plain sight,' Natalie's late husband Anton had said. Anton didn't only run the Prince Albert; he also ran escape routes from London to Liverpool and from there to Belfast and Dublin, en route to New York. Without the help of George's father, whom Ena had never met but whose death she had investigated, those students would have been sent to concentration camps and eventually to gas chambers. Ena shuddered at the thought.

There was still a brass plaque outside dressing rooms seven and eight at the Albert Theatre. Now, the rooms were only used when a show had a large cast but, during the war, number seven had been Natalie's private sitting room, a place where she went when she didn't want to be disturbed, and eight was Anton's room, used for the same purpose. If he worked late or the roads were closed after a bombing raid, Anton slept at the theatre; at least, that's what he told the theatre company and staff. The real purpose of dressing rooms seven and eight was to keep Jewish students safe while waiting for work permits and travel documents.

As the applause died down, Natalie hugged George and took centre stage again. 'Most of you know the musical *Tribute* is in memory of the West End's most beloved wartime dancer. Not only did she become the leading lady at the Prince Albert Theatre, she was also top of the bill at the Talk of the London, a favourite at the Albert Club, and the sweetheart of our armed services after she joined ENSA to entertain our troops before they went overseas. That is why this year, twenty-five years after Victory Europe Day, the Young Albert Theatre will open with a show in honour of someone many of us know and have worked with: Margot Dudley.'

Leaving the stage to applause and whistles, Natalie stood behind the table of raffle prizes. 'Ladies and gentlemen, have you bought raffle tickets?' A cheer went up. 'Have you bought enough? You don't want to miss your chance to win one of these wonderful prizes! In case you have been too busy to buy tickets, let me tell you there are bottles of port, brandy and whisky, a dozen bottles of red wine, and a dozen of white. Tickets to see shows in the West End, dinner for two at the Albert Club and lunch for two at Dooley's on the Strand.' Natalie picked up a card and read, 'A year's subscription to *The Stage*, and, as you can see, many more prizes.'

She paused for a few seconds. Then she said, 'As you know, we are here tonight to raise money to replace the theatre sound system, which was stolen last week. The first night of *Tribute* is less than a week away, and this is our only chance to raise enough money to buy or hire a new system. Any donations would be gratefully received, so please be generous, my friends.'

CHAPTER THIRTY-FIVE

With its sweeping drive, manicured lawns, pruned trees and beautifully shaped shrubs, the house Connor and Scarlet Wolf lived in looked like something out of *Homes and Gardens*. It wasn't one of the biggest properties in Hampstead, but with three bay windows downstairs, two on the left of a solid oak door and one on the right, six windows on the first floor, which Ena assumed were bedrooms, and three garret windows above them – and all with a view of Hampstead Heath – the house was bigger and grander than most family homes.

Ena pulled up in front of one of the two garages attached to the house. His and hers, she thought. As Scarlet wouldn't be able to drive herself, someone else would have to drive her when Wolf was working. Ena guessed she had a chauffeur. From the look of the house and grounds, the Wolfs could afford any number of staff.

With the anonymous letter sent to Rose in her shoulder bag, Ena mounted the three semi-circular steps leading to the front door and rang the bell. When there was no reply, she retreated and casually walked along the side of the house. Drawn by the sound of music to the second window along, Ena flattened her back against the wall and looked over her shoulder. A piano was playing a slow melodic tune that she recognised from Tchaikovsky's *Swan Lake*. No surprise there. The surprise came when Scarlet, holding onto a ballet exercise barre with her right hand, began practising pliés.

Ena put her hand up to her mouth and stifled a gasp. Scarlet was bending at the knee with her feet turned out as if nothing was wrong with her legs. It was as Ena expected, but she was shocked all the same.

Scarlet suddenly spun around and held the dance barre with her left hand. Ena ducked down, hoping she hadn't been seen. Still flat against the wall, she sidestepped back to the drive at the front of the house, flew up the steps to the front door, and rang the bell again. She didn't have to wait long before the door opened, and Scarlet, in leotard, vest and cotton shirt open at the front, stood before her.

'Hello, Mrs Wolf, I wonder if you remember me, Ena Green. We met at Natalie Goldman's fundraiser.'

'Of course, Mrs Green.' Scarlet offered Ena her hand, and Ena shook it. 'What can I do for you?'

Ena was expecting the frosty spoilt woman she'd met at the fundraiser, not the amenable woman who stood before her. 'I hope it isn't inconvenient, but I'm making enquiries about letters sent to the Prince Albert Theatre. I wonder, could I ask you a few questions?'

A tall, handsome man with dark wavy hair came into view from a room on the right of a large circular hall, which Ena thought was the right direction for the exercise room where she had just seen Scarlet. 'Is everything alright, Mrs Wolf?'

'Yes, thank you, James. Mrs Green wants to speak to me about something. I'll take her through to the sunroom. I'm sure we won't be long.'

Ena followed Scarlet through the spacious hall to a room with a wall of windows overlooking a well-kept garden. 'Take a seat, Mrs Green.'

'Call me Ena.'

'And I'm Scarlet, but then you know that. So, how can I help you?'

'This may seem a little strange, but could I ask you which newspapers you read?'

Scarlet laughed out loud. 'It does seem a little strange, but I expect you have a reason for asking. I don't read newspapers as such. I occasionally scan the *Evening Standard*, if my husband brings one home with him, but I prefer magazines. I have *Vogue* and *The Stage* delivered by the local newsagent.' She sighed. 'Can I ask what this is about?'

'Rose Allen has been receiving anonymous letters.'

'What has that got to do with me? And why are you asking me which newspapers I read?'

Ena took the letter from her shoulder bag and gave it to Scarlet.

'Good lord.' She picked up her stick and limped to the window to see the letter more clearly. 'Now I see why you asked.' Holding the letter at arm's length, Scarlet shook her head. Then she marched across the room to Ena. 'You think I had something to do with this?' she shouted, pushing the letter into Ena's hand. 'It was sent to Rose Allen, you said. Well, was it?' she shouted again.

'Yes, it was.'

Scarlet shot Ena a scathing look. 'You have a very low opinion of me, Mrs Green. You don't know me; you don't know anything about me, yet you think I am capable of sending this disgusting filth?'

'I'm sorry,' Ena said, standing up and wishing she'd never heard of Scarlet Wolf, let alone confronted her about Rose's threatening letter. 'Please accept my apologies, Mrs Wolf, I shouldn't have come.'

'No, you shouldn't.' A voice came from the hall. Scarlet ran to the man, and he put his arms around her.

'I am truly sorry that I have upset you,' Ena said. She looked at the man called James. 'I'll leave.'

'No!' Scarlet spun round. 'You have come all this way. The least you can do is explain yourself.' James helped her to the nearest chair, then sat on the arm, his hand resting on her shoulder. 'Take a seat, Mrs Green, and tell me why you think it was me who sent the letter.'

'I'm sorry,' Ena said. 'Your husband is working with Rose Allen, and I thought, because she and Connor were in a relationship in the past, you might have worried that Rose would try to...' She searched for the right words. 'I thought you might think you had reason to distrust Rose, that she might try to rekindle the friendship that she and your husband once had.'

'Love, Ena. That's what Rose and Connor once had. They loved each other and I ruined it for them.' Scarlet put her hand up to James's.

Ena gave her a puzzled look. 'So, it wouldn't matter to you if Connor and Rose struck up a friendship again?'

'If only that would happen,' Scarlet said. 'Ena, you don't know how much I have prayed that one day Connor will find someone to love. When he was asked to direct *Tribute* at the Prince Albert, where I knew Rose worked, I thought it would at last happen and he would be happy, that they would both be happy – and then perhaps...' Her voice trailed off.

CHAPTER THIRTY-SIX

Scarlet looked up at James, her eyes brimming with tears. 'Connor doesn't love me,' she said. 'He has never loved me. Since the accident – that bloody accident! – he has been kind and caring, but that isn't love. Not the love he wants, the love he deserves. It isn't the love I want either. Connor married me because he felt guilty. He did his duty by me because of this,' she said, hurling the stick across the room. 'But I don't need the damn thing. I don't need it mentally *or* physically.'

She looked up at James again. 'It's a cliché that the wife of the house falls in love with the chauffeur, but not for me; for me, it's true.' He put his arm protectively around her shoulder and kissed the top of her head. Her eyes softened and sparkled with tears. 'I love James. We love each other,' she said, the hard, brittle edge to her voice giving way to softness as she touched his cheek.

'I denied Connor of love and now I too am being denied love. Ironic, isn't it? If only my mother and father hadn't covered up the accident, paid to hush up yet another problem their daughter brought to their door, life would have been very different.'

Ena already knew the answer, but she asked the question anyway. 'Why did your father have the accident hushed up?'

'Because our injuries were not consistent with the

way they claimed the accident happened. If the police had been involved, they'd have known I was driving and that I was drunk. They insisted that Connor was the right husband for me, so they made him believe he was responsible. If they hadn't done that, we might both be happy now. A life of love instead of a life living as brother and sister.'

'Does Connor remember anything about the accident?'

'Yes, his memory came back slowly.' Scarlet burst into tears. 'He has never told anyone that he knows the truth about what happened that night. But it was when he remembered that he stopped being my husband. Neither of us has told anyone that I was driving the car that night – until now.'

Ena knew that wasn't true, but there was no point telling Scarlet she knew differently. It would seem that Ena had caught her out in yet another lie.

Suddenly, Scarlet put her hand to her mouth. 'Oh my God. I did tell someone. I confided in my best friend, Sylvia.' She slumped forward. 'Another good person I offloaded my troubles onto and then abandoned. I told Sylvia that I was driving the car that night and that I didn't want to marry Connor.'

'And you haven't seen her since?'

Scarlet looked down and shook her head. 'When I married Connor, I was too embarrassed to see her again. She was a kind and loyal friend who I ignored because I was ashamed.'

'Maybe it isn't too late to put that right,' Ena said. 'Right the wrong you feel you did her.'

'It is too late.'

'It's never too late, Scarlet. If she was as good a friend as you say, she'll understand why you haven't been in touch.'

'She wouldn't want to see me after all this time.'

'She might. But you'll never know unless you try.'

'I would love to see her, but–'

'She sounds like the kind of woman who doesn't hold grudges.'

'She wasn't,' Scarlet said, her eyes sparkling with tears.

'Well, you know where she lives. You may be surprised.'

Ena turned at the sound of someone entering the room. 'I thought you might like a cup of tea, Mrs Wolf.' A woman of about sixty, stout with a kind, round face and red cheeks, crossed the room and placed a tray on the coffee table.

'Thank you, Mavis,' Scarlet said, as the housekeeper, or whoever she was, left. 'Ena?' she added, pouring three cups of tea.

'Thank you, but I ought to be going–'

Scarlet added milk and sugar to James' tea, milk to her own, and passed Ena a cup of tea, the milk jug and the sugar bowl.

Ena added a little milk and sipped the welcome beverage. 'It isn't too late for you to be happy, Scarlet. There is still time for you all: you and James, Connor and Rose.' She put down her cup and looked at James, who gave her a pale smile.

'Is there, Ena? Do you honestly think there's still time?' Scarlet asked.

'I'm sorry to interrupt.' James looked from Ena to Scarlet. 'You'll be late for your appointment,' he said, consulting his wristwatch. He didn't say what the appointment was for, but added, 'It's in half an hour.'

He put his cup on the tray next to Ena's. 'I'll get the car and see you outside. Goodbye, Mrs Green.'

'Goodbye, James.' Ena watched Scarlet's lover leave the room. The way he said goodbye to her was a clear indication that she should leave, and she stood up. 'I'm sorry I've caused you pain today.'

'You haven't caused me pain, Ena. I have done that to myself by not being honest. One day!' Scarlet said. 'One day I will be brave enough to stand up to my mother.' She lifted her head high. 'And I'll be honest enough to tell her about James.'

Ena wondered whether she dared advise Scarlet. She decided she would tell her what she thought and be damned. 'I think you should tell your mother how you feel. It isn't fair on you, and it isn't fair on James. You both deserve to be happy. I hope one day you'll believe that.' She picked up her bag and put the strap over her shoulder. 'I had better go so you can get to your appointment.'

Ena followed Scarlet to the door. James was sitting in a car with the engine ticking over. The two women began to walk down the steps, and then Ena stopped. The car looked remarkably like the one that almost ran her and Rose down on their way to Dooley's. She turned to Scarlet. 'It was you! You were a passenger in a car that narrowly missed Rose Allen and me as we crossed The Strand. I *knew* I'd seen you somewhere before. Was James driving? Did he drive at us on purpose?'

'Of course not!' Scarlet stumbled down the last step. 'I was in the car, yes, and I wanted to stop and go back to make sure you were both all right–'

'Scarlet?' James called, getting out of the car and running to her. 'What have you said now?' he said, glaring at Ena. 'Haven't you upset her enough?'

'Ena recognised the car from that day on The Strand,' Scarlet said.

James took her by the arm. 'There's nothing we can do about that now,' he said. 'I need to get you to your appointment. Goodbye again, Mrs Green!'

CHAPTER THIRTY-SEVEN

Ena had been to Somerset House many times when she worked for the Home Office and several times since working for herself. Despite being a woman, it had been easy to obtain information when she flashed her Home Office security card. Depending on the registrar on duty, her private investigator business card didn't carry the same kudos.

One of three middle-aged registrars in the General Register Office took a form and a pen from a shelf at the back of the counter and, with a professional smile, said, 'How can I help you today?'

'I'm trying to find a young woman.'

'Well, you've come to the right place,' the registrar said, her pen poised. 'What's the young woman's name?'

'Orla Tyler.'

'Date of birth?'

Ena frowned. 'She's in her early to mid-twenties, so she would have been born in the mid to late forties.'

The registrar stepped back from the counter. 'I'm afraid you'll need to be more precise than that.'

Damn! Ena knew this was the case from previous visits. 'I understand you need a specific date, but I don't have one. I know how important it is, but I can't tell you more than I know.' The registrar put down her pen and opened her mouth. 'I wouldn't ask for your help, but it's imperative that I find this young woman,'

Ena said, cutting her off before she had time to speak. She wondered if she should show her old Home Office ID card. It was years out of date, but the print was so small it was hardly readable. Thinking better of it, she decided to play on the woman's conscience first. 'It's imperative that I find this person,' she said, pausing for a beat to give gravitas to her next statement. 'It's a matter of life and death.' It could be, Ena thought. 'Would you please help me to find her?'

The registrar picked up her pen and began to write. 'Between 1945 and 1949. Where was she born?'

'Ireland. The south,' Ena said, recalling the soft lilt and the distinctive pronunciation of certain vowels. She didn't know the difference between the accents of Dublin and Limerick, and sighed with relief when the registrar didn't ask her to be more precise. 'I think she lives in Surrey now.'

The registrar shook her head. Then her face lit up. 'Does she drive?' Ena scrunched up her shoulders and nodded. 'You don't know the registration of her car?'

'No, I'm sorry.'

'If you'd like to take a seat, Mrs…'

'Green.'

'Mrs Green. I'll see what I can do.'

Ena crossed the room to a wating area and sat down. She could have kicked herself. She was nothing if she wasn't meticulous about details, and failing to take down the registration of Orla's car was sloppy work. Angry with herself, she grabbed a leaflet from a table next to her chair. *How to Tax Your Car.* She dropped it back onto the pile of how-to brochures.

An hour later, which felt to Ena like six, the registrar returned. 'I'm sorry, Mrs Green, there wasn't enough information.'

'I understand.' Ena thanked the registrar and turned to leave. 'Oh!' she said. 'Would the local register office in the area where Orla Tyler lives be able to help?'

'They would, but only if you can provide them with the relevant details, which–'

'I don't have,' Ena said, finishing the registrar's sentence for her. Thanking her again, she left Somerset House, crossed The Strand and walked through Covent Garden to her office.

CHAPTER THIRTY-EIGHT

Artie pressed the entrance buzzer for Jim Bonner, Theatrical Agent.

'Yes?' came the reply.

'It's Artie Mallory, from Dudley Green,' he said, purposely leaving out "Investigations".

A second later, there was a loud click, and a metallic-sounding voice said, 'Come on up.'

Bonner met Artie at the top of the stairs. 'Hello again,' he said. 'What can I do for you now?' He ushered Artie into the cosy sitting room, where he interviewed artists. 'I can only give you ten minutes; I'm going to see a new show in the fringe. A young actress invited me. She sent me her CV and photograph – and a ticket, of course. We have to go to fringe shows. It's where the young talent is. You never know, this one could be the next Susan George. Have you seen her new film, *All Neat in Black Stockings*?'

Artie pressed his lips together tightly to stop himself laughing. 'It's not my type of film,' he said, eventually giving in to a broad smile that was lost on Jim Bonner.

'So, young man, what can I do for you?'

'When we last met, you told me about an actress called Sylvia August.'

'Oh, yes. Very sexy girl. Tight arse, big...' Bonner cupped his hands at his chest. 'If you know what I'm saying.' He laughed, showing tobacco-stained teeth. 'Drink?'

'If you're having one, thanks.'

Bonner poured two glasses of Chablis and slid one across the coffee table to Artie. 'Now, where were we?' he said, gulping his wine.

'Sylvia August. I have copies of her Spotlight photograph, CV, and newspaper cuttings.' Artie took them from his briefcase and pushed them across the coffee table to Bonner.

'What do you want me to do with these?' he said, pushing them back.

'I'd like you to look at them, read the list of work she's done and the reviews she's had, and represent her.'

Bonner stood up. 'I don't know who you are, but you'd better leave.'

'Leave before you've even considered representing Miss August?'

'Who are you, and why would I want to consider representing someone who hasn't done any work of note for more than a decade?' he asked, sticking his chin out mockingly.

'Because you owe her.'

'I owe her nothing!'

'Oh, but you do. You tried it on with her, and when she rejected you, you panicked in case she told people the truth about you. You told your pals in the West End that she came onto you and when you rejected her, she tried to blackmail you. If you hadn't lied then, Sylvia wouldn't have been ignored by the likes of Michael Brookes for the last ten years; she'd have a CV as long as your arm and she'd still be working as an actress. With her talent, she could have been as famous as Janet Leigh, Deborah Kerr, or any other well-known forty-year-old actress by now.'

As if distancing himself from the pain he had caused Sylvia, Bonner backed away from Artie. 'I can't take her. There was someone the year before her who went to the union and complained about me. Lies, of course, but my wife threatened to leave me.'

'What has that got to do with Sylvia?'

'I went home to Kent after Sylvia August had been to see me. I told my wife it had happened again, that another unknown actress had tried to seduce me and threatened to go public when I rejected her. My wife believed me. Well, I think she did, because she said I should ignore her and brave it out, that it was her word against mine, a bit part actress and a respected theatrical agent – and that, like last time, no one would believe her.'

He took a glug of wine. 'I told Michael Brookes. He said she wouldn't risk getting herself a bad name when everyone found out she was lying. He said he'd see to it that no one would touch her in the business because they'd worry that she would do the same to them if she didn't get what she wanted.' Knocking back the last of his wine, he added, 'I'm sorry, but if I took Sylvia on now, my wife would know I was lying about her all those years ago.'

'I'm sorry too, Jim. I'm sorry that I have to do this.' Artie took a Dictaphone from his open briefcase and pressed the stop button. It made a loud click. 'Do you need me to play what you just said back to you?'

'No!' Bonner jumped up. 'That's a rotten trick.'

'Trying to seduce young actresses isn't too wholesome either. The thing is, Sylvia August is a decent person. Pulling the rug from under her career was a cruel thing to do. She was and still is a very good actress.'

Bonner paled. 'She might be, but I can't represent her.'

'We'll see.' Artie put Sylvia's photographs back in his briefcase and closed it. Then he laid the Dictaphone on the top.

'All right, all right! Tell her I'll help her to get a good agent.'

'Thank you.' Artie smiled. 'Oh, I didn't say. Sylvia August is a friend of my colleague. Neither she nor Sylvia know that I've come to see you, and I'd rather they didn't find out.' He glared at Bonner, who put his forefinger up to his lips and shook his head. 'Sylvia is going to be sending her CV out to agents, and my colleague and I are hoping you'll put in a good word for her if you're asked. I'll give you a call and let you know which agents she's going to approach, and you can take them to dinner or to see a show. It's delicate; we don't want Sylvia to know we are... how can I put it? Helping her. She's a proud woman.'

'I'll do as you say,' Bonner said, hastily. 'I won't tell anyone that we've had this conversation if you don't tell anyone what I said on that!' He flicked his hand towards the recording device with a look of disgust.

'You have my word,' Artie said. 'I'm not in the business of hurting people, Mr Bonner. I leave that to philandering husbands, and theatrical agents who take advantage of young women.' Crossing the office to the door, he added, 'Thanks for the wine. I'll see myself out.'

CHAPTER THIRTY-NINE

'Can I help you?' Ena heard Artie say.

'Is Ena Green here?'

'Yes, she's here. She won't be a minute, she's–'

'Tell her I wish to speak to her.'

Artie jumped up from his chair and, giving the woman his most practised smile, crossed the room to greet her. 'It's Mrs Brookes, isn't it? I'm Ena's associate. We met at the fundraiser for the Young Albert.'

Ignoring him, Elsbeth Brookes marched into the room. 'Well, is she here?'

Artie closed the door, crossed to Ena's desk, and pulled out a chair. 'If you'd like to take a seat, I'll tell Ena you are here.' She didn't reply, nor did she sit down, so Artie left her standing and hopped up the steps to the kitchen, where Ena was making drinks.

'Who the hell does she think she is?' he hissed. 'Did you hear her?'

Ena closed her eyes in exasperation, expelled a lung full of air and began to laugh. 'Shush! She'll hear you. Sorry,' she said, biting her bottom lip. 'I'm going to get both barrels, aren't I?'

'Yes! So compose yourself,' Artie instructed.

Ena poked her head around the door jamb. 'I'm making a cup of tea, Mrs Brookes. Would you like one?'

'No, thank you!' Elsbeth Brookes said, before

sighing loudly.

Artie's mouth gaped open. 'What are you playing at, Ena?' he whispered.

She grinned at him. 'Here's your cuppa. Come on, let's go in and face the music.'

'After you,' he said, standing back.

Ena put on a smile and almost skipped down the steps from the kitchen to the office. 'How can I help you, Mrs Brookes?'

'I don't need your *help*, Mrs Green. I have come here to say you have ruined my daughter's life. Her marriage is in tatters, as is her standing in the theatre.'

'Oh, I don't think that's true, is it now? I think it was you who ruined your daughter's life by manipulating her and her career and deciding who she could and couldn't have as friends. You took your daughter's life from her and moulded it into what you wanted it to be. Were you such a poor dancer that you needed to be famous through her?'

'How dare you speak to me in this way!'

'Because it's your need to reflect in Scarlet's glory that has driven you to make her life a misery,' Ena continued, unperturbed. 'And when she wasn't a good enough dancer, you saw a way to get that reflected glory using Connor Wolf, who you and your husband believed would be the next great director.'

'My daughter would have been the main dancer if Connor Wolf had not been drinking and crashed her car!' Elsbeth exclaimed. 'I wanted what was right for her. She could no longer dance, which was *his* fault. He had to pay for what he'd done to my daughter.'

Ena smirked. 'I think you have told so many people the story of how Connor Wolf was driving Scarlet's car on the night of the accident that you actually believe it.'

Looking defiant, her eyes half closed in anger, Elsbeth Brookes stood ramrod straight and didn't reply.

'And so she married Connor Wolf, who you knew your daughter didn't love. Did you know Connor's memory of that night returned?' Elsbeth took a short, sharp, involuntary breath. 'No? I didn't think so. You not only denied Scarlet the chance to meet someone else, fall in love, and be happy, you also denied Connor of that – but then, you know that, don't you? You knew at the time of the accident that he was in love with Rose Allen, and you couldn't bear it. The accident was convenient, Elsbeth. You knew by then your daughter wasn't good enough to make it as a lead dancer, so you manipulated a tragic situation.'

'I refuse to be subjected to any more of your lies and insinuations,' Elsbeth Brookes barked, turning and marching towards the door.

Before she got there, Ena said: 'It isn't too late to put things right with Scarlet.'

Elsbeth physically stiffened. Keeping her back to Ena, she spat, 'I know what's right for my daughter, and it is *not* living with a chauffeur!'

'And that's the crux of it, isn't it?' Ena said, going to the filing cabinet and taking out the anonymous letter that had been sent to Rose. 'You are embarrassed by your daughter's love for James. What would your friends say if they knew the daughter of the famous impresario Michael Brookes and his sophisticated wife was living with her chauffeur?' She put the threatening letter on the edge of her desk. 'I wonder what they'd say if they knew you were the author of this creative missive.'

Elsbeth gasped. 'How dare you accuse me of sending anonymous letters to that woman!'

'How do you know the recipient of this *anonymous* letter is a woman?'

She caught her breath. 'It says–'

'You can't read what it says from where you're standing, Mrs Brookes.'

'These kinds of letters are always to women.'

'And are they always *from* a woman, Mrs Brookes?'

'How would I know?'

'Oh, I think you know because you sent it.'

Elsbeth turned on her heels. 'How dare you accuse me of such things?'

'I dare because your fingerprints are all over it.' Ena held up the letter. 'That woman, as you know, is Rose Allen. She has done nothing to deserve being threatened by you, Mrs Brookes.' She returned the letter to the filing cabinet.

'I don't have to listen to your slanderous accusations! Good day, Mrs Green. You'll be hearing from my solicitor!' With that, Elsbeth stormed out of the office.

CHAPTER FORTY

Ena followed Elsbeth out of the office to the front door. She stood to one side, so the self-important woman had to let herself out. She pulled on the door but it didn't open.

'Let me, Mrs Brookes.'

Ignoring Ena, Elsbeth yanked the door with such strength that it swung open, almost knocking her off her feet. Cursing under her breath, she fled across the street.

Ena was about to close the door when she stopped. She recognised the model of car parked opposite the office. It was the same one James drove. Elsbeth and Scarlet had the same cars. She ran across the road and took hold of Elsbeth by the arm. 'Your car is remarkably like the one that almost hit Rose Allen and me when we were crossing The Strand some weeks ago,' she said. Seeing the panic in Elsbeth's eyes, she continued, 'It was you! You were driving this car on that day, weren't you?'

Elsbeth held Ena with a cold stare. 'I have no idea what you're talking about. Take your hand off me!'

'I knew I'd seen Scarlet before when I met her at Natalie Goldman's fundraiser, and now I know where. It was that day when Rose and I were almost knocked down. I didn't see who was driving the car; I only saw Scarlet because she was in the passenger seat. Did you drive at us on purpose?'

'Of course I didn't.'

'It was a coincidence, was it, that you almost ran down the woman your son-in-law once loved, and you feared might love again?'

'Yes, and that was all it was. I was at my daughter's house, and she needed to see her husband urgently, so I drove her to the theatre. As you know, my daughter hasn't driven since she was injured in a car accident.'

'You drove Scarlet? Isn't it usually James, her chauffeur, who drives her?'

'I was coming into London, anyway–' Looking drawn, Elsbeth stopped speaking and leaned against the car. Taking her leather driving gloves from her handbag and slowly putting them on, she said, eventually, 'I fail to see what my daughter's domestic arrangements have to do with you, Mrs Green.'

Ena felt angry that Elsbeth appeared to care more about smoothing the leather of her gloves between her fingers and over the backs of her hands than she did about taking responsibility for almost running over two people. 'You could have killed us!' she said. 'You do know that, don't you? Or doesn't it bother you?'

'I had no choice. A car coming from the opposite direction was driving recklessly. I put my foot down to avoid an…' Elsbeth took a deep breath. 'Accident. I'm sorry I caused you distress. It wasn't intentional. I was shocked to see Rose Allen and didn't turn the steering wheel quickly enough. Scarlet wanted me to stop, to go back to make sure you were both alright, but I thought Rose would make a fuss to Connor, and it would make things worse for Scarlet.' She pulled open the car door and slumped down into the driver's seat. 'I'm sorry. I don't know what has happened to me, how I've become so bitter. My daughter has moved out of the home she shared with Connor and won't speak to me.'

'For your sake as well as Scarlet's, put the situation right before you lose your daughter for good,' Ena said. 'You have the power to make both your daughter and Connor happy. And by making them happy, you'll be surprised how much better you'll feel.'

'You're right, Mrs Green.' With gloved hands, Elsbeth dabbed at moisture beneath her eyes. 'May I ask a favour of you?'

'Yes,' Ena said, tentatively, dreading what the favour might be.

'Would you tell Rose how very sorry I am that...' She wiped away the involuntary tears that now flowed freely onto her cheeks. Hardly able to articulate the words, she continued, 'Would you tell her I didn't drive at her on purpose.'

'I will, but you know, I don't think it would have crossed Rose's mind that you did,' Ena said. 'Elsbeth, why don't you come back into the office and sit down for a few minutes? I'll make you a cup of tea. I think you're too upset to drive.'

She shook her head. 'I'll be fine, Ena, but thank you.' She swung her legs into the car and when she put the key in the ignition, Ena shut the door. 'Oh, Ena,' Elsbeth called, rolling down the window, 'thank you. I'll tell Scarlet and my husband everything. I have no idea where to begin, but I'll tell them, and I'll do my best to make it up to them. To Connor too.'

'Perhaps you could start by accepting that your daughter and James love each other.'

Elsbeth smiled. 'I will.'

Ena watched her drive away and went back to the office. 'Is she alright?' Artie asked. 'I came to the door, but you were almost hugging her.'

She tutted. 'Don't exaggerate! But, yes, I think they'll all be alright in time.' She crossed to the filing cabinet, locked it and took the dirty mugs to the kitchen. After leaving them in the sink, she flicked off the light. 'Have you got anything to get home for tonight?' she asked him.

'No, why?'

'Come on, then,' she said, taking her coat from the back of the door. 'I need a drink. Lock up, and I'll go up to the flat and pour us a couple of large ones. Scotch okay?' She didn't wait for Artie to answer.

CHAPTER FORTY-ONE

'Cheers!' Ena said, when she and Artie were relaxing on the sofa with their drinks.

'Did you enjoy putting the witch Brookes in her place?'

'I did when she first arrived all hoity-toity,' she said, 'but I felt sorry for the silly woman by the time she left.'

'I could see you were deep in conversation outside.'

'She wants her daughter back in her life and she knows for that to happen she has a lot of bridges to build – and not only with her daughter. She must make amends for the hurt she has caused. And she has to accept her daughter's choice of partner.'

'She's too arrogant to do that,' Artie said. 'People like Elsbeth Brookes never admit to being wrong and they rarely apologise.' He knocked his whiskey back. 'You know the old saying, Ena: leopards don't change their spots.'

She laughed. 'You're full of advice today. Old saying, indeed.' She poured another drink. 'But I think you're wrong, Artie. I think people *can* change. I'd have said Rupert was more Elsbeth Brookes' type than ours, but he's changed.'

'He has, hasn't he?' Artie said. 'Good lord, he'd be impossible to live with if he hadn't!'

Ena heard the front door bang shut. 'Now, my

Henry has never changed his spots. He's still my reliable old rock.'

'Here's to Henry,' Artie said, raising his glass.

'What are you two cooking up now?' Henry said, sticking his head around the living room door.

'Cooking? I'm afraid there isn't anything cooking,' Ena said. 'Take your coat off and come and join us. Artie and I are celebrating leopards changing their spots.'

Henry laughed. 'Pour me a drink, darling,' he said, leaning through the hatch between the sitting room and kitchen. 'Cold meat and cheese alright, or were you going to cook me dinner tonight?'

Ena looked at Artie and pulled a face. Artie giggled. 'I thought you'd have eaten by now. You have eaten, haven't you, Henry?'

'Yes, Ena, I had lunch at one o'clock. Here, put these plates of meat on the dining table,' he said, placing one of ham and one of beef on the counter before taking cheese from the refrigerator. Slicing a loaf of bread, he added, 'We'll put all the food we have on the table and help ourselves. Butter!' he announced, putting it on the counter.

'Food!' Artie said, jumping up from the settee. Cutting a wedge of cheese from a slab of cheddar, he carried the cheeseboard and the bread to the table, then returned for the butter. 'I'm starving!'

'Help yourself,' Ena said, pushing the cold meats towards him. While Artie buttered the bread, she went to the sideboard and refreshed their drinks.

'Anything else?' Henry asked, placing dishes of pickled onions and gherkins in the middle of the table. 'No? Right, don't stand on ceremony, Artie. Tuck in.'

'Thank you, darling,' Ena said, as she sat down at

the end of the table.

'I'm ravenous,' said Artie. 'Thanks, Henry.'

'My husband is an excellent cook,' Ena said. 'None of this everything with chips malarky, oh no. He cooks sliced potatoes in a gorgeous sauce – though don't ask me what it's called. And his buttery mash is scrumptious. Oh, and he makes perfect roast potatoes.' Artie laughed. 'I'm being serious!' she said. 'Henry's roast potatoes are better than any I've tasted anywhere. They are brown and crispy on the outside and soft and fluffy on the inside. I either burn them, or the insides aren't cooked enough and they're rock hard.'

'I was a bachelor for a long time, Artie, and if I hadn't learned how to cook, I'd have starved,' Henry said, taking two slices of bread and putting ham on one and beef on the other. 'Who does the cooking in your house?'

Artie feigned shock. 'Me, of course! Rupert can't boil an egg.'

Henry chuckled. 'Rupert was a bachelor for long enough; I'm surprised he never learned.'

'I don't think he was interested. Besides which, he didn't need to cook. He was a member of so many clubs he was able to eat out every night.'

The three friends chatted and laughed while they ate their meal. When they had finished, Ena cleared the table and Henry made coffee.

'So,' Henry said, when they were settled in the sitting area of the room, 'how are you getting on at the Young Albert? What are the chaps you're working with like?'

'They are a mixed bunch,' Artie said. 'Ben Wilson – the foreman – seems like a decent enough bloke. He's fair and he knows his job. One chap's a family man. He's nice enough, talks about his wife and kids most of the time. Another is a bit older. He's quiet. He's married, but he doesn't talk much about his family.'

'He likes a bet on the horses,' Ena added, 'but you don't think he's the thief, do you?'

Artie shook his head. 'He's decent enough. From what he says, the most he bets is a shilling-each-way. The youngest of us is David. He doesn't say a lot. He hasn't mentioned a girlfriend or wife, so I assume he has neither. There are two painter-decorators, but I don't know anything about them. I only see them at lunchtime. One or other of them comes to the green room and makes tea around eleven and takes it to wherever they're working. They bring a pack-up for lunch, which they usually eat with us in the green room. But they don't say a lot. They keep themselves to themselves. You met them, didn't you, Ena?'

'I didn't meet them,' she said. 'They were painting the dressing rooms when I was there.'

'Do you suspect anyone of the thefts?' Henry asked.

'I'm not sure about Ben. What do you think, Ena?'

'I don't think he's involved. He's too proud of what he's achieved.'

CHAPTER FORTY-TWO

'Good morning, Stan.'

'Morning, Mrs Green,' the doorman replied. 'Mrs Goldman is in her office if you would like to go through.'

'Thank you.'

The passage at the back of the stage was as busy as Paddington Station. Male artists in a variety of American military uniforms were streaming from their dressing rooms and heading for the wings to await their cue to go on stage, followed by girls waving flags.

'It's VE Day!' a young actor dressed as an American airman shouted, and the ensemble piled onto the stage.

'Natalie,' Ena said, seeing her niece returning to her dressing room. 'Don't tell me there's a scene in this extravaganza that you're not actually in?'

Natalie laughed. 'I'm in it, alright, Auntie, but they're blocking the crowd scene first. It's the big one, Trafalgar Square on VE Day. They'll call me when they're ready for me.'

'You look tired, darling.'

'I am. We all are.' She looked at Ena. 'I have loved every second of dancing and singing in the show. The director said I have exceptional talent, and I won't find it difficult to get work when I've finished my studies and I'm ready to go into the business full time. I hope Mum will see that.'

'Of course she will. She'll be very proud of you.'

Ena's niece inhaled and said, 'I mean, see that I'm good enough to be a professional dancer. Perform in shows. Go on tour. It's what I want to do more than anything in the world.'

Ena laughed. 'You remind me of your mum when she was young. Being in musicals, dancing and singing was all she wanted to do, too. If you want it badly enough, you'll do it, Natalie.' She put her arm around her niece's shoulders. Noticing tears in her eyes, Ena said, 'What is it, darling?'

'You mustn't say anything, Auntie Ena. Promise?' Ena nodded. 'Mum wants me to take over the running of the dance academy. I've been studying business at night school and shadowing Dad and the academy's administrator during the day. When I get my Higher Certificate in office studies in the summer, she wants me to become an apprentice, and eventually, when I have enough experience in the business side of things, she and Dad are going to take a step back.' Natalie sighed. 'When Mum thinks I'm capable of running the academy the way she wants it to be run, she and Dad are going to retire.'

'But you don't want to run it?'

'No. I know I'm twenty-four, but I feel too young for that kind of responsibility.' Tears filled her eyes. 'Auntie Ena, I want to have some fun before I settle down. I want to experience what it's like to live and work away from home. I want to get a job in a musical, go on tour, live in other cities, and share digs with other dancers. *The Stage* is full of adverts for auditions. I want to go to those auditions and try for those jobs. I want to experience what it's like to be free. I want to be a professional dancer and singer, like Mum was.'

'I think when your parents see how brilliant you are on that stage, they'll think as I do: that you need to have a career of your choosing, have some life before you settle down to run the academy.' Ena put her arms around her niece. 'You're a natural,' she said, 'as your mother was.'

'Thank you.'

A voice came from the wings. 'This is your five-minute call, Miss Burrell.'

'Oh, heck! I had better prepare for singing to the troops!'

'I'll leave you to it,' Ena said. 'Bye, love.'

'Auntie Ena!' Natalie called as Ena was leaving the dressing room. 'Don't say anything to Mum, will you?'

Ena shook her head but, as she walked away, she wondered if she could say anything to her sister without breaking Natalie's confidence. Then again, she was sure that once Margot saw for herself how alike she and her daughter were, how beautifully her daughter sang and danced, she would know how talented Natalie was. Although a nudge in the right direction never hurt where Margot was concerned...

CHAPTER FORTY-THREE

Ena knocked on Natalie Goldman's office door.

'Come in.'

'Sorry I'm late, Natalie. I've just been speaking to your talented young namesake.'

'She's her mother's daughter, isn't she?' Natalie said. 'She is every bit as talented as her mother was at that age.'

There was another knock at the door, and Hilda entered carrying a tea tray. 'Hello, Ena,' she said, putting the tray on Natalie's desk.

'Hello, Hilda.'

The secretary set two cups on the desk. 'Are you not joining us?' Natalie asked.

'I hope I haven't taken your tea?' Ena said, at the same time.

'No, I took my tea to my office before bringing yours,' Hilda said, smiling at Ena. Then she turned to Natalie. 'If you don't need me for anything else, I'll get on. I don't like large amounts of cash hanging about. The sooner it's safely deposited in the bank, the better.'

'I agree. Thank you.'

When Hilda had left the office, Ena said, 'This was her tea, wasn't it?'

'No. Stan rang through to say you were here, and I asked Hilda to get drinks for the three of us.' Natalie put milk in each cup and poured the tea. 'I wanted to fill you in on the donations made at and after the fundraising evening. Almost two thousand pounds was promised, and every penny came in.'

'I thought you were looking happy!' Ena said. Then she noticed a flicker cross Natalie's face. 'Is that not enough to replace the sound system?'

'I am happy. It's a huge amount – except we were still a thousand pounds short for even the basic equipment.'

'So, how will you get the rest of the money?'

'That's just it. I don't have to,' Natalie said.

'I'm confused. If you're a thousand pounds short…'

'I met with the theatre's main sponsors – Michael Brookes, George Derby Bloom, and my son, who represents his late father's estate – and told them that we were a thousand pounds short of purchasing the new equipment. I also told my other children; I thought it only fair to do so if I had to use my money as a stopgap because it is *their* inheritance I'd be spending. The next day, a parcel containing exactly one thousand pounds in five- and ten-pound notes was left on the shelf of Stan's hatch at the stage door.'

Ena was speechless. When she finally found her voice, she said, 'Was there a letter with it?'

'Nothing formal. Just a note inside that said, "I hope this helps."'

'Was the note handwritten, or were the words cut out of *The Times* newspaper?'

'*The Times*?' Natalie queried.

'Sorry, that was a joke – and not a very good one.' Ena took a sip of her tea, wondering if it was Elsbeth Brookes who had left the money. It might have been her way of trying to make amends. It wouldn't be

George, Natalie would know if it was her son, and Michael Brookes would want such a generous gesture plastered all over the front page of the daily newspapers.

'I've wracked my brains, but I can't think of anyone who would give away a thousand pounds,' Natalie said. 'I don't know anyone who could afford to give away that kind of money.' Her brow furrowed. 'A thousand pounds is a huge amount. An investment, yes, but to give it away, anonymously? If it wasn't someone at the meeting, then who?'

'Sounds to me as if someone at the meeting spoke about it afterwards, which is why the person wants to remain anonymous.'

'You're right, of course.' Natalie shared the last of the tea in the pot between them.

'So, now you have three thousand pounds. That's surely enough for a new sound system,' Ena said.

'It is. Unfortunately, it takes a lot longer than two weeks to build a system, even a basic one. Strand Electrics, who built our system here and the one at the Young Albert, are booked until after the summer. They can't start work until September at the earliest.'

'After all you've done to raise the money,' Ena said, feeling sorry for Natalie, George, and everyone else involved. Then she noticed her friend's eyes sparkling. Unable to stop herself, Natalie burst into laughter. 'What is it?' Ena asked. 'What aren't you telling me?'

'The boss at Strand Electrics has offered to loan us everything we need for the run of *Tribute*!' she exclaimed. 'By the time they are free to build our new system, the Young Albert will have taken money at the box office to pay the theatre's running costs, so I shall invest the three thousand pounds, ready for when they can build the replacement.'

Ena clapped her hands in excitement. 'The show must go on! Isn't that what you say in showbusiness?'

'It is, and it will,' Natalie said, smiling. 'And the house is almost full.'

'Already?'

'Yes. I have what they call "papered the house". There won't be an empty seat. I've sent tickets to every newspaper and every theatre reviewer in London and the Southeast, and every member of the company, including the kids of the youth theatre, have been given two tickets each. Some will bring their parents; others will invite agents and casting directors. I've sent tickets to the sponsors and patrons – your friends, the Galbraiths, have become patrons, so they have been sent tickets – and it goes without saying that there are two boxes for you and your family. And,' she said, handing Ena an envelope, 'tickets for Artie and his friend, and three complimentary tickets for you to give to anyone else. One seat in the box, and two in the stalls.'

'It must have cost you a fortune,' Ena said.

Natalie nodded. 'Speculate to accumulate, Anton used to say. And he was right. It encourages bookings. If the public can't get a seat on the first night, they will want to see the show even more. The box office staff tell me that advance bookings are coming in at such a rate that half the seats in the house are sold for the first two weeks. At this rate, by the time *Tribute* opens, we'll need to extend the run.'

CHAPTER FORTY-FOUR

Artie read the note Ena had left on his desk. *Natalie tells me the sound system is going into the Young Albert, and Strand Electric's engineers are installing it. So, as your electronic expertise is not needed, and Somerset House couldn't tell me anything about Orla Tyler, I thought I'd drive down to Brickham and talk to Mrs Thornton again. Sorry to leave you holding the fort. I'll be back as soon as I can, E.*

Hearing the doorbell, he put down the note and hurried into the hall, cursing himself that he had forgotten to turn on the light, an indicator that Dudley Green Associates was open for business and potential clients could walk in off the street.

Standing on the doorstep was a striking-looking woman in a black baker boy hat, white PVC jacket with upturned collar, and white patent leather high-heeled boots. Tall and slender, with large hazel-coloured eyes, she was soaked through, having been caught in a heavy rainstorm. She looked at Artie over the top of a huge bunch of flowers. 'Hello! I'd like to see Ena Green.'

'She isn't here at the moment,' Artie said. 'I'm her associate, Artie Mallory. Perhaps I can help you. Come in out of the rain.'

He ushered the woman into the hall and shut the door. 'Let me take your flowers and your coat,' he said, making them both laugh. 'Okay, flowers first.

Hold on. I have just the thing to put these in.' He opened the door of the cleaning cupboard and took out a bucket. 'Not very pretty–'

'But practical,' the woman said.

'There are a lot of flowers here,' Artie commented as he placed the bouquet in the bucket. 'There, just right. Come into the office.'

After putting the flowers near the door for easy access when the woman left, Artie took his coat from the hook and hung it on the back of a chair at the conference table. 'Let me help you out of your coat,' he said. Spreading her wet coat across three coat hooks, he showed the woman to his desk and pulled out a chair. 'Take a seat. Would you like a cup of coffee, or perhaps tea?'

'Coffee, please. Milk, no sugar.'

'I'll be back in two minutes,' he said, mounting the steps to the small kitchen. 'Would you like a biscuit?' he asked, looking back over his shoulder through the arched doorway.

'No, thank you,' the woman replied.

'Coffee with milk, no sugar,' he recapped, returning and giving the woman her coffee before sitting down with his own. 'I'm not sure how long Ena will be, but we work together on all Dudley Green investigations, so, if you'd like to tell me how we can help you, Miss…?'

'August. Sylvia August.'

Artie leaned back in his chair and laughed. 'Forgive me! Ena has told me so much about you. I am so pleased to meet you at last.' He looked across at the flowers. 'I take it they are for Ena?'

Sylvia nodded. 'I wanted to say thank you to her. She helped me so much when she came to see me.'

'So, everything is going well?'

'You wouldn't believe how well! I don't know whether Ena told you, but I was probably at my lowest when she came to see me about Scarlet Wolf.'

Artie gave Sylvia a warm smile. 'She told me she'd been to see you.'

'She did, and she gave me such encouragement. I think it was the first time anyone had actually listened to me and been genuinely interested in me.' Sylvia cleared her throat. 'When Ena left, I decided I was no longer going to be a victim of the Brookes dynasty. I was going to get back out there, and I did. I booked myself into some workshops at the Actors' Centre and started applying for all the auditions I could find. I wasn't sure whether I could find the truth in the characters I played, or remember my lines – but I could.' She took a handkerchief out of her handbag and wiped her eyes. 'I could!' she said again. 'Sorry. For a long time, working as an actress again was something I only dreamed about.' She laughed. 'I had lived a lonely existence, except for the odd bottle of whiskey,' she said, laughing again.

'And now?' Artie asked.

'I haven't had a drop of the hard stuff since Ena came to see me.'

'And now you're ready to go back on the stage?'

'Yes, and I can't wait. That's what I came to tell Ena. I have been offered a play at the Citizens Theatre in Glasgow. I auditioned one day, and the next day I got a call asking me if I'd like to go back and read for the part of Livia in *Women Beware Women*. I did – who wouldn't? Livia is a great part – and almost immediatcly, I was offered the role. The assistant director told me on the QT that the director was considering asking me to join the company for a season. So, fingers crossed *Women Beware Women* goes well.'

'I'm sure it will. You must have impressed them if they want you for a season.'

'I'm only being considered; nothing is set in stone, but I'm excited, and yes, it sounds hopeful.'

'Ena will be delighted for you.'

'I'm just sorry I won't get to the opening night of *Tribute*. I'm going up to Glasgow this weekend; rehearsals start on Monday.'

'Ena won't mind,' Artie said. 'She'll be over the moon that you are working.' He wondered whether Sylvia had an agent and if Jim Bonner had kept his word. As she hadn't volunteered that piece of information, he said, 'What about an agent? Did you need one to get the job?'

'No, it was advertised in *The Stage*. I walked in off the street. Would you believe I was brave enough to go to an open audition? There were hundreds of actors and actresses there.'

'So, do you or do you not have an agent? Come on, I'm dying to know.'

Sylvia tilted her head and smiled. 'Yes, a woman, Harriet Malone. I wrote to several agents, told them I was going up to the Citizens to do *Women Beware Women*, and asked if I could meet them when I returned to London. Harriet Malone phoned and asked me to go to her office the day she received my letter. She said she had an opening for an actress of my age. She agreed that, as I had a gap in my CV, a leading role would be good for me, especially at such a prestigious theatre as the Citizens. Good for my CV and my self-esteem. Most actors would give their back teeth to work there.' Sylvia looked at her watch. 'I wish I could wait for Ena to get back, but I can't. Do you have a sheet of paper? I could leave her a note.'

Artie took a fountain pen and a pad of Basildon Bond from his desk drawer. While Sylvia wrote the letter, he took their teacups to the kitchen.

Folding the sheet of paper in half, Sylvia said, 'Oh, I forgot. Will you tell Ena that Scarlet Wolf came to see me? She is at last free of her mother and she is very happy.'

'She apologised to you then?'

She put her hand up as if to say an apology wasn't important. 'So many wasted years. But, yes, she was genuinely sorry. Whether I see her again is up to her. She knows where I live. Or will be living, after Glasgow.' She sat upright. 'I need to think of the present, not the past. I'd better get a move on. I have an appointment with a photographer at twelve. My agent set it up, so I daren't be late.'

'This agent sounds a hell of a lot better than Jim Bonner,' Artie said.

'Who?' Sylvia grinned. 'Harriet said he gave me a glowing reference when she bumped into the old letch at a first night. Odd that, since the last time we met, I kicked him in the…' She laughed, and Artie laughed with her. 'Thank you, Artie,' she said.

She got up and crossed the office to the door. Artie followed and helped her on with her coat. 'Thank Ena for me, won't you?' she said. 'And thank you again.' She leaned forward and kissed him on the cheek. 'Tell Ena I'll see her when I get back from Glasgow. And Artie,' Sylvia said, as he opened the door to Mercer Street, 'put some water in the bucket, or Ena's flowers will die.'

209

CHAPTER FORTY-FIVE

As Ena pulled in to park the car outside Mrs Thornton's house, a red Mini with Orla Tyler at the wheel sped out of the drive and turned a sharp left away from the centre of Brickham. Ena drove behind the Mini at a discreet distance. When the Mini took the first turning off a roundabout, Ena followed. She slowed down at the first junction and held back, allowing a car coming from the right to go in front of her. At the next junction, she didn't leave space. Ena was not familiar with the roads; fall more than two cars behind and she might lose the Mini. With Orla's car in her sights, she cruised at forty miles an hour until, at the next junction, she saw a sign for the Hibbert Psychiatric Hospital. Ena watched as the Mini's left indicator began to flash. After hanging back, she turned left too.

Parking some distance away, Ena watched Orla get out of the Mini and cross the car park to the hospital's main entrance. She didn't want to risk Orla seeing her, so she sat on a bench outside the main doors for ten minutes until she felt sure she'd given the girl enough time to pass through the foyer to wherever she was going.

The large reception area was unfurnished except for two reception desks, one on either side. Above the desk on the left hung a sign saying "Enquiries"; the desk on the right was labelled "Visitors". As people were queuing at enquiries, Ena went to the visitors' desk. 'I arranged to meet a friend who is visiting someone today,' she said. 'Her name is Orla Tyler. Could you tell me if she has arrived yet?'

'I'm sorry, madam,' the receptionist said, 'but I can't give out the names of visitors.'

'No, of course not. I understand,' Ena said. Then she coughed. 'Thank you.' She put up her hand and coughed again. 'I'm sorry,' she spluttered. 'I've driven a long way and–' As if on cue, a sudden hot flush washed over her, and she choked. Sweating and coughing, she gasped, 'I don't suppose I could have a glass of water?'

The receptionist didn't respond to her request immediately but, seeing how red-faced and sweaty she was, she turned on her toes and left through a door behind the counter.

Ena looked across the room to the enquiries desk. Everyone was deep in conversation. Quick as a flash, she turned the visitors' book around and scanned the page. The last but one person to sign in was Orla Finnegan. Running her finger across the page, Ena was unsurprised to see the inmate Orla was visiting was Andrea Thornton. She returned the book to its original position and coughed again, this time for real.

The receptionist appeared with a glass of water and handed it to Ena, who took several sips. 'Thank you,' she said, not yet on the other side of the hot flush but no longer sweating as much. Soon the blush of the menopause would fade, and Ena needed to leave before it happened. More importantly, she needed to leave before Orla Finnegan, aka Tyler, returned from visiting Mrs Thornton's granddaughter.

She handed the empty glass back to the

receptionist. 'Thank you, I needed that!' she said, which was true. Then she looked around. 'As there are no seats, I'll wait for my friend outside.'

'I'd get a chair for you, but…'

Ena waved away the suggestion. 'You've been kind enough. Thanks for the water.' And with that, she left the cold, sterile waiting area.

From her car, Ena saw Orla leave the hospital. She was in tears. Instead of going to her car, she dropped onto the bench that Ena had sat on earlier. 'Orla?' Ena said, approaching the young woman. 'What on earth's the matter?'

As she looked up and recognised Ena, a look of surprise crossed the girl's face. 'Who *are* you, Mrs Green?' she said. 'Why are you following me? I've done nothing wrong – I… I haven't, and I wouldn't do anything to hurt Mrs Thornton or Rory. Never!'

As Ena comforted her, Orla sank into her arms and sobbed, as if she was letting go of all the hurt inside her.

Ena held her until she had calmed down. Taking a couple of shaky breaths, Orla stared at the ground and said, 'I was an inmate at the Hibbert. I was here for eighteen months.' She paused and took another long breath. 'Until I began my treatment, I didn't realise that the breakdown I had at twenty-one was because of the abuse I suffered at the hands of my stepfather when I was a teenager. He used to come into my bedroom at night. He said if I told anyone, he'd kill my mother. I loved Mum, so I let him do it to me.' She lifted her head and looked at Ena. With tears rolling down her cheeks, she whispered, 'He promised he wouldn't hurt Mum, but he killed her in front of me.'

'I am so sorry, Orla,' Ena said. 'It's no wonder

you spent time in the Hibbert.'

'I didn't come here then, though it was a contributing factor to me having a nervous breakdown later, a big factor,' Orla said. 'After my stepfather was arrested, I was sent to live with a foster family. They already had a girl and a boy who were older than me. They were the three happiest years of my life.' She wiped her face with her hand and, smiling now, said, 'I got on well with my foster brother and sister, and my foster parents were loving and kind. I loved them, and they loved me.' Seeming surprised that anyone could love her, Orla stared at the ground again. 'My foster mum died of cancer, and my foster dad couldn't look after us, so we were put into care.'

Ena wanted to cry for the poor girl, but she knew she had to stay strong for her.

'When I turned eighteen, I had to leave the care home. It was fine. I lived in a hostel with other young women. One of them got me a job in the office where she worked. I started as a junior, picking up after everyone and making the tea. Then one day the woman who ran the department asked me if I'd like to learn how to type, which I did. She lent me an old typewriter and gave me exercises to do at home. When I could type, she taught me shorthand and soon after I got a job in the typing pool. A couple of the girls I worked with were looking for a flat to rent and they asked me if I wanted to go in with them. Everything worked out well. We shared everything. We even took driving lessons at the same time. I was happier than I'd been since my foster mother died.'

Orla swallowed hard, took a calming breath and resumed her story. 'I was the happiest I'd been in years until the boyfriend of one of my flatmates came into my bedroom drunk. He got into my bed and tried to… It was as if my stepfather was abusing me all over again. I screamed, but he wouldn't get off me. He pinned me down, but as he was pulling up my nightgown, he loosened his grip for a split second. It was long enough for me to raise my hand and scratch his face. He yelled, I began to scream, and his girlfriend came in. He told her I had asked him to come to my room and then began to scream. I tried to tell my flatmate what had really happened, but she didn't want to know and told me to pack my bags and get out. I had nowhere to go, so I lived on the streets.'

'I am so sorry, Orla. Turning you out at night is a wicked thing to do. You must have been terrified.'

'I was often terrified. On their way home after a night in the pub, men would stop and bully people living on the streets.' Orla shrugged. 'I was frightened for my life once, and then a homeless man, about the age my father would have been had he lived, took me to a courtyard at the back of a parade of shops. There were other homeless people there, men and women, and I felt safer. The old man was kind. He looked out for me. I think it was him who called an ambulance when I took ill.' She sighed. 'And I woke up, here,' she said, looking up at the sterile windows of the Hibbert Psychiatric Hospital. 'I'd had pneumonia, and they kept me sedated because I was delirious.' Suddenly, Orla began to shake.

'What is it?' Ena said, putting her arm around her as she tried to calm her.

'I can't–' she said, gasping for breath. 'I… can't… breathe.'

'Breathe for me, Orla,' Ena said, Ena leaning away so she didn't crowd her. 'Don't hold your breath;

you must breathe. Come on, Orla, breathe for me.' Ena wondered whether she should get a doctor or nurse from the hospital but decided against it. If she had been in Orla's place, medical staff from a mental hospital would have been the last help she wanted. 'Come on, breathe for me,' she said, again.

Orla did as Ena asked and took a shallow, shuddering breath. 'That's it, now take another breath, Orla, and again.' The girl looked at Ena and took a deeper breath, followed by another. 'That's right. Keep breathing, love.'

'Thank you, Ena,' Orla said, once her breathing had become more normal. 'There's something else I need to tell you. Apart from the doctors, Andrea was the first person I met at the Hibbert. She visited me when I was on the hospital wing. She said she was my only friend.'

CHAPTER FORTY-SIX

'Are you sure you feel up to talking about Andrea?' Ena said, unsure whether it would be a good idea.

'I need to talk about her,' Orla said, her voice no more than a whisper. 'I *want* to tell you. I need to exorcise her, get her out of my system.' She nodded as if to affirm her decision. 'At first, Andrea was kind to me. She listened to me and seemed interested in what I had to say. She was like those girls at school who had the rest of us running around after them. She was the leader, the one the other women looked up to. She had a clique of women who would have done anything for her. When she asked me to sit at her table in the canteen, I suppose I was flattered. I honestly thought she liked me.'

Tears filled her eyes, and she blinked them back. 'Now I know she only wanted to get information out of me to use against me. She asked me about my family. I told her that my stepfather killed my mum, and she said something similar had happened to her. She said because I had no family, she would be my family. She said she had a wicked grandmother and a spoilt brother who had disowned her. She said because we were both alone in the world, we should watch out for each other. She called me her sister, and I liked it. I liked having a big sister.'

'Did Andrea tell you what happened to her parents?' Ena asked.

'She said they were killed in a car crash. It was after the accident that she'd had a breakdown. She said we had a lot in common. I suppose we did: we'd both lost our parents, and both had nervous breakdowns. She said she and her brother were sent to live with their cruel grandmother, who hated her; she said she gave her nothing, but she loved and spoilt her brother. She said her grandmother used to enjoy setting them against one another.'

'Did she tell you why she was in the Hibbert?'

'Yes. Her grandmother was in a nursing home, recovering from an operation, and there was an old man in there who had known her when she was a young woman. Andrea said the man knew things about her grandmother that would send her to prison for a long time if they got out. He said what he knew would help Andrea to claim the inheritance her grandmother had stolen. The old man said he'd tell her everything the following day. Andrea told the people at the care home she was visiting her grandmother, but instead of going to her room she went to see the old man, and when she got there, he was dead, poisoned. Her grandmother told the police that Andea had tried to poison her for her inheritance but had killed the old man instead. Andrea said her grandmother had poisoned the man and then told the police it was Andrea that killed him; that he had accidentally drunk cordial Andrea had poisoned that was meant for her. She said her grandmother had stolen her inheritance and then set her up for murder.' Orla sighed. 'Because Andrea had had a breakdown in the past, her grandmother persuaded the authorities she was mentally ill and had her committed to the Hibbert. She said if she'd been given the chance of a trial, she would have been proven innocent and her grandmother would have been sent to prison.'

Ena wanted to tell Orla what had really happened at The Willows – how Andrea had planned to poison her grandmother in cold blood but instead killed George Derby Bloom's father – but she bit her tongue.

The two women sat in silence. After a few minutes, Ena said, 'Now you've met Mrs Thornton and Rory, and you've got to know them, what do you believe now?'

'That everything Andrea told me was a lie!' Orla put her head in her hands and wailed.

'I'm so sorry she has hurt you,' Ena said.

Orla lifted her head. 'I was stupid to believe her.'

Ena cupped her face in her hands and looked into her eyes. 'Listen to me. You are not stupid. Andrea Thornton manipulated you. She saw a vulnerable girl who had been hurt, and she used that to control you. None of what happened was your fault. Do you understand?' Orla nodded. 'You mustn't blame yourself. You are no match for Andrea; few of us are.' Taking a handkerchief from her bag, she pressed it into Orla's hand. 'Now, dry your eyes.'

Orla nodded. 'Thank you,' she whispered. Closing her eyes, she lifted her face to the warm sun and took several calming breaths. Then she turned to Ena and gave her a pale smile.

'Was it Andrea who told you to befriend Mrs Thornton?' Ena asked.

'To my shame,' Orla said, nodding.

'Did she ask you to do anything specific?'

'Not at first, but a week ago she asked me to take the jewellery box from Mrs Thornton's dressing table. She said it was hers by right. That her late mother had bequeathed it to her. I didn't do what she asked. By then, I had become fond of the family and I knew they weren't the type of people to do the things Andrea said. She was furious, but I didn't care. I had already decided to move out of the flat and stop visiting her.'

'So, what are your plans?' Ena asked, a lightness in her voice that until now had been missing.

'I thought about getting into the car and just driving until I ran out of petrol, but Mrs Thornton has been very good to me and I owe her and Rory the truth. So, tomorrow I shall see her, and I'll tell her how sorry I am for lying to them. And,' she said, wringing her hands, 'I want to say goodbye properly. But that's tomorrow! Tonight, I need to find somewhere to stay.'

'To stay? Don't you have anywhere to live?'

'Not anymore.'

'Where have you been living?'

'When I was given my release papers and left the hospital I didn't have anywhere to go. My mother left me the house she and my father bought when they were first married, but my stepfather sold it before he was arrested and sent to jail.'

'So, you were left with nothing?'

'No, my mother had made a will. She didn't have much money, but what she had she left to me. I think she knew my stepfather wouldn't treat me fairly. I was a child when she died, so it was in trust until I was twenty-one. My uncle, who I had only met once, was a trustee. He and Mum's solicitor looked after my assets until I came of age. When I met with Mum's solicitor, he persuaded me to file a lawsuit against my stepfather in the civil court. I did, and I got back most of the money from the sale of the house. But until then, I had very little money of my own and nowhere to go.'

'What about your uncle?'

'I didn't know him. To me, he is a signature on a piece of paper. I didn't understand the legal ramifications. I didn't know I could have asked for money to tide me over until I came into my own.'

'So, Andrea offered to help you?' Ena said.

'Yes,' said Orla. 'I don't know how she did it – I didn't question it – but she arranged somewhere for me to stay.' She looked into the mid-distance, thoughtfully. 'About once a month she had a male visitor. At first, I thought the man was her boyfriend. If he was, he was also letting out her flat for her, because the same man was waiting for me outside the hospital on the day I was released. He drove me to a flat in Brickham, which he said was Andrea's. He showed me around, told me he'd collect the rent on the last Friday of every month, and gave me a set of keys.'

CHAPTER FORTY-SEVEN

Orla looked exhausted. Her face was pale and tear-stained, and her eyes, dull and swollen, had dark rings under them. She had been through so much in her young life that it was all Ena could do to stop herself from hugging the girl.

'That's why I came here today,' she said. 'To give Andrea back the keys to the flat and to tell her I'd left next month's rent on the kitchen table. I also left the keys to the Mini with her. The guy who collected the rent loaned me the car. I assumed it was bought with money from the rent paid by previous tenants, but where the money or the car came from is none of my business – I want to wash my hands of both him and Andrea.' She sighed with relief. 'I told her the car was in the car park. I wanted to tell her how disappointed I was that she used me and that I wanted nothing more to do with her, but before I got the chance, she said, "Have you finished?" She looked straight through me. It was as if I was nothing – I was nothing to her. I felt a dull pain in my chest and I thought my heart would break. I had loved her like a sister, and I believed she loved me. The pain was so strong, it was like losing my mother all over again. It was then that I suddenly saw her for what she was: cold and vacuous. I was ashamed of myself for being taken in by her – and I was angry. I wanted to scream, but I couldn't find my voice, so I left.'

Ena gave her a sympathetic smile. She admired her for standing up to Andrea and wondered how long she would blame herself for the time she had spent doing Andrea's bidding. 'What happened wasn't your fault, Orla. You mustn't blame yourself.'

Orla shrugged her shoulders. 'Mustn't I?'

The two women sat on the bench in the pale sunshine for some time. It was Ena who broke the silence. 'So, what now?'

'Tomorrow, I will go to see Mrs Thornton and Rory and tell them everything. They won't want to see me again, and I can't blame them.'

'Mrs Thornton knows her granddaughter. I think she'll understand,' Ena said. 'Where will you stay tonight?'

'I'll walk to the nearest telephone box and call a cab. Taxi drivers know where there are decent hotels or B&Bs that aren't expensive. I'll book somewhere for a week. A week should give me time to look for somewhere more permanent.'

'I know just the place!' Ena said. 'A friend of mine and her husband have a hotel in Waterloo, the Duke of Wellington. It's clean and comfortable; the food isn't fancy, but it's good, and it's reasonably priced. The Duke is the kind of place where you'll be left alone if that's what you want.' She looked at Orla, her head tilted to one side as she waited for an answer.

'Thank you, Ena, that sounds perfect.'

'What about your luggage?'

'I have my toothbrush with me!' Orla patted her handbag. 'Everything I own is in the luggage store at Woking station.'

'Come on then. We'll pick up your luggage and get you to the hotel.'

While Orla retrieved her suitcases, Ena went to the bank of booths just inside the station's main entrance and telephoned her old friend Doreen Hardy. There was no need to go into detail other than to say that Orla needed a room for a week to recover from an abusive experience. Ena had helped Doreen through a similar encounter and she knew her friend would look after Orla.

Driving past the public entrance of the Duke of Wellington on Waterloo Road, Ena turned left opposite the Old Vic to The Cut, left again onto Cornwall Road and into the car park at the rear of the hotel. After she'd parked, she helped Orla carry her suitcases to the back door. Ena knocked, and after a few moments, her old friend Doreen Hardy opened the door.

'Ena!' she said, hugging her. 'And you must be Orla. Come in, love.' Doreen took one of Orla's cases and, leading the way along a passage not used by the public, took the stairs to the second floor, to a room at the far end of the corridor. 'We're quiet with it being mid-week. Most of our regular guests are on the first floor. You won't be disturbed in this room.' Opening the door, Doreen placed Orla's case next to the wardrobe. 'The bathroom is opposite.' She drew back the curtains. 'There isn't much of a view, I'm afraid, but in the afternoons, when the sun comes round, the room is light and cheery.' She pointed to a washbasin next to the window. 'Fresh towels on the stool under the sink.'

'Thank you, Mrs Hardy.'

'How would you like a nice cup of tea and sandwich in, say, a quarter of an hour?'

Orla's eyes filled with tears. She put her hand up to her mouth and whispered, 'Yes, please.'

'Now, love, don't get upset,' Doreen said. 'You're among friends here. I'll leave you to unpack, and when I come back with your tea, if there's anything else you need, you just let me know.'

'Thank you,' Orla said again as Doreen left. Looking across the room to Ena, she exhaled loudly and dropped onto the bed. 'I don't know how I shall ever be able to thank you for what you've done for me today.'

'I do,' Ena replied, smiling. 'Forget about Andrea Thornton and the Hibbert Hospital. Don't worry about anyone or anything. You just look after yourself.'

Orla jumped off the bed and threw her arms around Ena. 'Now,' she said, 'haven't you got an office to go to?'

Ena laughed. 'I have, haven't I? My colleague will wonder where I've got to. Are you sure you'll be okay if I leave?'

'Yes. I'll be fine. I think when I've unpacked, I shall fall into bed.'

'Not before you've had a cup of tea and a sandwich,' Ena reminded her. She took a card from her bag and gave it to Orla. 'Telephone me anytime. So,' she said again, 'if you're really okay, I'll–'

'I am fine. I feel safer than I have done for a long time,' Orla said, opening the bedroom door for Ena to leave.

'Okay. Right, then. Goodbye.' As she left, Ena added, 'Ring me?'

'I will,' Orla said, waving the business card.

CHAPTER FORTY-EIGHT

As Ena entered the office, she spotted a large bunch of flowers in a bucket on the conference table. 'Artie, you shouldn't have,' she said.

'I didn't. Read the letter.'

Taking the bouquet from the bucket, she inhaled its fragrance. 'Mm... I love the scent of old English roses. If not you, then who–? Not Henry, it isn't my birthday.'

'Read the letter!' Artie said again.

'Alright, alright.' Ena sat at the conference table and picked up the letter. 'Oh, it's from Sylvia August,' she said, smiling.

'Er, yes, she wrote it when she brought you the flowers.'

Ignoring him, she read the letter out loud. 'She says, in a nutshell, she's going up to Glasgow to do a play. That's wonderful! Oh, and Scarlet Wolf called to see her. She has left Connor!' Ena bit her bottom lip. 'Sylvia says it was amicable. Oh, and she has a theatrical agent.' She looked at Artie. 'She says you'll fill me in on the agent.'

'Her agent is a woman. She mentioned Sylvia to Jim Bonner at the opening night party of some play or other in the West End – Sylvia didn't say which – and he gave her a brilliant reference.'

'Well, I never! The old creep kept his word. Well done, Artie.'

'For what? For threatening to expose him for trying it on with Sylvia?'

'Yes. If you hadn't got him to admit on tape that he'd offered her representation in return for sexual favours, he would never have kept his word. But now that the investigation is over, we need to destroy the tape. We can't risk it getting into the wrong hands.'

'There was no tape.'

'What?' Ena said, shocked. 'You mean you were bluffing?'

Artie shrugged. 'I meant every word of what I said to Jim Bonner. I would have used the tape if the thing had got one in it.'

'What thing? What are you talking about?'

'Didn't I say? It was a spook's gadget. Something Rupert used when he was with MI5. It no longer works; it hasn't done since Rupert did his last covert op. He was going to throw it out, so I borrowed it. It looks like a Dictaphone. It's a bit bigger, but the con worked. Jim Bonner fell for it.'

'You clever old thing. I knew you hadn't lost your touch.' Ena picked up the office diary and flicked through the pages. 'Next week, I'll telephone the theatre in Glasgow to find out when Sylvia's opening night is, and we'll send her a good luck telegram.'

Artie nodded in agreement. 'How did you get on today? Did you find out anything about Orla Tyler?'

'I did. I followed her to the Hibbert Hospital. Her name isn't Tyler, it's Finnegan. She was an inpatient at the Hibbert and she was manipulated by Andrea Thornton and a man who Orla thought was Andrea's boyfriend. She was scared and confused. She has been renting Andrea's flat, but she gave her the keys today and had nowhere to stay tonight.'

'You haven't put her in your flat, have you?'

'No, of course not. We don't have room. I took her to the Duke of Wellington. Doreen's looking after her.' Ena looked at Sylvia's note again. 'Anything else happen while I've been out? Any phone calls, post?'

'No to both.'

'What's going on at the Young Albert?'

'Engineers from Strand Electrics went in today to fit the new soundboard and speakers, and Ben Wilson has brought in a night watchman.'

Ena laughed. 'There's nothing like locking the stable door after the horse has bolted. Still, at least it won't bolt twice.'

'He isn't taking any chances so close to opening night.'

'Are you there tomorrow?'

'I don't know if he wants me, but I think I'll show my face to see what mood the chaps are in. The decorators didn't care about the Strand engineers; they couldn't have done the job anyway. The two older guys weren't happy, but they were getting paid for the day, so they accepted it. At first, David said Strand were doing them out of work, and then he offered to help them, but they said they didn't need him, which he took personally. I was pleased. It meant I could spend the rest of the day in the office. A closed sign isn't good for business.'

Ena, knowing it to be true, chose to ignore his comment and quickly changed the subject. 'I ought to telephone Jeanie McKinlay and tell her about Orla.' She looked at the telephone. 'However,' she said, rotating her shoulders, 'I'm shattered. I'll phone first thing in the morning.' She left the table and took her coat from the back of the door. 'Henry has a meeting in Cheltenham tonight. He won't be home for dinner, so I don't have to cook.'

Artie laughed. 'Rupert's in the same meeting. He said he'd be late and not to wait up for him.'

'So, shall we go out and have a drink and something to eat?' Ena said. Then she looked back at the telephone on her desk.

Artie laughed. 'Go on! Telephone Jeanie now and put her mind at rest.' He picked up the bucket. 'I'll take the flowers up to the flat.'

'You're a star, Artie Mallory. What would I do without you?' Ena took the flat keys from her coat pocket and dropped them into Artie's outstretched hand.

'I dread to think,' Ena heard him say as he exited the office.

Returning to her desk, she dialled Jeanie's number. She didn't have to wait long for her friend to answer. 'Hello Jeanie, it's Ena. I can't stop, but I wanted to let you know that I went to see Orla today.' She heard Jeanie take a sharp breath. 'You were right to be concerned, but everything has been resolved. Orla isn't dangerous, so don't worry. It's a complicated story that Orla wants to tell Mrs Thornton herself.'

'Was Andrea involved?' Jeanie said.

'Yes, she was. Andrea manipulated Orla. She'd had a rough time, culminating in her having a breakdown. She had no family and was sent to the Hibbert, where Andrea took advantage of her. As I said, there's no need for you to worry. Orla is free of Andrea. She is going to see Mrs Thornton to tell her what happened, and she said to say goodbye.'

'Thank you for letting me know.'

'Give my best to Gerry, and don't worry, alright?'

'I won't. Goodbye, Ena.'

'Good timing,' Ena said, putting down the telephone as Artie returned.

'So, shall we go for that drink?'

'And something to eat. I'm starving!'

'It's the Lamb and Flag then,' Artie said, laughing. 'How about chicken in a basket?'

Ena shook her head. 'You can have a rubbery chicken breast and the thin chips they call French fries. I am going to Café Romano. I need pasta – and lots of it. And Chianti.'

'And lots of it!' Artie said, laughing.

CHAPTER FORTY-NINE

Having sorted the Old Cases/Resolved files into alphabetical order, Ena had changed her mind and rearranged them according to the date of the investigation, putting the oldest folder at the back of the bottom drawer of the filing cabinet and working forward to the most recent. Each folder had two name tags, one with the date of the case and one with the client's name, so it made sense. Or did it?

She emptied the second drawer – Recent Cases/Resolved – and lined up the folders on the conference table.

There were only five folders in the top drawer: one case she had yet to work on, a current case that had not yet been resolved, and three resolved cases (Sylvia August and Jim Bonner, Rose Allen and Connor Wolf, and Mrs Thornton and Orla). On the front of each of these folders she wrote *PROBONO*. On the folder of the case that had not yet been resolved – and the only one likely to bring in some much-needed revenue – she wrote *Natalie Goldman, Sound System, Young Albert Theatre. CASE OPEN*. The final folder she labelled *Charles Galbraith. Investigation to find a missing family member. FUTURE CASE*. Tearing a sheet of A4 paper from her notepad, she wrote, *Dinner with Charles and Priscilla Galbraith as soon as possible*. After slipping the sheet of paper into Charles Galbraith's folder, she laid the three recently resolved folders on the table with the current folders, Case Open and Future Case, first.

Ena was fond of Charles and Priscilla. She first met them when Charles commissioned her to investigate a girl who claimed to be Priscilla's daughter. The girl was an imposter, but while investigating her, Ena found Priscilla's real child, who had been taken from her at birth. Now, she had been asked to find one of Charles's family members.

Pondering what the investigation would entail, Ena had just picked up a Recent Cases/Resolved file when there was a knock on the office door, followed by, 'Hello, Ena?'

'Orla?' Ena jumped with surprise at the sound of the young woman's voice. 'I didn't expect to see you so soon. Is everything all right?'

'Yes, everything's fine.' Orla looked past her to the pile of folders. 'I can see you're busy. I shouldn't have come.'

'This?' Ena said, following Orla's gaze to the chaos on the conference table. 'This is a mess of my own creating. My colleague is working out of the office today, so I decided to catch up on some paperwork and, as you can see by this lot, do some filing. I should have started with the paperwork.' Sensing something was wrong, she put down the file she was about to open. 'What is it, Orla?'

'I… I'm going to see Mrs Thornton, and I was wondering, well, hoping really, whether you would come with me. But I can see you're busy.'

Ena brushed away the idea of being busy with a wave of her hand. 'I can do this anytime. You never know, my colleague might be back and do it for me.' After checking that everything in the kitchen was switched off, she took her keys from the desk drawer, picked up her shoulder bag and put on her coat. 'Let's go,' she said. 'My car is the old Sunbeam in the car park opposite.'

They were soon out of London and, in less than fifteen minutes, over the county boundary into Surrey. Ena turned off the main road at the sign for Brickham and took the B road through town. 'Orla, I won't sit in on the meeting you have with Mrs Thornton,' she said.

Orla took a shaky breath. 'Why?'

'Because it's your business. It's personal, love. What you say to Mrs Thornton should be between you and her.'

'And Rory, if he's there.'

'You like Rory, don't you?' When Orla didn't reply, Ena glanced sideways at her. She was deep in thought.

'It doesn't matter how I feel about him now. I've ruined our friendship and anything else there might one day have been between us. He won't want to know me when he hears what I have done, and I don't blame him.'

'From what I know of Rory Thornton, he won't judge you,' Ena said. 'Like his grandmother, he will listen to what you say, and he'll make up his own mind as to whether he wants to see you again or not.' No one knew better than Rory how manipulative Andrea could be. Ena wondered whether she should tell Orla how Rory had suffered at the hands of his sister. She decided against it. It wasn't her story to tell. If Rory wanted Orla to know, he would tell her when he was ready. 'Rory is his own person,' she added. Ena looked at Orla again. The love she felt for Rory emanated from her sad eyes.

They turned into Mrs Thornton's drive. Ena stopped the car and pulled on the handbrake. 'Are you ready?'

'As I'll ever be.'

The two women mounted the steps to the front door. Orla stood so close to Ena, she could feel her shaking. Ena rang the bell, and a minute later, the door opened. Mrs Thornton stood in the open doorway with Rory by her side. 'My dear, we've been so worried about you,' she said, wrapping her arms around Orla. 'Rory, take Orla to the sitting room.'

She shot Ena a concerned look. Smiling, Ena nodded that she would be all right, and she left with Rory guiding her by the arm.

Mrs Thornton looked concerned. 'Jeanie told me that the poor child was in the Hibbert Hospital after having a breakdown, and Andrea befriended her.'

Ena nodded. 'Orla felt alone in the world, and Andrea made her feel wanted. Once she'd reeled her in, she told her a pack of lies about her life with you and why she was in the Hibbert. The poor kid believed Andrea – until she met you and Rory.' Ena placed her hand on the old lady's shoulder. 'Let's go inside. I'll make us all a cup of tea while Orla tells you what happened.'

Mrs Thornton crossed the hall to the sitting room, and Ena went on to the kitchen. After making tea, she took a tray for three to the sitting room and returned to the kitchen. Pale rays of sunshine shone through the glass in the door, as it had done the first time Ena came to the house. She took her cup outside and sat on the low wall that separated the patio from the garden. When she had finished her tea, she took the empty cup back into the kitchen and, going out again, strolled across the lawn.

There was a light on in Gerry's studio, reminding her of his and Jeanie's engagement party. Ena recalled how excited Jeanie was when she told her that Mrs Thornton had converted the old summerhouse into a physiotherapy practice for Gerry. The conversion was also for Rory, who, since the car accident that killed his parents, had been confined to a wheelchair until Gerry worked with him. In just a few months, with Gerry's help, Rory had gone from sitting in a wheelchair to walking with crutches. Ena breathed in the fresh air. 'So much has happened since then,' she thought. Rupert Highsmith, having almost been killed in a hit-and-run the same year, was Gerry's first paying patient.

As she passed the old Anderson shelter, Ena remembered the bonfire and the fireworks display, which reminded her that the engagement party was on Guy Fawkes night. 'Oh my... November 5th, 1960. Almost ten years ago,' she said out loud.

Hearing someone calling her name brought Ena out of her reverie. 'Jeanie!' she said, as she returned to the kitchen. 'Have you seen Orla?'

'Yes, in the sitting room. I've just come from there.'

'And?'

'She is tearful, as you'd expect. She's told them about Andrea wanting her to steal the jewellery, and they have forgiven her.'

'Have you forgiven her?'

Jeanie didn't answer straight away. When she did, she said, 'It isn't up to me.'

'No, but it took strength of character for Orla to face them and confess what she had done.'

'It did, and I respect her for that,' Jeanie said. 'Mrs Thornton has invited Orla to visit them again. She said she'd be happy to see her anytime. And I know Rory would like to see her.'

'What about you?'

'It isn't me she'll be coming to see, but if I'm here, I will make her welcome.'

CHAPTER FIFTY

Hitting the rush hour traffic made it a slower drive back to London. Orla spent most of the journey looking out of the passenger window. Ena, concentrating on the busy road, didn't feel the need to speak. If Orla wanted to tell her about her time with Mrs Thornton, she would when she was ready. If she didn't, that was alright too. Ena wasn't going to push her.

'I'll drop you off at the Duke of Wellington, but I won't come in,' she said.

'I don't want to go to the hotel and be on my own,' Orla replied. 'Can I come to the office with you? I won't get in the way,' she added.

Ena drove past Waterloo Station and over the bridge to Covent Garden and Mercer Street. 'I won't be able to take you back to the hotel though,' she said. 'My husband Henry and I are going to dinner at a friend's house tonight. It's a special celebration for my sister Margot. She was a singer and dancer in the West End during the war. Before your time, of course, but in the forties, she was famous. My brother and his wife and my sisters and their husbands will be there. The family is in London to see a musical tribute in honour of Margot. It's a play that has been written specially for her.'

Ena unlocked the door to Dudley Green Associates, switched on the hall light and led the way to the office. 'Make yourself at home, and I'll put the kettle on. Tea or coffee?' she asked, going through to the kitchen. Getting no reply, she flicked on the kettle and poked her head around the arch between the two rooms. Orla was looking at the files on the conference table. She picked up the file labelled Mrs Thornton and Orla – PROBONO, and gasped.

Ena felt the blush of embarrassment rising in her cheeks. 'I'm sorry. I should have told you there was a folder with your name on it.'

Orla shook her head. 'I shouldn't have looked without asking. I wasn't being nosey. Because I interrupted you earlier, I thought I'd do some filing to make up for it, and to say thank you for taking me to Brickham. I'm sorry.' She sighed. 'I shouldn't have started without asking you if it was alright first.' Scrunching up her shoulders, she said, 'Is it?' Ena nodded, and Orla took her file and, without opening it, placed it in the middle drawer in front of the resolved cases. Picking up the current and future files, she put them in the top drawer of the filing cabinet.

Closing the drawer and opening the second, labelled Recent Cases/Resolved, she said, 'I'm guessing what's left on the table belongs here. Is it okay if I carry on?'

Ena laughed. 'If you can bear to, please do.'

While Ena was making tea, she heard Artie arrive. 'Hello... Oh!' he said, surprised to see a stranger at the filing cabinet. Before he had time to ask who she was and why she was looking through the agency's confidential files, Orla had closed the cabinet and crossed the room to him.

'Good afternoon. Can I help you?'

'Er, yes, good afternoon. Is Mrs Green about?'

'She is.' Looking from Artie's desk to Ena's, Orla turned back to the man and said, 'If you'd like to take a seat, I'll tell Mrs Green you're here. Who shall I say wants to see her?' As he looked past her and spotted Ena leaning against the arch between the office and the kitchen, she followed his gaze and bit her lip. 'I've done it again, haven't I? You're Mr Mallory?'

'I am,' Artie said. 'And you are–?'

'Orla.'

'Ah! Hello, Orla. For a minute, I thought Ena had employed a secretary without telling me.'

'I wish! But no, I was just doing a bit of filing.' Orla made a wide sweep of her arm, indicating the pile of folders on the conference table.

'Tea?' Ena placed a mat and a mug of tea on the table for Orla. 'And here's one for you,' she said, giving Artie her mug and returning to the kitchen to make another drink for herself.

'Have you had a successful day out of the office, Mr Mallory?' Orla asked, resuming her filing.

'Yes, thank you,' he said. When Ena returned from the kitchen and took her seat at her desk, Artie added, 'I presume that you have also been out of the office today?'

'I have. And it was a successful day, all told. Wasn't it, Orla?'

Nodding, her eyes moist with tears, Orla continued to file. Without looking at Ena, she whispered, 'Yes.'

Artie mouthed, 'Ah!'

Ena nodded. 'Do you have anything to report?'

'Nothing much,' he said. 'There was a rehearsal at the Young Albert. Ben Wilson said if we wanted to watch it, we should go through the foyer and sneak into the auditorium at the back of the stalls. Harry wasn't interested, but Doug and David went to see it. I wanted to make sure Harry wasn't involved with the thefts, so I said I wasn't interested either. When the other lads left, I asked Harry about his gambling, and he said he had been addicted to all sorts when he was young. He said he was what they call a compulsive gambler and had spent years at Gamblers Anonymous. He stopped gambling for ten years but said he had recently fallen off the wagon and was trying to ween himself off by limiting himself to one bet a day and only placing a shilling or two each way.'

'Trying to ween himself off gambling without professional help won't work, surely?' Ena said. 'It'll be too hard without support.'

'Which is why I suggested he went back to Gamblers Anonymous.'

'And will he?'

'He said he would. The poor bloke is desperate for help. The reason he's been trying to stop gambling on his own is that he hasn't told his wife he's started again. He's terrified that she'll leave him if she finds out.'

'She'll find out if he starts going to meetings,' Ena said, 'which he should do. I think a white lie is needed. Have a quiet word with him and suggest he tells his wife that he has felt the urge to gamble and has joined Gamblers Anonymous because he doesn't want to become addicted again.'

Ena wondered if the gambler was the thief.

CHAPTER FIFTY-ONE

'Harry might have debts, Artie. Are you sure he isn't our thief?'

Artie nodded. 'I'm certain he isn't. He's a bob-each-way man.'

'What about the other two?'

'When they came back from watching the rehearsal, Doug said he was going to take his wife to see the show for her birthday.'

'And David?'

'Not his cup of tea. He said it sensationalised things, and it didn't ring true. I'm afraid we're no nearer to finding out who stole the sound system than we were yesterday.'

Ena became aware that Orla was sitting quietly at the now empty conference table. She laughed. 'Have you filed all those folders?'

'Yes. I hope it's okay. I saw the bottom drawer was filed in date order, so I've done the same: first date and then name. Is there anything else I can do?'

'A dozen things!' Ena laughed again. 'But no, what you've done is wonderful. It would have taken me all day tomorrow to sort that lot out. Get your coat. Now Artie's here, I can take you back to the hotel.'

'You've done enough for me today, Ena,' Orla said. 'I'm going to walk. I need to think, and I do that best when I'm walking.' She grabbed her coat and, putting it on, said, 'I enjoy walking over Waterloo

Bridge and looking at the boats moored along the Embankment. I love the bridge at this time of day. Lights will soon be coming on in the buildings, yet it's still light enough to see St. Paul's on one side and the Houses of Parliament on the other.'

'If you're sure?' Ena said.

'I am. Goodbye, Mr Mallory.' Orla shook Artie's hand and said, pointedly, for Ena's benefit, 'If Dudley Green Associates ever needs someone to answer the telephone while you're out investigating cases, a secretary who can write letters and invoices – and do the filing,' she added, with a cheeky grin, 'would you put in a good word for me with Mrs Green?'

Ena laughed. 'You'd be an asset to any company, Orla.' She walked with her to the front door.

'Thank you for today.'

'I'm glad I was able to help. Do you plan to see Mrs Thornton and Rory in the future?'

'Yes. I'm going to look for a small flat and try and find a job. Once I'm settled, I shall visit them with the good news.'

'With your qualifications, you'll get a job in no time,' Ena said, doing her best to give the young woman reassurance.

'I don't know. I have an eighteen-month gap on my CV. I kept up with my secretarial skills helping in the administration office at the Hibbert, but I don't want the hospital on my CV, or the manager as a referee.'

Ena opened the door, and Orla stepped out into the afternoon breeze. 'Give Doreen my best wishes.'

'I will,' Orla replied as she set off along Mercer Street.

'She's a nice kid,' Artie said, when Ena returned

to the office.

'She is, and she deserves a break.'

'Then why not give her one? We could do with someone like her.'

'Employing someone isn't that easy.' But Ena knew Artie was right; the agency needed an extra pair of hands, especially someone trained in office administration who could type. 'I'll think about it.'

'This week we've been out of the office more than we've been in it,' Artie said. 'There's no telling how much work we've lost. And when we start investigating Charles Galbraith's missing family member, we'll both be working on the case, and the office will be closed again. We need Orla in the office when we're out.'

'I agree, but how are we going to pay her?' Ena didn't want to remind Artie that the agency wouldn't be paid until Charles's missing family member was found, alive or dead, which could take weeks. 'One investigation won't bring in enough to pay the wages of three people, and there's no money left in the reserve kitty. We need another case. I'll put an ad in *The Times,* and as soon as we get some work in, we'll talk again.' Collecting the empty coffee mugs, she went into the kitchen.

Artie leapt out of his seat and followed her. 'Aren't you forgetting something?'

'The Young Albert's sound system?'

'Exactly!'

'It might have slipped your mind, but we haven't found it.'

'Yet!'

'Well, let's hope we do.' Ena washed the mugs and dried them. 'Are you okay to hang on in the office until five-thirty in case anyone calls? It's Margot's surprise dinner party tonight at Natalie Goldman's house in Hampstead.' She looked at her watch. 'Natalie wants us there for seven. Margot and Bill are arriving at seven-thirty. If it's okay with you, I'll go up and get ready.'

CHAPTER FIFTY-TWO

At the sound of the doorbell ringing, Ena's sisters fell silent. 'That will be Margot and Bill,' Ena said, looking at her family.

'I can't believe she has actually made it!' Bess whispered.

Ena looked questioningly at her older sister, but before she had time to ask her what she meant, Natalie Goldman said, 'Right, everyone. Quiet. Hilda?'

Her secretary had been invited to stay for dinner after helping to prepare a bedroom downstairs. She was also there to help with anything the caterers weren't employed to do, like answering the door. She left the gathering and crossed the hall to the front door, while Natalie switched off the dining room light. 'Shush, everyone, or she'll hear you.'

Margot's daughter giggled. 'I can't wait to see Mum's face when she sees us all.'

Ena put her arm around her niece's shoulder and drew her close. 'She'll love it.'

Once Natalie had stepped into the hall, closing the dining room door behind her, Hilda opened the front door. 'Margot, Bill, how lovely to see you both. Come in,' Natalie said, hugging her friends and kissing them on both cheeks, as was her custom. 'I am so pleased to see you.'

'I wouldn't have missed spending time with you, or the opening of the theatre, for anything,' Margot said. 'It's wonderful to see you, Natalie.'

'It's wonderful that you were able to come down tonight and spend a little time with me. I've missed you! I see George and Betsy often. As you know, it's George's father's money that has allowed us to build the Young Albert.'

'I can't wait to see them.'

'And they can't wait to see you,' Natalie said. 'And Bill? Lovely to see you. It has been too long.'

'It has,' Bill said, hugging Natalie. 'You look well.'

'And so do both of you.'

'I'm kept on my toes by this one,' Bill said, nodding at Margot and smiling lovingly.

'Natalie, you should see what we've done at the academy and how it has developed and grown,' Margot said.

'You are not still working?' Natalie asked.

'I wouldn't call what I do work. We have wonderful teachers – academic and artistic – but I still like to keep my finger on the pulse. Well, darling Bill runs the academy; he's the power behind the throne.' Margot looked up at her husband. 'Keeps him out of trouble,' she added, winking.

'Talking about power behind the throne, I don't think you've met Hilda.' Natalie turned to her secretary. 'I'm sorry, Hilda, I was so excited that I completely forgot to introduce you. Margot, Bill, this is Hilda, my secretary – without whom the Prince Albert would have fallen to pieces after Anton died.'

They shook hands and Hilda whispered, 'I think you know Natalie better than to believe her when she says that.'

Margot laughed. 'Lovely to meet you.'

'Hilda has been helping me with some last-minute arrangements–'

'Details about the opening of the Young Albert,' Hilda cut in. Taking the large suitcase from Bill, she stood it at the side of the stairs. 'How are you at climbing stairs, Margot?'

Margot looked at the winding staircase in front of her. 'Because the treads are wide and not too steep, and there's a good strong stair rail to hold onto, I'll be fine if I take it slowly.'

'There's a bedroom downstairs if you prefer.'

'Perhaps that would be better,' Bill said. 'And as Natalie has gone to the trouble…'

'Down here would be best,' Margot agreed. 'Thank you, Natalie.'

'I'll take your case to your bedroom, but first, let me take your coat.' While Natalie helped Margot out of her coat, Hilda helped Bill out of his.

'My hands feel grubby. Could I use your downstairs washroom?' Margot asked.

'Of course.'

'Follow me,' Hilda said. 'There is a downstairs washroom, and there's also an en suite in your room. I'll show you where it is.' She picked up Margot's suitcase and led the way.

'I remember the downstairs bedroom,' Margot said. 'It's where the children's nanny slept. It's hardly a bedroom,' she told Hilda, 'it's more like a suite!'

When the two women returned, they joined Natalie and Bill outside the dining room. Natalie looked up at the grandfather clock. 'It's almost time for dinner. Shall we go straight in?' Without waiting for a reply, she opened the door and flicked on the light.

'Surprise!' everyone shouted.

Overwhelmed, Margot stumbled. For a moment, she looked unsafe. Tears pricked at the back of Ena's eyes to see her sister so unsteady on her feet. Bill stood behind Margot and, with a hand either side of her waist, held her until she nodded. Moving to her side, he offered her his arm and she grabbed it. Now she was holding onto her husband, Ena saw the worry lines on her sister's face relax.

Smiling, her eyes sparkling with surprise and happiness, Margot looked from one to the other of her family and friends. Then she looked up at Bill. 'I'm okay now, darling,' she said, gently removing her hand from his arm. Bill watched Margot make her way slowly towards the gathering. He stayed close to her, all the time watching and making sure she didn't fall. Margot was soon enveloped in the middle of all those who knew and loved her, and she shone with joy as everyone greeted her with hugs and kisses.

Ena was shocked to see how thin Margot was, and how bent she was with arthritis. Margot had never been overweight, but she had never been this thin. As Ena watched her smile, she realised she might have lost weight and height, but she hadn't lost the sparkle in her eyes or the sheer joy that emanated from them. Ena swallowed hard to move the emotion that was stuck in her throat. Her sister could still light up a room.

'I'd like to make a toast,' Natalie said. 'To Margot!'

'To Margot!' the Dudley clan shouted, with raised glasses.

Margot shook her head. 'Did you know about this?' she asked Bill, who put his hands up and shook his head.

When everyone had settled, two waiters brought in more wine and topped up their glasses while they stood around chatting. 'Madam?'

'Thank you.' Ena held her glass out, and the waiter refilled it.

'Sir?'

Henry did the same. 'When was the last time all the Dudley clan got together?' he asked Ena.

'My sisters came to London when you were accused of killing Helen Crowther. Tom and Annabel didn't come then, but we've seen them since. We've all seen each other at different times, but we haven't all been together at the same time, not like this. This is a very special occasion.'

Bess came over to Ena's side. 'In future,' she said, 'why wait for a special occasion? We should make an effort to see each other more often.'

Ena nodded. 'Before we all leave London, let's arrange to meet up once a year at least. We could come up to Foxden for Christmas or New Year. The hotel would be ideal. It's easy for everyone to get to.' She put her hand up to her mouth. 'The last time the whole family were together was at Mam's funeral. It's been eight years.'

CHAPTER FIFTY-THREE

'If you'd like to take your seats, everyone, dinner is about to be served,' Natalie called above the chatter and laughter of her guests. When everyone had found their seat, she took her place at the top table, opposite her eldest son Benjamin. Soft music began to play in the background, and waitresses brought in the starter course of pâté and toast.

Ena looked across the table at her oldest sister, Bess, who was the strongest of all her siblings. Bess had held the family together many times and in many ways, and Ena had always looked up to her. She also looked up to Claire who, during the war, had been recruited by the Special Operations Executive and sent to France to work with the French Resistance. She never talked about that time in her life.

Claire's husband Alain, or Mitch, as everyone called him, caught Ena's eye. 'You look miles away.'

'I was thinking how wonderful it is that we're all together.'

'It has been a while. How many years?'

'Too many.' Ena looked again at Bess. Life had thrown so much at her. She'd had her heart broken when she lost her fiancé in the war. Then she met Frank and was loved as she deserved to be loved. Bess didn't have children of her own but she and Frank had adopted Nancy – and what a beautiful and talented woman she had turned out to be.

That Ena didn't have children was something she thought about more and more as she got older. Recently, she had wondered what it would have been like to be a mother. Ena was the youngest of five, but Henry was an only child. He didn't seem to mind not having children. In all the years they'd been married, he had never said he wanted to be a father.

Looking around the table again, her eyes settled on her handsome brother Tom and his beautiful wife Annabel. They were a match made in heaven, but from two very different worlds. Tom was the son of a groom, Annabel the daughter of a lord – but they fell in love the moment they met. The war had blurred the boundaries in society and narrowed the gap between the upper and middle classes and the working class.

As she watched Tom laugh at something his niece Nancy said, Ena was reminded, as she was every time she saw him, what a loving husband and father he was. 'My handsome big brother,' she used to call him, and he was still handsome. He always combed his hair back off his forehead, and silver at his temples gave him a maturity she hadn't noticed before. He had no frown lines, just laughter lines at the corners of his eyes. His face was rounder, and he carried a little more weight now, but it suited him. It suited Annabel, too. Neither of them had changed much over the years. Annabel had a fuller figure, but she was still tall, still elegant, and still very beautiful. Ena looked at their daughter and wondered which of her parents she looked most like. Tall and elegant like her mother, Charlotte had her father's dark hair and kind brown eyes.

And Margot! Margot was still beautiful. Everyone said Margot Dudley could conquer anything, and she did. During the war years, Ena's talented sister had many demons to slay – and slay she did, with the help of Natalie Goldman. Margot and Bill's path had not been smooth. There were many obstacles in their way, and none bigger than the theatre. But, when the glitz and glamour of showbusiness faded, there was still a strong love between them. Bill was devoted to Margot and their daughter, Natalie, whom they had named after Natalie Goldman. Without the Goldmans, Margot may not have lived to have a daughter.

Ena suddenly felt hot as a flush of heat washed over her. She needed air. Putting her napkin at the side of her plate, she began to get up from the table. 'Thank you,' she said to a waiter, who pulled her chair back so she could stand. 'I'm going outside for some air,' she added, feeling that any second she would spontaneously combust.

Natalie's garden comprised a large, neatly cut lawn and colourful flowerbeds. The lawn was as big as a bowling green and surrounded by tall fir trees to keep it private. On either side of the lawn were rose beds, and further down were swings and a slide. Ena sat on a swing and walked backwards until she was on tiptoe. Then, lifting her feet, she let gravity propel her forward. Feeling refreshed by the evening air, she lifted her face, closed her eyes and enjoyed the cool breeze blowing across her face until the swing slowed to a standstill.

'I wondered where you'd got to,' Henry said, taking off his jacket and putting it round Ena's shoulders.

She looked up at her husband. 'Thank you.'

'Want a push?' he asked.

Ena lifted her feet again, and Henry, pulling the chains on either side of the wooden seat, took several steps back before letting go of the swing, thrusting Ena forward. Catching her on the backward swing, he pushed again, this time harder, and she began to laugh.

'Higher!' she shouted. Henry, laughing with her, pushed Ena until his jacket flew from her shoulders onto the nearby slide.

After retrieving his jacket, he sat down on the slide and watched as she leaned backwards and forwards, moving the swing higher and higher. Taking a packet of cigarettes from his pocket, he took one out and lit it. 'Want one?'

Using her feet as a brake, Ena brought the swing to a standstill. 'Please,' she said, joining her husband on the slide.

Henry lit a cigarette and passed it to her. 'Are you going to tell me why you left the party and came out here?'

'I was hot, and everyone chatting at the same time gave me a bit of a headache.'

'Are you sure that's all it was?'

'Of course!' Ena said. 'What else would it be?'

Henry stubbed out his cigarette. 'You looked sad, and you were quiet. That isn't like you.'

She slapped him playfully on the arm. 'Cheeky! I was not sad; I was thinking.'

'Alright, thoughtful then.' She nodded. 'We've never kept secrets from one another, have we?' Henry said. She shook her head. 'We've always told each other everything, always been honest with one another, haven't we?'

'Y-e-s,' Ena said, slowly. Then she tutted and rolled her eyes as she rested her head on Henry's shoulder.

He pulled her close. 'Ena, you would tell me if you were ill, wouldn't you?'

CHAPTER FIFTY-FOUR

'What makes you think I'm ill?' Ena asked, sitting up.

'Well,' Henry said, 'recently, when I try to hold you in bed, you push me away. You've been getting up in the middle of the night and walking around the flat. You've been having headaches, and you've been irritable.'

She leaned forward and kissed her husband on his cheek. 'More irritable than usual?' she asked, laughing.

'I'm being serious, Ena. You've bitten my head off a couple of times. Something's wrong, I know it is.'

Ena took a deep breath. The time had come to have the conversation she knew was inevitable but had hoped to avoid. 'There's nothing wrong with me, Henry, not in the way you think,' she said, forcing back tears. 'I'm going through the menopause. "The change of life", they call it. I'm sorry if I've been miserable. I sometimes get anxious for no reason. It comes on suddenly. I feel fine one minute, and then my mood changes and I'm irritable. It's worse when I haven't had much sleep and I'm tired. When I don't want to be cuddled or made love to, it's because I'm hot. I get hot flushes. They suddenly sweep over me. That's why I get out of bed in the night and walk around the flat. It's nothing to do with you, and I'm certainly not ill in the sense of having something medically wrong with me. Although I suppose hormonal changes are medical.'

'Isn't there something the doctor can give you?' Henry asked.

'I'm not sure. My doctor told me about something called hormone replacement therapy. When I have time, I'll make an appointment and discuss it with him.'

'And that's the only reason you came outside tonight?'

'Yes. It's embarrassing when you start sweating and go tomato red!' Unable to hold her tears any longer, Ena let out a sob. Henry went to put his around her but quickly retracted it. She edged along the slide to be closer to him. 'You can put your arm around me. The hot flush has passed.'

'I'm sorry you have to go through this,' he said, taking a handkerchief from his pocket and dabbing at her tears. 'I wish there was something I could do.'

'So do I,' Ena said, laughing through her tears. 'Come on, let's get back to the party. They'll wonder where we are.'

As they walked back to the house, Henry said, 'I know you, Ena. I could see you were sad before you came out here. I'm not trying to make light of what you're going through, but it wasn't just the hot flush, was it?'

There was a pause. 'I was thinking how lucky my sisters and our Tom are to have such lovely children. Did you ever want children, Henry?'

'Once, when I was young. There was a time when it seemed that all my peers talked about was finding a girl, getting married and having a family.'

'But you didn't want to settle down?'

'It wasn't that I didn't want to settle down. It wasn't a conscious choice; it just didn't happen for me. At university, I led a solitary life. By the time I left, the talk was about the war and which of the services to join. Then I was recruited to Bletchley Park, and the long hours we worked weren't conducive to having a wife, let alone a family.'

'I guess not.' She looked up at him and laughed. 'I remember when we first met. I didn't think you liked me.'

'Like you? I fell in love with you the first time I saw you. But you were so much younger than me. You were beautiful and intelligent. You could have had any man you wanted.'

'But I wanted you. I loved you.'

'A boring bachelor who liked working out puzzles and deciphering codes.'

'You're only ten years older than me!' Ena laughed. Then she looked serious. 'But when you finally gave in and we married, I didn't think you wanted children because you were older.'

Henry sighed. 'Looking back, I don't suppose I thought about children because of my age. You were all I wanted. I didn't think beyond my love for you and making you happy. I'm sorry if you're unhappy now.'

'I'm not unhappy.' Ena stopped walking and stood squarely in front of Henry. 'I love you. It's just that going through the menopause has brought it home to me that it's too late; that we won't ever have children now.'

He pulled Ena to him. 'Do you regret that?' he asked, looking into her eyes.

She shook her head. 'It isn't regret that I feel. I wouldn't change a day of my life with you. But I feel a kind of defeat. This change has defeated me as a woman because, suddenly, it's too late. The choice has been taken from me. From us. I'm too old now – we are both too old – but the possibility that it might happen has gone.'

'I understand now why you were sad,' Henry said. 'I'm sorry, Ena.'

'Don't be, darling. It just wasn't meant to be.'

'It wasn't as if we ever took precautions.'

'No.' Ena laid her head on his shoulder. 'I love you. You're all I need.'

'And I have everything I want in you,' Henry whispered.

CHAPTER FIFTY-FIVE

As Ena watched with excitement, she was relieved that, after so many delays, the opening night of *Tribute* had arrived and, so far, it was a success. She had seen the first act several times in rehearsal but hadn't yet seen the nightclub scene.

On stage, the band leader asked the young Margot, 'Will you sing for us?'

Margot's daughter Natalie, playing her mother when she was her age, looked around the stage, which had been changed to a nightclub during the interval. 'Yes,' she said, dreamily. Looking up at the bandleader, she let him take her by the arm and lead her across the set to a raised stage.

'What's your name?' the bandleader asked.

'When I was a child, I named myself after famous film stars. Sometimes I was Myrna Dudley, and sometimes Greta Dudley. My favourite name was Marlene, but tonight I am Margot, a shortened version of my real name, Margaret.' She looked up at the bandleader. 'My name is Margot Dudley,' she said, with confidence.

The bandleader whispered into her ear again, and she replied, 'They can't take this – I mean, that – away from me.'

When she had finished singing the famous Gershwin song, applause and calls for more rang around the auditorium. The stage lights dimmed to dark and the curtains closed. A spotlight followed a newspaper boy as he walked across the apron, calling, 'The Yanks are here!' and 'GI Joe has come to town.' As the newspaper boy disappeared stage left, the spotlight moved to centre stage, and the orchestra struck up. The heavy stage curtains parted as three young men dressed as American airmen and three girls in pumps and swing skirts danced to the *GI Jive*.

The stage went dark once again. The spotlight picked up the newspaper boy, stage left. He turned his placard to the front and began to walk back across the apron. 'Margot Dudley to stand in for Miss Goldie Trick! Margot Dudley to take the place of injured dancer Goldie Trick!' As he arrived at the far right of the apron, a queue of city gents and shop girls were buying newspapers from a street vendor. When the shocked gathering disappeared into the wings, the spotlight dimmed to blackout, leaving the stage in complete darkness.

'Margot Dudley, your friend Goldie Trick has been badly beaten up!' a man's voice echoed around the auditorium. 'She is not able to dance. You must take her place in the show tonight.'

A soft, wide spotlight shone on Margot as she entered the stage wearing her usherette uniform, followed by two wardrobe assistants. The first had a collection of costumes draped over her arm; the second carried a selection of headdresses. Margot stopped three-quarters of the way downstage.

'Every design of costume and every type of shoe,' the first assistant said.

'Hats, masks, feathers, fans, parasols, we've got all manner of paraphernalia,' added the second.

'Your face won't be seen clearly,' they said in

unison.

Margot turned her back to the audience and the wardrobe mistresses, one on each side of her, pulled off her usherette uniform to reveal a short, above-the-knee gold dress, straight and slim-fitting with a fringe at the hem and a low neckline, and a long string of pearls. Margot turned around and looked with amazement at her costume transformation. One of the assistants dressed her in a short blonde wig in the style of a 1920s bob and added a headband covered in rhinestones. After Margot had slipped her feet into a pair of high heels, the first wardrobe mistress held out a tray of makeup, the second a mirror. Margot dabbed her face with powder before applying bright red lipstick.

Without warning, an explosion of jazz music rang around the auditorium and bright lights came up on a 1920s speakeasy, complete with two gangsters in charcoal grey and white striped suits, black shirts, black fedoras with white bands around them, and white ties. Margot and the young actress playing her friend Betsy, also dressed as a flapper, shimmered from head to foot in golden tassels as they danced the Charleston with the gangsters. When Betsy circled her hands to the right, Margot mirror-imaged her, circling her hands to the left. At the end of the dance, before Margot's friend Goldie Trick made her exit, she struck a pose, held it for two beats, then blew a kiss to the middle of the first row of the balcony before taking an exaggerated bow. Margot, eyes closed, did the same.

CHAPTER FIFTY-SIX

Ena and Henry had never been theatregoers, but she found the buzz of the audience thrilling. Having seen how hard the director, dancers and singers had worked in rehearsal, and how hard everyone backstage had worked to get the show ready in time for the anniversary of VE Day, she had nothing but admiration for everyone involved.

As she looked along the box at her sister Margot, anticipation fluttered in her stomach. The happiness that shone from Margot's eyes made Ena wish she had seen her onstage in her heyday. Even now, crippled with arthritis, Margot had a theatrical way about her. She had a classic bone structure, her makeup was always perfect, and her hair was always skilfully coiffured. Margot still had style, and she was still beautiful.

An influx of excited theatregoers returning after the second interval took her attention as they found their seats. She looked up at the boxes opposite. Artie was waving at her and she waved back. He shook his head and beckoned to her. 'He isn't waving,' Ena thought, 'he's trying to attract my attention!' She lifted her hands, palms up, and Artie pointed to the exit and stood up. She saw him whisper something to Rupert, who frowned and looked worried. He caught hold of Artie's hand and said something, and Artie nodded. Then Ena watched Artie make his way out of the box.

'Henry, swap seats with me,' she said. 'I need to sit on the end, so Margot won't see me when I slip out.'

'Where are you going?'

'I don't know, darling, but Artie has just signalled that he needs me.' Keeping as low as she could, Ena crossed in front of Henry, and he slid into her empty seat. Margot turned and smiled at her, and Ena smiled back. When her sister's attention was focused on the audience, she whispered, 'I'd better see what's happening. I won't be long.'

'Where are you going, Ena?' Claire whispered, reaching past Henry and grabbing her hand.

'Artie wants me. It'll be something and nothing, I expect,' Ena said. 'Don't tell Margot. I don't want to worry her.'

'I'll come with you,' Claire said, taking hold of the arms of her seat in readiness to stand up.

'No, stay here, love. I won't be long.'

Grateful that the auditorium lights were on, Ena slipped through the exit curtain and down the narrow stairs to the ground floor. Passing through the door to the stalls, she walked swiftly between the sound box and the last row of seats. As the audience, chatting and reading programmes, made themselves comfortable, Ena went unnoticed.

The house was full. She began to feel anxious. She tried to shake the feeling from her mind. But as much as she tried to put the hollow feeling in the pit of her stomach down to the changes that were happening in her body, she knew something was very wrong. She arrived at the end of the back row of seats, turned quickly and walked down the side aisle, all the time saying, 'Excuse me,' but not giving way to people entering the auditorium through the same exit.

The corridor was busy with people coming from the bar and toilets. Artie was nowhere to be seen. The door leading backstage was open and Ena passed through it, pulling it shut behind her. It was mayhem. All around her, people were dashing from one place to another. ASMs were setting out props while others carried out checks to ensure everything was in the right place for curtain-up. Dressers hurried back and forth with costumes, and performers who needed to be on stage before the curtain went up were heading into the wings from every direction.

Ena looked around. Where would Artie have gone? She doubted he'd have been able to get backstage to the dressing rooms, and the double doors to the scene dock at the back of the stage were blocked by two burly stagehands waiting to put a flat in place. One door led to the fly tower and grid, where the fly crew flew in curtains, lights, scenery, stage effects and, sometimes, artists. Would anyone be allowed up there? Ena thought not. She tried the door anyway but it didn't open.

The third door had a brass nameplate labelled "Trap Room". The trap room, she remembered Ben Wilson telling her, was a large preparation room beneath the stage, mostly used to store unwanted flats and furniture. The door was ajar.

Slowly, she inched the door open and stepped inside. It was dark, and she waited for her eyes to adjust. A steep staircase led below the stage and she began to descend, aided by small green lights either side of the steps. Halfway down she heard voices, and she stopped and listened. She recognised Artie's voice. The other voice was male but sounded younger than Artie. Ena couldn't hear what either man was saying, but the younger voice sounded distressed.

Taking each step carefully, placing her feet in the middle of each tread, Ena reached the bottom of the stairs. Her view was blocked by large items of furniture. Quietly, she crossed from the bottom of the stairs to a tall stage flat. Standing in its shadow, she looked around the side of it and heard Artie say: 'Come on, David, put the can down.' She heard liquid splashing against the side of what sounded like a tin container. 'David, think about it, mate. There are a lot of people up there in the theatre. You don't want to be responsible for their deaths, do you?'

'No, of course I don't!' shouted the man she now knew to be one of the electricians. 'I just want to stop the show. I want it all to stop!'

'I know you do,' Artie said, 'but there are better and safer ways to stop it. I'll help you if you put the can down.'

'Did I tell you my mother died after my father left her for that dancer?'

'Yes, you told me,' Artie said, sympathetically.

'I try so hard to see Mum's face, but I can't. When Mum died, I was sent to live with my gran. She was bitter and strict. Her favourite saying was "Spare the rod and spoil the child." I wasn't spoiled, that's for sure,' David said, a bitter edge to his voice. 'She didn't believe in giving me love or comfort – and she didn't spare the rod.'

Ena, hearing the trap room door open, held her breath. Seconds later, the theatre fireman stepped into view. She waved at him to go back. He began to retreat up the stairs, but it was too late. David had already heard his heavy footfall.

He spun around. 'Who's there?' If it came to it,

the fireman was more capable of handling a fire than she was, so Ena stepped out of the shadows. 'Who the fuck are you? Get over here!' David shouted, raising the cigarette lighter so she could see it. He looked beyond Ena. Satisfied that she was on her own, he shouted, 'I'll flick it, and we'll all go up. Is that what you want?'

'No, David,' Ena said.

'Get over here!' She moved further into the room as David ordered. 'Who else is there?' he shouted, holding the lighter at arm's length.

'No one. I'm on my own. No one knows I'm here.' Ena looked at Artie. 'I came to see if my friend was all right.'

David tilted the petrol can towards Artie. 'You!' He stabbed his forefinger at Artie. 'You shouldn't have followed me.' Gripping the cigarette lighter in his hand, he made a fist and began to beat his forehead. 'You shouldn't have followed me!' he shouted again. 'This isn't how it's meant to be. You're not part of the plan.' Then he slumped against the wall. 'It's all going wrong. And you!' he said to Ena, 'coming down here... It's all wrong.'

Ena took a couple of steps towards David, and he pushed himself off the wall. 'Stay where you are!' Rolling his shoulders as if to release tension in them, he said, 'You think I'm stupid, don't you?'

She shook her head. 'I don't think you're stupid, David, far from it. I think you've been lied to, and you're hurting.' She took another step towards him.

'I told you to stay where you are!' David opened his hand and struck the wheel of the lighter. It didn't ignite. He struck it again; it sparked, but again, it didn't ignite. The third time he struck it, a small blue flame appeared. 'If you come any closer, I swear I'll–'

Ena took a step back and put up her hands to show him she understood. 'Alright, I'll stay here. I won't move.'

'Close the lighter, David, and put down the petrol can.'

Ena turned at the sound of her niece's voice. 'Nancy, go back. Get out of here, it's dangerous.'

Ignoring her aunt, Nancy walked up to David. 'Give me the lighter, David.'

Confused, he said, 'Who are you to tell me what to do?'

Nancy held his gaze. 'I'm your sister.'

CHAPTER FIFTY-SEVEN

In shock, David looked at Nancy. His mouth dropped open, and his eyes were disbelieving and wild. 'Liar!' he spat. 'You're the daughter of the Donnelly woman. She was the first woman to take Dad away from my mother and me.'

'I'm adopted, David,' Nancy said. 'My birth mother was a young dancer called Goldie Trick.'

'Goldie? It's because of her that my mother died.'

'Goldie didn't know about your mother, David. She was just a young woman who dreamed of being a dancer and came to London to fulfil that dream. When she met your father, she didn't know he was married with a son. She fell in love with him. It was Goldie that your father came to London to be with. Goldie was my birth mother, and your father, Dave Sutherland, was my father.'

David began to rock backwards and forwards. 'No, no, no…' he said, shaking his head violently. 'I've seen your parents. They're up there!' He pointed at the trap room ceiling.

'Bess and Frank Donnelly are kind and caring. I couldn't wish for a more loving mother and father, but they are not my birth parents. It was Doreen Trick – Goldie – a young dancer that fell in love with your father, who gave birth to me.' Keeping eye contact with David, Nancy took a step towards him. She reached out and took hold of his hand. 'One day, I will tell you what happened.'

David pushed her hand away. 'Tell me now!' he demanded.

'I'm sorry, David, I can't tell you here, not like this. It will be difficult for you to hear. You won't like what our father did. Let's get out of here and–'

'No! I'm going nowhere until you tell me. Tell me now!'

Nancy looked into David's eyes. A caring smile spread across her face, emanating compassion. Ena watched as her courageous niece took a deep breath. 'Alright, David, I'll tell you. Our father beat up my mother, Goldie, and almost killed her. He left her to die in an alley opposite the theatre where she worked. My aunt, Margot, found her and managed to get her to the theatre and safety. She had been beaten so badly that she almost died. It took a long time, but eventually she was well enough to travel and was taken to Ireland to be with her mother and her sister, Maeve. Aunt Margot went on stage in Goldie's place. Every night, she wore her costumes, sang her songs and took her curtain call. Even after she was followed, had her life threatened and was sent a bunch of dead arum lilies, she performed in the show as Goldie. My Aunt Margot was very brave.'

Hearing Nancy talk about Margot brought tears to Ena's eyes; knowing the danger she had put herself in night after night to help her friend escape from Dave Sutherland reaffirmed how brave her sister was. Considering the constant pain Margot was in now, and how she rarely complained, she was still brave.

'Goldie – my mother,' Nancy continued, 'could hardly walk, but she was determined to get out of London and save the child she was carrying, and she did. I was born in Ireland. Goldie died after giving birth to me, and my Aunt Maeve looked after me. When I started school, I was the only one in my class who didn't have a mother or father. I asked my aunt why it was, and she told me that my father had been a brave airman in the RAF. She said he was killed when his plane was shot down. When I asked about my mother, Aunt Maeve told me that she loved me very much and she didn't want to leave me, but she had been very poorly, so, once she knew I was safe and would be loved by my aunt and my grandmother, she went to heaven.'

'It was her fault my mother died,' David said again, but with less conviction. 'Gran told me that when Goldie Trick took Dad away from us, Mum died within weeks of a broken heart.' He began to sob.

'I'm so sorry, David.'

'I was only four years old, but I remember Mum telling me that Dad had died a hero fighting for his country.' He wiped tears from his eyes. 'When my gran died and I found her diaries, she said Dad was controlling and he had bullied Mum. Gran hated him. She said he wasn't good enough for her daughter. She said she despised my father because he was a Nazi sympathiser. But he couldn't have been a Nazi. Gran lied. Everyone has lied to me.' David looked bewildered. Like a frightened child, his eyes searched Nancy's face. 'You lied!' he spat. 'You're all liars.' Suddenly, he stopped talking and looked hard into Nancy's face. Shaking his head violently, he shouted, 'You and those other women who came here when you were writing the show made the whole thing up. I heard you. I heard you and them telling lies about Dad. If you are my father's daughter, why do you want the world to know that your father was a Blackshirt, a Nazi sympathiser that beat women up, eh?'

'I'm sorry, David. I helped to write the history of my Aunt Margot and her love of dance. The first time she went on stage was in the place of Goldie Trick. It's part of the reason she is being honoured now. It's part of her life story, her history in the theatre.'

'No! It can't be. You've got it wrong! Dad never laid a finger on Mum or me.'

Nancy reached out to David again, and again he backed away. 'I'm sorry. David, just because our father hurt my mother doesn't mean he would have hurt your mother or you.'

He shook his head. '*Our* father?' he snarled. 'There's no mention of Dad having another child in Gran's diaries.'

'Why would I lie about who my real father is? I'm not proud of Dave Sutherland; I hate him.' David swept tears from his eyes with a swipe of his free hand and opened his mouth to argue, but Nancy didn't give him time to speak. 'I promise I'm not lying to you. We had different mothers, but we had the same father.' She held out her hands. 'Close the lighter, please, David.'

With tears rolling down his face, David stared at the cigarette lighter as if mesmerised by its blue flame. Then he turned his gaze to Nancy, flicked the lid of the lighter with his forefinger, extinguishing the flame, and gave it to her.

'Thank you.' Nancy passed it to Ena. 'Will you give me the petrol can, David?' she asked, sympathetically. 'Please give me the can.'

'I'm sorry,' David whispered, handing it to Nancy.

Passing the can to Artie, Nancy took David gently by the arm. 'Come with me, David. Let's go outside and get some fresh air.'

Like a compliant child, he followed Nancy across the trap room and up the stairs.

CHAPTER FIFTY-EIGHT

When she was sure Nancy and David had left, Ena gave the lighter to the fireman, and Artie did the same with the petrol can. The fireman nodded. 'Will you have to evacuate the theatre?' Ena asked.

The fireman sniffed the almost empty can. 'No need for that, miss,' he said. 'It isn't petrol in here, it's water! I'd have been surprised if anything inflammable had been left down here with all this wood and fabric about.' He picked up a tin of paint. 'This shouldn't be here, though. It should have been cleared out long before the theatre company came in, let alone the public. I'll have a good look around and make sure there isn't anything else that's flammable, and I'll get some buckets of sand brought down as a precaution. Best be on the safe side.'

Ena exhaled with relief. 'So, it's safe for the show to continue?'

'Oh, yes. You go back and enjoy it, miss.'

'How did you know David was in the trap room?' Ena asked Artie when they were back in the entrance hall.

'He was in the foyer when Rupert and I arrived. Harry, who I'd been working with, said he was going to take his wife to a matinee in a couple of weeks' time, for her birthday, and David said nothing would persuade him to see the show, it was rubbish, so I thought it odd that he was here. Then I saw him in the side aisle of the stalls. Something didn't feel right, so I watched him, and when he left the auditorium, I alerted you. He had a head start on me because he was already on the ground floor. It was mayhem backstage, but by a process of elimination I went through the only open door that no one else was going through.'

'It's a good thing you did,' Ena said.

'It is,' said Artie, 'but I should have known something wasn't right with David before tonight. A few days ago, he said he'd overheard the show's writers talking about a scene about a bloke who had beaten up his girlfriend. He was quite uptight about it, said it wasn't right blackening a man's name when he wasn't there to defend himself.' Artie shook his head. 'His personality seemed to change after that. And then when the replacement sound system was brought in and the Strand engineers came to set it up, David complained. He went from saying the engineers were doing him out of a job to offering to help them. The other guys weren't bothered as long as they got paid, but David was really angry. I should have suspected then that something was wrong.'

'Well, you were there when it mattered,' Ena said. 'And now you'd better get back to Rupert before he sends out a search party. Oh, Artie,' she added, 'Dan Powell's in the box next to yours; ask him to come down, will you?'

As Artie left, the fireman appeared with an extinguisher and a bucket of sand, followed by one of the stagehands carrying a pile of fire blankets. The fireman pushed open the door to the trap room with his foot and held it for the stagehand. 'You go and enjoy the rest of the show, love. Everything's in hand,' he said, disappearing through the door and letting it swing shut behind him.

'Ena?' Dan Powell had appeared suddenly at her side.

'Dan, we had a problem. It has been dealt with, but my niece Nancy is outside with one of the lads who worked here. His name is David. I don't know what he called himself, but David Sutherland is his real name.'

'Is he related to *Dave* Sutherland who–?'

'His son. He threatened to set fire to the place.'

'What?'

'He didn't,' Ena said. 'He was bluffing. He had a petrol can, but he'd put water in it. The theatre fireman has checked everything thoroughly. The building is safe and precautions have been put in place; the fireman is down there now. I'm asking for your help because David needs delicate handling. I think he is more of a threat to himself than to anyone else. Apart from that, I don't want uniformed policemen all over the building tonight. Could you arrange for a couple of your officers to come down and take him to Bow Street – discreetly?'

Dan nodded. 'I'll get a couple of plainclothes chaps down, Ena. Leave it with me.'

They parted company, Dan to the foyer at front of house to telephone the police station, and Ena upstairs to watch the rest of the show with her family. Taking care not to let light from the corridor creep through the door, she slipped behind the blackout curtain and, crouching low, slid into her seat.

Her family were singing along to the celebratory wartime songs. Only Henry and Claire knew she'd been gone. Henry nodded towards the box on the opposite side of the auditorium. 'Artie's been back in his seat for ten minutes,' he whispered. 'Where have you been?'

Putting her hand to her mouth, Ena said, 'Dave Sutherland's son has been working here. He turned up tonight and threatened to set fire to the building.'

'What?'

'Shush!' she said, looking past Henry to make sure he hadn't been heard. 'There's nothing to worry about. It's safe now.'

'Where's the lad now?'

'Outside with Nancy.'

'What?'

'Darling, do stop shouting what! The family will hear you. They'll want to know what's happening.'

'Aren't you worried that Nancy is outside on her own with a man who threatened to set fire to the theatre? He's clearly dangerous!' Henry said, pushing himself up from his seat. 'I'm going out to make sure he doesn't hurt her.'

Pulling him back by the sleeve of his jacket, Ena hissed, 'Sit down!'

Thankfully, her family was so engrossed in the nostalgic songs that they didn't notice the raised voices. Only Claire, who was sitting next to Henry, heard. 'Is everything alright, Ena?' she asked, leaning forward.

'Yes,' Ena said, 'there's nothing to worry about. I'll tell you about it later.' Turning to Henry, she said, 'Dan Powell is with Nancy. He has the situation under control. He's called for a couple of plainclothes coppers to escort David to Bow Street.'

'Good. Hopefully, they'll have taken him away by the time the show ends. Which won't be long now.' Henry looked at his watch. 'You were gone ages.'

'Well, I'm here now.' She took his hand and gave

it a squeeze. 'Let's enjoy the rest of the show.' Ena looked past Henry again. Margot was in her element, singing along and applauding with the rest of the audience. 'I don't want Margot worrying about anything tonight.'

CHAPTER FIFTY-NINE

For what seemed like an age, Nancy and David sat in silence on the low wall in front of the theatre. Every few minutes, the still, quiet May evening was disturbed by a passing car or the distant hoot of a barge sailing up the River Thames.

It was David who spoke first. 'How did you know I was in the trap room?'

'I didn't at first,' Nancy said. 'I'd seen you earlier wandering around in the stalls. I thought it was strange. I knew you hadn't been given a comp, and you wouldn't have bought a ticket to see the show. The day I was here with George and Betsy, discussing Margot's debut performance when she'd taken the place of a dancer who'd been badly beaten up, you were putting up light fittings, and you dropped something and raced out of the auditorium. The other electrician said you'd told him the show was slanderous because the man they accused of being a Nazi was a war hero. I thought that was odd, because we'd spoken several times before that day and you hadn't said anything like that to me.'

'I didn't know the truth about him then,' David said. 'I didn't know what he was or what he'd done until tonight. I didn't know who you were when I talked to you at the theatre. I thought you were just one of the show's writers.' His brow furrowed. 'How did you know who I was?'

'I didn't, not at first. Not until I heard you talking to Artie in the trap room. I was backstage speaking to one of the dancers, and I saw my aunt looking around. I saw her open the door to the trap room and go inside, and I followed her. When I heard what you said about a dancer taking your father away from you and your mother, I knew you were talking about Goldie, my birth mother, and it hit me that we had the same father.'

'I didn't want to hurt anyone,' David said, his voice no more than a whisper.

'I know you didn't.'

'That day, when I heard you and your friends talking about what Dad had done and asking each other whether it could be written into the show without upsetting the audience, I convinced myself I had to stop the show from opening.'

'I'm sorry you had to find out about your father like that,' Nancy said. 'If I'd known who you were then…'

He lifted his shoulders in a shrug. 'You couldn't have known.'

'No,' Nancy agreed. Giving David a warm smile, she said, 'We both had a shock tonight, didn't we?' Nodding, he returned the smile. 'How did you get the job here?' she asked him.

'It was the name: Dudley. In my grandmother's diaries, she'd written about a woman called Bess Dudley who my father had been seen with at a party that was something to do with theatre, at the beginning of the war. She said Bess Dudley was a friend of people called Goldman who owned the Prince Albert Theatre in the West End of London. So, when I heard that electricians were wanted to work on a new theatre in the East End called the Young Albert, and there was

278

to be a tribute to Margot Dudley, I got Gran's diaries out and read them again. I didn't believe it at first, but it was all there in black and white. Gran had written about a dancer called Goldie, who Dad had run off with when he left Mum and me. Gran wrote that when Dad went away with the dancer, it was Margot Dudley who covered for her, and she blamed Margot Dudley as much as she blamed the dancer.' Tears fell onto David's already tear-stained face. 'Except he didn't go away with the dancer, did he?'

Nancy shook her head. 'No, David, he didn't.'

'Then why didn't he come back to us?'

'I don't know.'

Turning to face her, David said, 'He's dead, isn't he?' When she didn't reply, he looked into her eyes and said again, 'He's dead, isn't he?'

'I'm sorry, David.'

'How? When did he die?'

Before Nancy had time to tell David about his father's death, Dan Powell came out of the theatre. At the same time, a car pulled up and two men got out. 'Hello, David,' Powell said. 'I'm DCI Powell and these gentlemen are Detective Sergeant Mainard and Detective Constable Towers.'

'We'd like you to accompany us to Bow Street police station to answer some questions,' Mainard said.

David gripped Nancy's arm. 'It's okay,' she said. 'Go with the detectives, and I'll get a taxi. I'll be right behind you.' She spotted one of the detectives take handcuffs from his pocket. 'Are those necessary?' she asked him.

'I'm sorry, miss, but they are,' he said. 'Mr Sutherland, if you'd come with me, please.'

As the detectives put David in an unmarked police car, Nancy turned to Dan. 'Excuse me, Inspector, I'm going to get my handbag.'

'Is it somewhere safe?'

'Yes, it's in the administration office, but I need money for a cab to Bow Street.'

He smiled. 'Leave your handbag. I'll take you. My car is across the road.'

*

As they turned onto Leman Street in Whitechapel and followed the road to Tower Bridge, Nancy said: 'Thank God the theatre fireman didn't stop the show.' She looked at her wristwatch. 'Evacuating the theatre would have taken hours. It would have been dreadful for the audience, never mind the artists, after all the work they've put in.'

'I'm sorry you had to miss the show.'

'It's alright. Considering the alternative, which I'd rather not think about, it isn't important.' Nancy shuddered. 'If tonight hadn't gone the way it did – if it had been petrol in David's can instead of water – there wouldn't have been a show to miss.'

The inspector nodded in agreement. 'Nevertheless, after all your hard work, it's a shame to miss opening night.'

'I don't mind,' she said. 'My work was done weeks ago. I've seen so many rehearsals, I could play every part!'

'I saw your name in the programme as one of the writers,' Dan said. 'I'd have thought being at the first night, seeing the performance after all your hard work would have been the cherry on the cake, so to speak.'

'I suppose it would have been, but I can see it tomorrow. I'll go to the Saturday matinee-'

The inspector put up his hand. 'Sorry,' he said, cutting Nancy off. 'We're here.'

CHAPTER SIXTY

The public waiting area of Bow Street police station was heaving with people, some there to report a crime, some having committed a crime. Petty thieves in handcuffs, locals worse for wear after a night in the pub and suited and booted city types who'd had one over the eight after work mingled with an array of plainclothes officers and detectives in suits with wide lapels, sporting fashionable sideburns and moustaches. Most of the Metropolitan police detectives were as smartly dressed as the city guys, but they looked tougher, more streetwise. It was an intense environment. The room was thick with cigarette smoke, the atmosphere hostile.

Inspector Dan Powell ushered Nancy through the crowded waiting area to a row of seats. A middle-aged man who looked as if he'd been sleeping rough for some time jumped up and offered her his chair. She shook her head. 'Thank you, but I'd rather stand.'

Dan didn't try to persuade Nancy. Instead, he led her to the glass hatch where the custody sergeant was dealing with a man who was drunk. They waited behind a constable in shirt sleeves and a young man wearing bright red lipstick, boxer shorts, a tie in a bow around his neck and the constable's dark blue jacket, who was singing *I'm Getting Married in the Morning.*

'Stag night!' the constable said when he reached the hatch. 'His mates stripped him but for his tie and boxers and tied him to a lamppost. They did a bunk when they saw me.'

'Any ID?'

'A note on a scrap of paper pushed down his shorts. James Calder. 54 Arndale Street, West Ham. And a telephone number.' He passed the note through the hatch.

'Hope it isn't the number of the bride-to-be. She won't be happy seeing him in this state!'

The young man lurched towards the glass, still singing. 'But I can't help falling in love with you...'

'Come on, Romeo, let's make that telephone call and get someone to bring you some clothes,' the constable said, pulling the bridegroom-to-be through the door marked "Private".

'Good evening, Sergeant,' Dan said to the man behind the hatch.

'Good evening, Chief Inspector.'

'Miss Donnelly is with me,' Dan said. 'She's a relative of a young man two of my detectives brought in a while ago. We'd like to see them.'

The custody sergeant consulted the logging-in book. 'David Sutherland? Yes, sir, if you'd like to go through.'

As Nancy and Dan turned to leave the waiting area, DC Towers poked his head around the door of the custody sergeant's office. He pointed at Inspector Powell, and the DC returned to the corridor. Opening the door, he stood to one side to allow his boss to go through. 'DS Mainard is in interview room two, sir. Second door on the right.'

Nancy began to follow the inspector along the corridor. 'I'm sorry, miss,' Towers said. 'You won't be allowed into the interview. I'll escort you back to the waiting room.'

'I'm responsible for Miss Donnelly, Constable,' DCI Powell said. 'It's bedlam out there.'

'Perhaps Miss Donnelly could wait for you here, sir. I'll get her a chair.' Before waiting for a reply, he disappeared into the interview room.

Nancy and the inspector stood with their backs to the wall to let a constable, a teenage boy with a cut eye and lip, and a worried-looking woman who looked like the boy's mother go past. 'You won't be safe sitting here,' Dan said.

He flattened himself against the wall again as an exhausted-looking man in a crumpled suit, with greying hair, a smoke-stained moustache and spectacles on the end of his nose, carrying files and a briefcase, bumbled through the pass door. He greeted Powell with a tired smile. 'Chief Inspector!'

'Mr Salt, thank you for coming out at this hour.'

'It's Friday night, sir. I've already been here twice this evening. I see more of this place at the weekend than I do my wife.' He cleared his throat, rapped once and opened the door to the interview room just as DC Towers appeared carrying a chair.

'Sorry, Mr Salt,' he said, almost knocking the duty solicitor over. Salt lumbered into the room without acknowledging the young detective.

'I don't suppose there's an interview room free where Miss Donnelly could wait?' Dan asked.

'Not tonight, sir.'

'There's too much human traffic; she can't sit out here,' he said. 'Take Miss Donnelly to my office. No, on second thoughts, take her to the canteen and get her a cup of tea and something to eat. I'm sorry, Nancy,' he said, turning to her, 'you can't sit in on the interview. Go with DC Towers. I'll fill you in when I've finished here.'

She nodded. 'Will you tell David I'll see him the first opportunity I get?'

*

The interview room was small and airless. Like most of the interview rooms at Bow Street station, it was windowless and had a fug of stale smoke. As the inspector entered the room, DS Mainard stubbed out his cigarette and stood up out of respect for his senior officer, offering him his seat. DCI Powell crossed to the table and nodded to his sergeant.

'This is Arthur Salt, the duty solicitor,' Mainard said. Powell acknowledged the solicitor with a nod and received a weary smile in return. The only other person in the room besides David was a uniformed WPC sitting at a small desk a few feet away, notebook and pen in hand.

'Have you charged David yet?' Powell asked Mainard.

'Yes, but we were waiting for you and the solicitor to arrive before we began the interview.'

Powell nodded. 'Thank you, Sergeant.' He leaned back in his chair and waited for the custody solicitor, who was taking a pile of papers from his briefcase, to settle down. When he looked up, DCI Powell began the interview.

CHAPTER SIXTY-ONE

'David, would you confirm your name, address, and date of birth?' DCI Powell said.

'David Sutherland. 23 Warren Gardens, South Croydon, Surrey. Twenty-fifth of January 1939.'

'Do you understand why you've been brought in for questioning?'

'Yes,' David whispered.

'Can you tell us what happened tonight?'

'I wanted to stop the show at the Young Albert Theatre.'

'And how did you try to do that?'

'I took a petrol can and a cigarette lighter to the trap room–'

'Trap room?' the inspector queried. 'Can you tell me what the trap room is and where it's located?'

'It's a room under the stage used to store furniture and equipment.'

DCI Powell nodded. 'Go on, David.'

'I said I was going to set fire to the can.'

'Why was that, David? Why did you threaten to set fire to a can?'

'It was a petrol can. I thought they would stop the show if they thought I had petrol in it.'

'Are you saying there was no petrol in the can?'

'No. I filled it with water. I didn't want to hurt anyone. I just wanted to stop the show.'

'What about the cigarette lighter, David? Did you

light it?' David nodded. 'Answer the question so the WPC can write your answer down.'

'Yes.'

'A bare flame in a storage room under a stage would have been very dangerous. You do understand that, don't you, David?'

'Yes.'

'Have you been involved in similar incidents before?'

'No, never. I...I took some light bulbs, and the office telephones – and,' David took a shaky breath, 'I took the sound system.'

'You stole these items, David?'

'Yes.'

Inspector Powell looked sideways at DS Mainard. 'Why did you steal the sound system?'

'Without it, they couldn't put on the show. The system controls all the sound.'

'So, you stole the sound system to stop the show from opening?'

'Yes.'

'Why didn't you want the show to open, David?'

David's eyes sparkled with tears. 'My father left me and my mother for a dancer in the war. In the show, they say my father was a Nazi sympathiser who beat up a dancer and almost killed her. When the dancer died, they blamed my father. I didn't believe it. My mother told me that Dad was a war hero who died fighting for his country. I thought they'd lied about him. I thought it was wrong to discredit an innocent man, a war hero, in a stupid musical show.'

'And that was when you decided to get rid of the sound system.'

'Yes, because it's a musical. They couldn't put

the show on without it.'

DCI Powell looked enquiringly at David. 'But the show did go on. Tonight.'

'They were all so pleased. When they came to do a dress rehearsal, they were all laughing. They went out afterwards to celebrate. It was like they were celebrating the death of my father. They didn't care that they were blackening a dead man's name. That's why I pretended I was going to set fire to the place! I only wanted the show to stop.' Tears filled David's eyes. 'I wanted my dad to be the dad I believed him to be,' he said, bursting into tears. 'But I put water in the can because I didn't want to hurt anybody.'

DS Mainard looked at DCI Powell. 'Presumably, there are witnesses to the events of this evening, sir?'

'Three,' Powell said. 'David's half-sister Nancy Donnelly, who is one of the show's writers, Ena Green, and her associate, Artie Mallory.'

Mainard raised his eyebrows. 'The writer of the show is the sister of–'

'Miss Donnelly is the daughter of the dancer who was beaten up in the war and subsequently died. David didn't know about that. And neither sibling knew about the other until tonight. It was Miss Donnelly who persuaded David to give her the petrol can and the lighter.'

'She's my sister,' David said. 'Tell her I'm sorry, Inspector.'

'I will, David.' Powell turned his attention back to Mainard. 'Mr Mallory was first on the scene. He and Mrs Green are private investigators. The theatre's owner employed them to find the stolen sound system. Mrs Green is also Miss Donnelly's aunt.'

'Quite a family affair,' David's solicitor said,

nodding his thanks for the information.

The inspector looked over at the WPC, who was taking notes. When she put down her pen, he turned his attention to David. 'We're going to keep you in overnight, David. Tomorrow, I shall examine the physical evidence and take eyewitness statements from the people who were with you earlier this evening.'

The duty solicitor, who had also been taking notes, put his notebook and pen in his briefcase. 'I'll see you tomorrow, Mr Sutherland. Ten o'clock.'

'There'll be a bail hearing tomorrow, David, and Mr Salt will represent you,' Powell said.

The solicitor got up from the table and closed his briefcase. 'That the petrol can contained water may help,' he said to the inspector. Then, turning to David, 'But your threat was serious. You do understand that, don't you?'

David nodded. 'Yes.'

'I'll see you tomorrow. Goodnight.'

'He's a good solicitor, David. He's a bit brusque, but he'll do his best for you.' DCI Powell looked at DS Mainard. 'If there's nothing else.'

'I'm sorry!' David cried, tears pouring from his eyes. 'Tell Nancy the sound system is in Gran's garage. It's safe. It's still in the boxes it was delivered to the theatre in.' He sniffed. 'Tell her I'm sorry.'

'I will, David. She said she'll come and see you at the first opportunity. Thank you, DS Mainard.' At the door, DCI Powell looked back to Mainard, who was explaining to David what would happen at Bow Street Court in the morning.

※

The atmosphere in the canteen was one of camaraderie. DCI Dan Powell entered to the clattering of cutlery on plates and the hum of conversation, punctuated by bursts of laughter and the occasional crackle of a radio. Officers of every rank were coming and going. Those who had finished work after a long day were there to unwind, while others were having a hot meal before going on night shift. Some were still high on adrenaline and were recounting their experiences, and others who were still working had missed their evening meal and were taking a quick break and a sandwich. The police canteen was a place where rank didn't matter much, a place where everyone could relax and join in the conversation.

Powell spotted Nancy and DC Towers at a table on the far side of the canteen. After queueing for a cup of coffee at a long stainless-steel counter, he made his way over to join them. 'Would either of you like another drink?'

DC Towers stood up. 'No, thank you, sir.'

'Nancy? Something to drink, or a sandwich?'

'No, thank you,' she said, lifting her cup and drinking the last of her coffee.

Once DCI Powell had sat down, Towers returned to his seat.

'How was David?' Nancy asked.

'Upset, as you can imagine. But he has been cooperative,' Dan said, taking a sip of his coffee.

'Good. When can I see him?'

'He is still being interviewed.'

'Will they let him go home then?'

'No, they'll keep him overnight in a holding cell. He's appearing before the magistrate at ten in the morning.'

'He will get bail, won't he?'

'I don't know. Holding hostages and threatening to set fire to a building is very serious.'

'He hardly held us hostage!' Nancy said. 'We could have left at any time. And it was water in the petrol can!'

'Technically, it was a hostage situation, so the judge has to take that into consideration.' Nancy started to interrupt, but Dan put up his hand. 'The judge will consider everything. It was an unusual situation, and it *will* be taken into account.' She didn't look convinced. 'The Bow Street magistrate is a fair man,' he said. 'Don't worry, and be patient. David is safe where he is. Tomorrow afternoon, telephone the station and ask to speak to him. He'll know more about what's going on by then.'

'I'm going to the court hearing,' Nancy said. 'I'll ask Mum and Dad to lend me the money to pay his bail.'

Dan nodded, not because he agreed with her going to David's hearing, but because he expected that she would. 'David asked me to tell you he was sorry,' he said. 'The sound system is safe. It's in the garage at his late grandmother's house in South Croydon.'

CHAPTER SIXTY-TWO

Ena sang along with her sisters, albeit quietly. She was the only member of the Dudley family that God forgot when he was dishing out singing voices.

On stage, the professional singers and dancers of the Young Albert Company, holding hands with the East End girls and boys, entered from the wings. It seemed the whole cast was on stage. A props girl pushed a hand cart along and, as the orchestra began to play *We'll Meet Again*, red, white and blue balloons were released from it and confetti fell from the sky.

Led by Margot's daughter Natalie, the company began to sing. 'We'll meet again, don't know where, don't know when, but I know we'll meet again some sunny day.

'Keep smiling through just like you always do, 'til the blue skies drive the dark clouds far away.

'So, will you please say hello to the folks that I know? Tell them I won't be long.

'They'll be happy to know that as you saw me go, I was singing this song…'

As Natalie and the company finished singing to rapturous applause, the lights dimmed until the stage was in darkness. In small groups, the chorus took their curtain calls, followed by the performers, with the solo artists taking the call one at a time. When everyone was back on stage, they took a final bow, and the stage lights dimmed to blackout.

Instead of the curtains closing as they always did after the last curtain call at the end of a show, a single spotlight lit Natalie Goldman as she entered back centre stage and walked to the apron at the front. 'Tonight we have paid tribute to a very special lady,' she told the audience. 'Not only was she the leading lady here at the Prince Albert from 1943 to 1946, but she was The Talk of London, a favourite of the customers at the Albert Club, and the sweetheart of the British and Commonwealth Army, Navy and Airforce during her time with ENSA.'

Natalie Goldman looked around the auditorium, smiling as she waited for the applause to stop. Eventually, she put her hands up. Slowly, the cheering lessened.

'But to us, ladies and gentlemen. To us,' she said again, as applause started up again, 'and to her sisters and friends, her husband and daughter...' The audience, one row after another, stood up and cheered. Natalie waited again, but the cheering didn't stop. She beckoned to the wings and Joe Singer brought her a microphone. 'Ladies and gentlemen, you know who I'm referring to.' By now, the audience was chanting, 'Margot! Margot! Margot!'

The curtains that hung across the back of the stage opened very slowly from the middle and the entire cast stepped back. A spotlight beamed a bright warm light into the darkness and Margot stepped into it. The audience went wild as she opened her arms and looked about her. Slowly, she walked through the sea of performers, applauding them and blowing kisses. As she passed through the guard of honour, the artists moved back into their curtain call positions and Natalie Goldman walked over to greet her. Handing her a microphone, Natalie led her to the front of the stage. 'Are you alright to stand?' she mouthed.

Margot nodded. 'Try and stop me!'

Natalie stepped to the side and applauded with the rest of the company. Margot, no longer able to curtsey, put her hands together and bowed. She began to speak, but the audience drowned her out. Eventually, she turned to Natalie and mimed for two more microphones. Natalie put up her thumb and left the stage. Margot then looked up at the box and motioned for George and Betsy to join her.

Once she had seen her two ENSA partners leave their seats, she waved to the leader of the orchestra. He went to her immediately and, after a short conversation, returned to his podium and started to play the introduction to *Burlington Berty,* which Margot sang on her own. When George and Betsy arrived on stage, the three friends sang *Puttin' On The Ritz*, which brought the house down.

After a standing ovation, the lights dimmed and a single spotlight picked out Natalie, who led three chorus boys, each carrying a chair, onto the stage. Placing the chairs downstage right, they beckoned to Margot, George and Betsy and, with sweeping gestures, offered them a seat. George looked at Betsy and lifted her shoulders. They had been asked to join Margot on stage – and, if she was happy to sing, to sing with her – but they hadn't been told what was going to happen next. By the look on Margot's face, she didn't know either.

'Ladies and gentlemen,' Natalie said, 'someone who knew Margot many years ago has popped in to say hello. Would you please give a warm welcome to… Mr Tommy Trinder!'

The famous comedian swaggered onto the stage wearing his trademark trilby. 'The name's Trinder. That's T-R-I-N-D-E-R, pronounced Chumley,' he said, laughing with the audience. 'Good evening, you lucky people.' Hearing Tommy Trinder's catchphrase, the audience cheered. 'What a lovely lot you are.' When the audience was quiet again, he said, 'This is a special night for me. Not only have I seen a wonderful show and been asked to say a few words about a wonderful lady, but I've got a date with three gorgeous girls later.' Laughter rang around the auditorium. 'And,' he said, putting up his hands to quieten the audience, 'if that isn't enough, I've come home. It was on this stage when it was Silver's Music Hall that I performed *The Load of Nonsense*. I was young and handsome in those days,' he said, putting the back of his hand under his chin and winking.

When the audience stopped laughing, he said, 'Happy days!' to cheers and applause. 'A lot of water has gone under Tower Bridge since then.' There was another burst of applause. 'But I'm not here to talk about me.' He turned upstage. Rose Allen appeared from the wings and put her thumb up.

'I first met Margot Dudley, George Derby Bloom and Betsy Evans in the war, when they called themselves the Albert Sisters,' Tommy said. 'We were in the same concert party, on tour with ENSA. The lads in the audience laughed at my jokes, but when the Albert Sisters came on stage in their short uniforms, they went wild, whistling and throwing their caps in the air.' Tommy looked around the audience. 'We all fell in love with the Albert Sisters,' he said. 'So, without further ado… you lucky people!' While the audience was laughing, Rose gave Tommy a selection of military hats. After distributing them to Margot, George and Betsy, he said, 'It is my pleasure to introduce you to The Prince Albert Theatre Conscripts, Misses WAAFY, WAACY and WREN.'

As the orchestra struck up the opening bars to *Boogie Woogie Bugle Boy*, the girls began to swing their hips. Just before the end of the song, Margot stepped forward and sang, 'In the army now!' George barked, 'In the navy now!' and Betsy followed with, 'And the 'RAF!'

When they had performed their song, Tommy Trinder bellowed, "Miss WAFFY and WACCY… Atteeeeeeeeention!' George and Betsy stood to attention. 'About turn!' They turned so their backs were to the audience, leaving Margot on her own. 'And… Left, right. Left, right.' Marching off, George and Betsy looked over their right shoulders, saluted, and held the pose until they were in the wings.

As the audience shouted for more, the girls turned, ran back to Margot and started singing *Run Rabbit Run*, followed by *Don't Sit Under The Apple Tree*. For the finale, they sang their interpretation of the Andrews Sisters' hit *Bei Mir Bist du Schoen* to rapturous applause and a standing ovation.

George and Betsy stepped away and joined Natalie and Tommy at the side of the stage, leaving Margot to take her curtain call.

CHAPTER SIXTY-THREE

For most of the journey from Bow Street to the Young Albert Theatre, Nancy was silent. DCI Dan Powell broke the silence. 'I'm sorry you've had such a tough night.'

'It was tougher for David,' she said, her voice hoarse with emotion. She looked out of the window. It had started to rain and the lights on Tower Bridge shimmered in the distance. 'David wanted to know what I knew about his father. He guessed that he was dead, and I have promised to tell him how he died.'

'How did he die?'

'He drowned in a frozen lake on New Year's Eve, 1948. It was the opening of my mother and father's hotel. How the hell do I tell David that?'

'Was it an accident?' Dan ventured.

'No one knows. Well, I say they don't know, but I expect they do; they just haven't told me. I don't expect they ever will.' She wiped tears from her cheeks.

Dan parked the Wolseley in front of the Young Albert Theatre. 'There aren't any lights on. I think we're too late to get your handbag.'

'The night watchman will be there.' She took a long breath. 'Are you going to the first night party at the Prince Albert Club?'

'I thought I'd pop in for a drink. You?'

'I have to. By now my mother will be worried sick

and Dad will be threatening to telephone Bow Street.'
Nancy opened the car door. 'I'll see if I can raise the
night watchman,' she said. 'I need to tidy my hair and
put some powder on. I expect the skin beneath my eyes
is red and blotchy. A dab of powder works wonders.'
She jumped out of the car. 'Thank you. I won't be
long.'

*

Feeling nostalgic, Margot looked around the foyer of
the Prince Albert Club. 'During the war, my mentor
was Nancy Diamond, the main dancer at the Prince
Albert Theatre,' she told Ena, who was walking
alongside her. 'Her fiancé, Salvatore Russo, was
manager of the club. He greeted everyone at the door.
Going to a restaurant in the nineteen-forties was like
stepping into another world.' She sighed. 'In those
days, men wore dinner jackets and women wore
evening dresses. Later, when material was limited and
clothes were rationed, the hemlines became shorter
and cocktail dresses were fashionable. Everyone
dressed for dinner in clubs like this, no matter what
was happening.

'Film stars and minor royalty used to come here,
and high-ranking military men and wealthy
businessmen entertained beautiful young women.'
Margot laughed, the memories bittersweet. 'I was so
naive in those days. Whenever I saw a glamorous
young woman in the club, I thought she was a starlet.'

As she moved from the foyer to the restaurant, she
continued. 'Each table had a lamp, and all around the
room were silver wall lights designed to look like half-
moons that shone upwards. And in the ceiling, right in

the middle above the dance floor, was a huge mirror ball.'

'Happy days,' Ena said.

'They were, but there were some unhappy days too.' Margot didn't elaborate but pointed to a table by the stage and said, 'I had my first taste of champagne sitting at that table. It was twenty-eight years ago!' She sighed again. 'Where have the years gone? No one greets you at the door anymore.'

Ena gently placed her hand on her sister's arm. 'No, darling. Times have changed.'

The moment was broken as several members of the Young Albert Company burst into the club, chatting and laughing. In unison, the sisters turned to see who had arrived. 'It's my daughter!' Margot said, beaming with pride. 'Wasn't she wonderful tonight?'

'Yes, she was,' Ena said. 'She reminded me of you when you were her age. She has the same love of dance, and she has inherited your beautiful voice.' Margot's brow furrowed, but she didn't reply. 'Natalie has experienced being a member of a theatre company, part of a dance troop, and she's loved it. Margot, did you hear me?' Ena touched her sister's hand, and she jumped.

'Sorry, Ena, I was miles away. What did you say?'

'I was trying to tell you that Natalie wants to audition for musicals. She wants to have a career as a singer and dancer, spread her wings, go on tour.'

'She has never said.' Margot looked at Ena, her expression a mixture of surprise and sadness. 'Did she tell you that? I didn't know she wanted to work in shows. I thought she wanted to teach at the academy.'

'She does,' Ena said, anxious not to upset her

sister. 'She wants to teach, but she has the same desire to go out in the world and make a name for herself as you had when you were her age. She's young; she wants to find her own way in the world and get some practical experience before she takes on the responsibility of the academy. She has your talent, Margot, your drive. It would be a shame if she didn't use it.'

'You're right,' Margot said. 'I thought the academy would be security for her, but seeing her tonight, watching her sing and dance, I can see now how wrong it would be to hold her back.'

'Mum?' Natalie called, waving her arm high in the air as she made her way across the room.

'Don't tell her we've spoken, Margot,' Ena whispered. 'I don't want her to think I've broken her confidence.'

'Of course not.' Margot kissed Ena on the cheek. 'Thank you, darling. I know where my daughter belongs.'

'But what about the academy?'

'We have half a dozen talented tutors and an amazing administrator. The academy will carry on as it is. And it will be there if and when Natalie decides to take it over. The academy isn't important; my daughter is,' Margot said, as Natalie joined them.

'Aunt Ena, do you mind if I drag Mum away? My friends want to meet her.'

'Be my guest,' Ena said. 'I'll see you later,' she called after her niece, as Natalie took her mother by the hand and led her across the room.

Ena joined Henry, Artie and Rupert at the bar. 'I might have known you three would be here. Thank you,' she said, as the barman passed her a flute of champagne.

'You just missed Bess,' Henry said. 'She's worried about Nancy.'

'Do you know where she is?' Artie asked.

'I left her outside the theatre with David and Inspector Powell. Dan was going to get a couple of his detectives to take David to Bow Street station. I expect Nancy went with them. She was adamant she was going to support David. She's probably still there. I'll have a word with Bess.'

No sooner had Ena said her sister's name than she saw Nancy and DCI Powell arrive. Ena watched her niece shake Dan's hand, turn and look around the room. Spotting Ena, they made their way over to her. 'Hello, Aunt Ena. I need to find Mum. If she's noticed I'm not here, she'll be going frantic,' Nancy said. 'Inspector Powell will fill you in with what happened with David.' She began to leave and then turned on her heels. 'Oh, the sound system is in David's grandmother's garage in South Croydon. It's still in the delivery boxes.' Before Ena could thank her niece, she had disappeared into a crowd of people to find Bess.

'You look as if you need a drink, Inspector,' Artie said to Dan. 'Will champagne do?'

Dan laughed. 'Anything cold and wet with a kick to it will do. Thank you, Artie.'

CHAPTER SIXTY-FOUR

'So what's happening to David?' Ena asked Dan.

'He's being held in custody overnight, to appear at Bow Street Magistrates' in the morning.'

'How do you think that will go?'

'Well, technically, it was a hostage situation, so the magistrate will have to consider that,' Dan said. 'If David's solicitor can convince the court that he didn't intend to harm anyone and he only wanted to stop the show, the magistrate might go easy on him. It's good that David gave himself up and confessed to the thefts. That will all go in his favour. The Bow Street magistrate is a fair man. Nancy said she was going to the court hearing, but I persuaded her to telephone the station tomorrow afternoon and speak to David. He'll know more about what's going on by then.'

'She told me about the sound system. So he'll be charged with theft,' Ena said. 'Will he be charged with arson too?'

'He's been charged with the potential to commit arson, but as it was water in the petrol can—'

'That proves he had no intention of setting fire to the theatre, doesn't it?'

'Yes, and no. He still had the cigarette lighter, and he did light it. As I said, I'll have a word with the magistrate tomorrow. I'll tell him about David's past – and I'll make sure his solicitor tells the court, too. It will all be taken into account.'

'Will he go to prison?' Ena asked.

'I doubt it. As it's his first offence he'll probably get a suspended sentence, and a couple of years' probation. Nancy says she's going to help him as much as she can. She wants to pay his bail if he gets it.'

'I'm not sure what her mother will say about that.'

'Nancy's a strong young woman. She's got a good head on her shoulders. Even so, it must be hard for her to live where her father was killed.'

'Drowned!' Ena corrected him. 'Fortunately, she doesn't think of Dave Sutherland as her father.'

'Okay, drowned,' Dan said. 'Nancy told me that David asked her about his father. He guessed he was dead, and she said she'd tell him one day how he died. She told me he drowned in a lake at Foxden Hotel. I asked her if it was an accident, but she said she didn't know, and that the family had never told her what actually happened.'

'We can't tell her what we don't know,' Ena said.

There was a pause. 'You knew Sutherland, didn't you?' Dan asked.

'Briefly. My sister Bess had dealings with him before the war, and Margot during the war.' Ena felt suddenly cold. 'You saw the show, so you know the story, at least part of it.'

'How did Sutherland come to be at Foxden when he died?'

'He was staying with an equally nasty piece of work and they gate-crashed the hotel's opening.'

'Was that a coincidence?'

'No. He knew what he was doing. Sutherland was a member of the British Patriots, a Nazi group run by a landowner called Sir Gerald Hawksley. Military intelligence had Hawksley in their sights. He'd evaded

303

the authorities for decades. He'd lived in London for some years before moving to the Midlands with his daughter. He bought a manor house in a village near Foxden called Kirby Marlow.' Ena laughed. 'He was a revolting man. He was pompous and arrogant. He swanked about like the lord of the manor, which I suppose he thought he was. Anyway, he wheedled his way into county society, joined the local Freemasons and the hunt, and bought stables in Kirby Marlow for his daughter. To those who didn't know him, Hawksley was a successful businessman who had moved to the country for a quiet life.'

'What business was he in?'

'That's a good question. I don't think he was in business. If he was, I doubt it was legitimate. No one knew what line of work he was in or where his money came from. As for leading a quiet life? Not with Dave Sutherland as a house guest.' Finishing her drink, Ena put the empty glass on the counter, and the barman refilled it. 'Another?' she asked Dan.

'Thank you,' he called after the barman, who had already poured a second glass and left to serve someone at the far end of the bar.

'For the first couple of years,' Ena continued, 'Hawksley played the part of local landowner and devoted father. So, while he wasn't stirring up trouble, the security services let him get on with it. Then the rumours started. Men began turning up at the manor house at all hours of the day and night and stayed for four or five days. As soon as they left, another group would turn up. Hawksley's gardeners and cleaners saw them in the grounds and the house. The staff didn't live in; they were local people from the village. Everyone knew someone and the rumours soon reached the police, and then the security services.'

'So, Gerald Hawksley was helping other British Patriots to spread their fascist hate in different parts of the country?' Dan asked.

'And worse. Some of his guests were Germans. Nazis. They came to Hawksley for fake passports and new identities.'

'Did the security services know Hawksley was helping Nazis?'

'Henry did, so MI5 must have.'

Dan looked puzzled. 'What I don't understand is, if the security services knew what he was doing, why didn't they stop him?'

'It isn't quite as simple as that,' Ena said. 'The fascist association that Hawksley ran had connections with groups all over the country. He had family in the north and MI5 was worried that if he got wind that the net was closing in on him, he'd do a moonlight flit and disappear to a bolthole in the wilds of northern England. Eventually, the major players in the fascist association were arrested and,' Ena said, smiling 'the security services found the names of hundreds of other British Patriots, along with the names of the Nazis who had escaped Germany. The escape route to South America was shut down, and every fascist who had helped them along the route was arrested.'

'I was wondering how Sutherland drowned,' Dan said. 'Because of his connection to Hawksley and the fascist movement, there might have been foul play.'

'It's more than likely, but the local police didn't find any proof,' Ena said. 'A local police constable, PC McGann, hated the Dudley family. He had a grudge against Bess, and he told Hawksley in front of his daughter Katherine that he intended to pin

Sutherland's murder on her. But he couldn't because Bess was never on her own that evening.'

'Was Hawksley's daughter with him the night Sutherland drowned?'

'Yes. Katherine was a pretty girl with fair hair and blue eyes. She was in her late teens. Hawksley had Katherine abducted from school and told her that her mother was dead. I found her mother living in Carlisle. She was a nice woman. She came from a well-to-do family. Hawksley married her for her money, not the other way around, which was what he told people. And she didn't abandon her daughter either. Hawksley was a big noise in the British Union of Fascists and he threatened to have her and her family killed if she didn't leave.'

Ena sighed. 'The first time I met Katherine, she was with her father on New Year's Eve at Foxden Hotel; Sutherland was there too. He was holding her hand. She looked petrified of him. She told me later that Sutherland had got into her bed when her father was away. She was a child, and that bastard raped her.'

'So Hawksley's daughter had a good reason to kill him.'

'Dan, I've known and respected you for a long time,' Ena said, sharply. 'How Sutherland died had nothing to do with any member of the Dudley family *or* Hawksley's daughter. It wasn't until his body surfaced when the lake thawed that we even knew he was dead. The last anyone saw of him, he was running through the estate grounds in a blizzard to a car parked in a lane beyond a small wood. Until his body was found, everyone believed he'd escaped in the car. The police investigated every angle, but eventually, as there was no evidence of foul play, they put his death down to an accident.'

'With his history?'

'It was a bitterly cold night. It was snowing heavily and blowing a gale. You couldn't see your hand in front of your face,' Ena said. 'So the police came to the only conclusion that made sense: he had slipped while trying to escape and fallen into the lake. The freezing water would have caused involuntary inhalation, and he would have died of shock. Case closed!'

'You're not going to tell me what really happened that night, are you, Ena?'

'No! Now, let me get you another drink. After all you've done for me, Nancy and that poor kid of Sutherland's, you deserve a large one. Another glass of champagne, or would you rather have a whiskey?' Dan chose whiskey, and Ena ordered two doubles. While she waited for the drinks, she saw Natalie Goldman welcoming Rose Allen and Connor Wolf. Taking a pound note from her purse and leaving it on the bar, she said: 'Would you excuse me, Dan? I'm going to tell Natalie the sound system has been found.'

'It's evidence, Ena. Tell her she won't be able to claim it yet.'

Ena nodded. 'Of course not, but she'll be thrilled to know she doesn't have to buy a new one.'

CHAPTER SIXTY-FIVE

By the time Ena had made her way through a crowd of young dancers, Natalie Goldman had left Rose and Connor and was walking towards her. She greeted Ena with her customary kiss on both cheeks. 'The sound system has been found!' Ena said. 'It hasn't even been taken out of its boxes.'

'Ena, you are a miracle worker,' Natalie said, kissing her again.

'I didn't find it; I'm only the bringer of good news. Nancy told me. She and DCI Powell–' Ena stopped explaining and said, 'It's evidence. You can't have it yet, but it's safe. Now you must mingle and enjoy the first night party and the success of the Young Prince Albert. I'm going to speak to Rose.'

She looked around and spotted Rose standing on her own. 'Rose?' she said. 'I thought I saw you with Connor. Is everything alright between the two of you?'

'Yes, it's wonderful,' Rose said, unable to stop herself grinning.

'So, where is he?'

'He's mingling.' Ena pulled a face. 'I insisted he spend time with the cast and crew,' Rose said.

'But–'

'We're taking it slowly.'

'Oh, right! That's good. I think,' Ena said, looking up at the ceiling and squinting thoughtfully.

Rose laughed. 'We're no longer teenagers.'

'I know.' Ena wrinkled her nose. 'I'm not usually a romantic. I think I've had too much bubbly, or maybe not enough.' They both laughed.

'Scarlet told Connor everything about the accident,' Rose said. 'I think he's still processing it. She has moved out of the house and is living with James, temporarily, until they find a suitable place of their own.'

'I expect she's waiting for Connor to sell the house.'

'I don't think so. Scarlet doesn't need any money from the house. She inherited a fortune from her maternal grandmother.'

'So, will you and Connor live there?'

'No. I don't want to live there, and nor does Connor. Too many unhappy memories. He plans to sell up and give Scarlet her share. He has always paid the mortgage and bills, but her parents gave them the deposit for the house as a wedding present, so he feels it's only fair.'

'I wonder what she'll do with her life now she's free of her scheming mother?' Ena pondered.

'She's looking for a studio,' Rose said. 'She wants to teach dance. I think she'll be a good teacher.'

'It was Elsbeth who sent you the threatening letters, you know.'

'That doesn't surprise me. Did Scarlet know?'

'Not at the time, but she does now. Never mind Scarlet, she has her life all mapped out by the sound of it. What about you and Connor? What are your plans?'

'Well, as I said, we're taking it slowly,' Rose said. 'He's been asked to direct a play in Manchester, and rehearsals start in a couple of weeks. It may or may not come into town. Either way, I shall stay at the Prince

Albert, and when Connor comes back to London, we'll start again.'

Ena smiled. 'I'm so pleased for you.'

Eyes sparkling with happy tears, Rose looked across the room at Connor. Surrounded by the cast of *Tribute*, he was nodding and laughing. 'He looks happy, doesn't he?'

'Yes, he does. And so do you.'

'I am. I'm very happy, Ena. Thank you so much for all you've done. I don't know how I'll ever repay you.'

'That you and Connor are together at last is payment enough.'

Rose put her arms around Ena and hugged her. 'Thank you.'

'Be happy,' Ena said, blinking back tears. 'Now, I must find Henry. I left him with Artie and a colleague. They'll be talking shop.'

Making her way to the table facing the stage, where her sisters were already seated, Ena found Henry, Artie, Rupert, and her brother Tom, deep in conversation. 'Ena?' Artie caught her by the arm as she passed and gave her an envelope. 'A cheque from Natalie Goldman.'

She looked at the writing on the front of the envelope. '"Thank you, Ena and thank you, Artie,"' she read out loud. 'And below, she's written, "PS Artie, if you ever want a job as an actor, come and see me."'

Artie laughed. 'I might take her up on that.'

'Don't you dare!' Ena slapped him playfully. 'Do you know how much the cheque is for?'

He shook his head. 'We can't really look now...'

'It doesn't matter.' She put the envelope in her

handbag. 'I'll bank it first thing tomorrow.'

'Now we're solvent, can we think about hiring a secretary?'

Ena laughed. 'We can think about it if there's any money left when the bills have been paid.'

*

The bandleader stepped down from the stage and made his way through dancers smooching to a slow song. He stopped behind Margot's chair and whispered in her ear.

'I'd love to. Natalie?' she called to her daughter. 'Would you sing a duet with me?'

'Of course, Mum.'

The bandleader led Margot and Natalie across the dance floor. At the front of the stage were two microphones. He called to a male singer and, after a short conversation, the microphones were lowered to the dance floor and placed side by side.

Involuntary tears filled Ena's eyes. She looked around the table to see Claire and Bess were wiping at their eyes. Henry gave her his handkerchief. 'This is going to be special,' she said. 'I wonder what they'll sing.'

The bandleader leaned forward and spoke into Natalie's microphone. 'Ladies and gentlemen, Miss Margot Dudley and Miss Natalie Burrell are going to sing the 1950s song made famous by Marlene Dietrich and Rosemary Clooney, *Dot's Nice - Donna Fight!'*

Before the song finished, the audience was on its feet. Natalie was laughing so much she could hardly sing. But it didn't matter, because the last lines, 'Dot's nice, Donna fight, everything's gonna be alright' were drowned by laughter and cheers.

Margot took her daughter's hand and kissed it. Then, turning back to the microphone, she said, 'Ladies and gentlemen…' She waited until the audience stopped cheering. 'Ladies and gentlemen, tonight I watched my beautiful daughter perform in the musical *Tribute*, and she showed me that she has what it takes to take any stage by storm.' Margot took a step back and, looking at Natalie, opened her arms. 'And just now, you showed me that you are a fabulous singer as well as a dancer. You should be out there using your amazing talents to entertain every night.' She turned and faced the audience. 'I had hoped my daughter would take over the Margot Dudley Dancing Academy, but after watching her tonight,' Margot turned back to Natalie, 'after watching you tonight, my wish for you is that you go out into the world and sing and dance, as I did. The academy will be there when you want it.'

When Margot finished speaking, Natalie threw her arms around her. The *Tribute* company leapt out of their seats, applauding. Margot said something to her daughter, and after kissing her, Natalie left the dance floor and joined her friends.

Standing alone, Margot looked into the audience and bowed her head to show her appreciation. Then, nodding to the musicians in the band, she said, 'Will you play *Moonlight Serenade*?' As the band began to play softly, Margot looked to where Bill was sitting. 'For you, Bill,' she said, before picking up the first line of the song. 'I stand at your gate and the song that I sing is of moonlight… I stand and I wait for the touch of your hand in the June night…'

EPILOGUE

As she returned to the sitting room after getting ready for bed, Ena picked up an envelope from the hall table. 'When did this come, Henry?' she said. She turned it over. It was postmarked Glasgow. 'Did you bring it up?'

'Sorry, darling, I forgot to tell you. It was on the mat this evening when I got home; must have come in the afternoon post.'

Ena ran her finger under the flap of the envelope and pulled out a letter. 'It's from Sylvia August,' she said, excitedly. '"Dear Ena. As you know, I had hoped to be invited back to the Citizen's Theatre in Glasgow for the autumn season. Well, today my agent telephoned to say they want me for the first three plays. I can't say anything to my fellow cast members of *Women Beware Women*, but I'm so excited I just had to write and tell you. I'll be in London when *Women* finishes, so there will be plenty of time to see you and Artie before I go back to bonny Scotland. I'll telephone as soon as I'm there. Love and peace, Sylvia."' Ena turned to see Henry reading a newspaper. 'Were you listening?'

'What? Yes, of course I was listening. Sylvia is going to–'

'Back to Glasgow!' Ena tutted. Leaning forward, she pulled on the newspaper's front page to read the title. 'Since when have you been interested in *The*

Stage?'

'Since today,' he said, thumbing through the pages until he came to the section on shows coming into London. 'There was a poster in the newsagent's window.' He folded the paper in half and passed it to Ena. 'Read *Brick by Brick*, halfway down the page.'

'"*Brick By Brick*, a new play penned by playwright Nancy Donnelly, will make its debut in Manchester before coming to London,"' she read. '"*Brick By Brick* will open the autumn season at The Young Albert Theatre in Whitechapel. Set in London's East End during World War Two, it's a play about courage in a working-class community blown apart in the Blitz. It tells the story of a family of four brothers who avoided gangs, survived the war, and, with strength and determination, built a better life for themselves and other youngsters in post-war London."'

Ena continued reading out loud: '"I was fortunate enough to be invited to some early readings of this refreshing play. *Brick by Brick* is Nancy Donnelly's first solo contribution to the world of theatre. It won't be her last."'

With a lump in her throat, she lowered the paper. Henry took it from her and continued reading. '"The box office is open for advance bookings, and tickets are selling fast."'

Squealing, Ena jumped onto the sofa and, putting her feet up, leaned back against Henry's chest. 'She told me she wanted to write plays for the Young Albert.' Ena made a steeple of her hands and put them up to her face. And she has! Who's directing the play?'

'It doesn't say. Perhaps they haven't found a director yet.'

'The guy who wrote the article said he'd been to some of the early readings, so there must be a director. What did it say on the poster you saw in the newsagents?'

'I don't think it said anything.'

'I expect it did. You just didn't look.' Ena yawned and sat up. Then she took *The Stage* from Henry, folded it and dropped it on the coffee table. 'Come on, darling, let's go to bed. We both have to get up early in the morning. You're driving to Cheltenham, and it's the first day of Orla's trial as our secretary.' She laughed. 'She's so eager she's bound to be here early.'

Pushing himself off the settee, Henry stood up and pulled Ena to him. He wrapped his arms around her and kissed her. Ena responded eagerly, leaning her body against Henry's and kissing him back. Taking her by the hand, Henry led his wife out of the sitting room.

As she closed the door behind them, Ena looked back at *The Stage*. 'I knew she'd do it.'

THE END

Dear Reader,

Thank you for reading Tribute. I hope you enjoyed Ena and Artie's investigation into the theft of the theatre's sound system and everything that unfolds afterwards. Was Nancy, being David Sutherland's half-sister, a surprise? It was a surprise to me when the idea woke me in the middle of the night. It worked for me because in the novel Legacy, Ena's sister Bess adopted Nancy, the child of Margot's dancer friend, Goldie Trick, who died after being beaten up by David's father.

I also hope you enjoyed meeting Sylvia. I loved creating Sylvia. I love her character. She's kind, witty, tells it as it is, and determined. I'm glad Sylvia decided to return to acting. She'll work hard to make her dream come true, and she'll succeed.

Rose Allen and Connor Wolf. Thanks to Scarlet's need to have what someone else has and her social-climbing mother, Elseth Brookes, years of happiness have been lost. They say it's never too late to fall in love. This trio is proof of that.

I couldn't resist introducing lovely Priscilla and Charles Galbraith. They have a cracking storyline in the next novel. Thanks to Jeanie McKinley, a favourite character of mine, we met Orla Finnegan. I am fond of Orla. Should Ena give her a job at Dudley Green Investigations? No spoilers… If you read the next book in the series, you'll find out.

I want to share with you what inspired me to write Tribute, but first, I'd like to tell you why writing Tribute was so important to me.

I love the Dudley sisters, and I have loved

writing every book in the Sisters of Wartime England series. However, just before I began writing Tribute, I had writer's block. After writing ten novels, I lost my confidence and spent months unable to write. So, in November 2024, I signed up for the National Novel Writing Month challenge of 50,000 words. I typed what had been in my heart and imagination for months, and eventually, I wrote Tribute. I hope you enjoyed reading it. If you did, would you spare a few moments to leave a review on Amazon? I would appreciate it. Even a short review can make all the difference in encouraging a reader to discover my books for the first time. Thank you, in advance.

I have always wanted to write a standalone sequel to Destiny, celebrating Margot Dudley's life as a dancer in a West End theatre during World War II. So, as 2025 is the eightieth anniversary of Victory in Europe Day, and as Justice, the last novel in the Sisters of Wartime England series, was set in the late 1960s, it made sense to set Tribute in 1970 – twenty-five years after the end of the war, and twenty-five years after Margot gave up her career.

I have always been fascinated by the achievements of women in wartime – some, like Claire Dudley, joined the armed forces. Claire was recruited by the SOE and spent her war years working with the French Resistance, other women, such as Ena, worked in factories. Ena's skills took her to Bletchley Park. Many women, like Margot, did war work as civilians. But Margot Dudley had a dream. She went to London, worked as an usherette and became a show girl, joined ENSA and toured with concert parties, entertaining the troops.

After the war, women who had known independence helped shape the modern post-war era of the 1950s and 1960s.

My mother told me that her sister, Marjorie, dreamed of being a dancer, but their father was a groom, and his wages didn't stretch to dance classes. I felt sorry that my aunt hadn't achieved her dream of being a dancer. So, because I had worked as an actress in West End theatres and fulfilled my dream, I wrote Destiny so that, in fiction, at least, my aunt could fulfil her dream. I wrote Tribute to celebrate her achievements.

I placed the Young Albert Theatre in Whitechapel because so much of the East End had been bombed in the war, and I based the building on The Young Vic Theatre in Southwark, where I spent a year as an actress in the late 1980s.

Thanks for being part of my writing journey. I hope you'll stay in touch, as I have many more stories and ideas to share with you!

Best wishes and happy reading,
Madalyn x

Website and Social media links

Website:
www.madalynmorgan.com

Facebook:
https://www.facebook.com/madalyn.morgan1

Twitter:
Madalyn Morgan (@ActScribblerDJ) / X

Instagram:
https://www.instagram.com/madalynmorgan1

LinkedIn:
https://www.linkedin.com/in/madalyn-morgan-b27317b

Bluesky:
Madalyn Morgan (@madalymorgan.bsky.social)

Printed in Dunstable, United Kingdom